MEGA 2
BAJA BLOOD
JAKE BIBLE

Chapter One: I Know A Guy…

It wasn't an actual forty foot whale that broke the surface of the water in the marina hangar bay. It wasn't alive in any way, but it could fool anyone, even the crew that developed and built it. Same with the second and third non-whales that surfaced next to it.

"How'd it go?" Jimmy McCarthy asked, looking over his shoulder at a woman standing a few feet away as he crouched at the edge of the dock, watching the non-whales, their backs splitting as hatches opened and wet suit clad men pulled themselves out of the machines.

Mid-fifties, white crew cut, muscled arms and legs under his t-shirt and Bermuda shorts, McCarthy looked and acted like a man that didn't take shit. Even crouched down so his flip-flops waggled beneath his heels, no one that knew him would ever mistake the man for anything but dangerous.

"Flying colors," Dr. Lisa Morganton replied, checking over a tablet she held. Streams of data and information flew by on the tablet, but her trained eyes missed none of it. Maybe late forties, with short, bobbed blonde hair and hazel eyes, Dr. Morganton was known as calm, cool and collected. A smooth operator and all business. She smiled and looked up, catching McCarthy's eye. "Everything in the green. Speed tests went better than expected. Detection is almost zero. These could swim right under a Coast Guard cutter and they wouldn't even know it."

"They'd know it, but they would think they were looking at adolescent blue whales," McCarthy grinned. "We still need them to see *something* so there are no alarming anomalies. Last thing we need is a sonar tech getting curious."

"Right," Dr. Morganton nodded. "They look to eyes and electronics like adolescent blue whales. Exactly as designed. They are the perfect stealth submarines."

"Good," McCarthy smiled as he stood up, watching the sub pilots crawl their way across the gangways that were extended to their masqueraded machines from the dock. Several techs hurried about the marina hangar, tossing lines to the sub. "How about you boys?"

"Ship shape, Jimmy," the first pilot replied.

Despite missing both legs below the knees, former SEAL John Sherman could never be mistaken for handicapped. Arms like trees and a barrel chest bigger than two men combined, John was in prime shape, and at thirty-two, he planned on staying that way. Just needed to sock away some cash so he could get his life back on track. And the gig with McCarthy allowed him to do just that.

"Any issues to report?" Dr. Morganton asked.

"None," John replied as he strapped on a pair of prosthetic legs one by one. "Smoothest SDV I've ever been in. Takes a little getting used to with the tail propulsion system and fin rudders, but after a few minutes I almost felt like a fucking whale myself."

"And you, gentlemen?" McCarthy asked the other two pilots.

Like John, they were also missing their legs below the knees. The wars hadn't been kind to young men in the US military, but they each had been given new starts by coming on board with McCarthy and Dr. Morganton.

Former SEAL Bart Stern was twenty-five and like John, was in amazing shape. He crawled across the gangway and a tech handed him his alloy steel legs, just like the ones John wore. He strapped them on then flipped over and pushed himself upright. He bounced on his "legs" a few times then gave a thumbs up to the tech who hurried off to help former SEAL Mike Pearlman.

Mike waved the tech off, preferring to hand walk his way over to a waiting wheelchair on his own. His torso wasn't thick and muscled like John's or Bart's, but long and lean with ropey arms that looked like they could twist and turn several ways at once. He climbed into his wheelchair, released the brake and wheeled over to McCarthy.

"You never get used to how populated the waters are in the tropics," Mike said to McCarthy. "There's more life down there than up here."

"It's Baja, baby," McCarthy smiled. "There's always more life here."

"What types of marine life did you encounter?" Dr. Morganton asked, her eyes drawn from her tablet to the former SEAL. "Can you identify them?"

"Fish," Mike smiled. "Lots of fish. A couple other whales."

"And something else, for sure," Bart added. "It was big. Did you catch it on the sonar?"

"I caught several big shapes, Mr. Stern," Dr. Morganton replied, watching the men carefully. "Can you describe what you saw?"

"Not really," Bart replied. "It was dark and the video cameras aren't the highest resolution."

"Why not?" McCarthy asked, looking at Dr. Morganton. "These things should have the best tech available."

"They do," Dr. Morganton replied. "But we are talking about conditions that are less than ideal. Submerged, moving, pilot error."

"Hey," John snapped. "Don't blame it on the operators. We did our jobs; we can't help it if the toys don't work right."

Dr. Morganton frowned at the man and looked back at her tablet. The men waited impatiently as she tapped at various applications then spun the tablet around.

"Is this what you saw?" she asked Bart.

Bart looked at the image on the tablet and nodded.

"Yeah," he replied. "That's it. Looks a lot better on your thing there."

"Must be the video monitor resolution, not the video cameras because the recorded feed is crystal clear."

"What is that?" McCarthy asked, walking over and taking the tablet from her. Dr. Morganton started to protest then remembered whom she was dealing with and let it go. "What kind of whale is that?"

"It is not a whale, Mr. McCarthy," Dr. Morganton replied. "It is a shark."

"Big fucking shark," McCarthy said. "That a great white?"

"I would guess so," Dr. Morganton responded, holding out her hand. McCarthy gave her back the tablet and smiled. She was not comforted by the smile in the least. "Although the water has distorted the image somewhat, so I can't say for sure. But this being the time blue whales migrate back to the area in large numbers, I would believe it is a great white looking for a meal."

"Ballsy," McCarthy smiled wider, looking very much like a shark himself. "Some of the whales out there are two or three times the size of great whites."

Dr. Morganton didn't reply as she was busy studying the image on the tablet.

"Doctor?" McCarthy asked. "Hello? I said a shark like that is pretty ballsy." He didn't like the puzzled look on the doctor's face and his smile dropped away instantly. "Talk to me. What is it? Something wrong with the subs?"

"I should hope not," a man said as a door to the marina hangar opened and he walked through, followed by eight heavily armed men. "You promised me they would be ready for delivery today. I hope that is the case, James. For your sake."

***

Max and Shane Reynolds sang along with the Beach Boys at the top of their lungs as they sped down I-5 in their Jeep Wrangler, top down, sun in their faces, life good.

The Wrangler was silver, but with the classic Rasta colors of Jamaica striped along the hood and doors. It was jacked up and looked like it had done some serious off-roading, which it had. The front and rear bumpers were reinforced, with the front having a good sized winch mounted to it. The side running boards were more than just stepping planks and had the same reinforced look as the front and rear bumpers.

The Rasta colors were more of a nod to their clientele- Northern California pot growers that hired the Reynolds so they could learn to protect their fields with more than just good vibes.

Since the Reynolds were both ex-Navy SEALs, they had the expertise to train anyone that wanted to learn. And wanted to pay. Which NorCal pot growers could easily do.

The Reynolds brothers were nine months apart and almost looked identical, both with yellow-blond hair, green eyes, and freckles across their noses. However, there was one easy way to tell the difference- Max was missing his left ear and had scar tissue running from his scalp, down his neck, and onto his shoulder while Shane was missing his left eye.

Shane sat in the passenger's seat, a joint firmly planted between his lips as he sang loud and proud. He lifted the black eye patch, which had a very prominent marijuana leaf stitched into it, and scratched at the empty socket underneath.

"Knock that off," Max said, slapping at his brother's hand just before he plucked the joint from his lips. "No scratching."

"But it itches," Shane whined. "It's like I have ants crawling around in there."

"Tell it to the doctors, bro," Max said. He took a long drag off the joint and handed it back to Shane. "What exit is the VA again?"

"Right there," Shane pointed as they passed the exit.

"Hold on," Max said casually. He hit the brakes, spun the Jeep to the right, slammed down the accelerator, and gunned it down the embankment of the off ramp. "There. Smooth as silk."

A multitude of horns blared around them, but the brothers didn't pay any mind to the angry drivers. They just casually passed the joint back and forth, as the next Beach Boys track came up.

"Thar she be, bro," Shane said, pointing to the large entrance of the San Diego Veterans Administration Medical Center. "Pull up front and drop me off."

"You sure you don't want me to hang?" Max asked. "I totally don't mind waiting."

"Nah," Shane said, giving his brother the joint back as they screeched to a stop in front of the VA building. "You know how long it takes before I get to see the docs. It could be an hour or two. Head to Gunnar's and wait for my call."

"Yes, master," Max said in a bad Igor voice. "Anything you say, master."

"Exactly, bee-otch," Shane grinned. He hoped out, stopped, turned around and grabbed the joint back. He sucked it almost dead before handing the roach to Max. "That'll help pass the time."

"Dude," Max frowned, looking at the spent joint. "Not cool. I don't have another rolled."

"You can roll one at Gunnar's," Shane said then slapped his forehead. "Shit, no you can't."

"Kinsey," Max said.

"Kinsey," Shane nodded.

"I'm way too stoned to hang with Kinsey right now," Max said. "I'll park and wait for ya."

"You sure?" Shane asked. "Like I said, bro, it could be a while."

"That'll give me time to sober up a little before we have to see Sis," Max said. "Probably not a good idea to walk in all blazed while Kinsey is only a year sober, right?"

"Good call," Shane said. "Park this bitch. I'll be in the always waiting room."

***

"Dammit, Gun!" Kinsey Thorne shouted as she tore back the covers and yanked Gunnar Peterson from his bed. "You aren't ready yet? They'll be here any minute!"

Gunnar's head slammed against his bedroom floor and he started swatting at Kinsey as she pulled him towards his bathroom.

Her blonde hair was cut short, but no longer spiked and colored like it had been several months before. But that wasn't the major difference in Kinsey's appearance. Instead of the strung out junkie with pallid skin that hung from her like damp clothes on a summer clothesline, Kinsey's frame was filled out and muscular. She'd been sober close to a year and turned her cravings for heroin, crank, booze, pills, whatever, into building her muscle mass back up to her fighting weight when she had been in the Marines.

At one time, she had been the first female candidate to make it through the Navy SEALs BUD/S training and move into the SQT portion. All she had to do was survive a little longer and she would have been assigned to a SEAL Team and made US history. But she broke, started using amphetamines, and when she was found out, she was dishonorably discharged.

That led to a downward spiral of drug abuse which resulted in her doing pretty much anything for a fix. Actually, there was no "pretty much" to it; Kinsey blew and fucked her way through most of the San Diego underground to stay high.

But that was before her father, former Navy SEAL Commander Vincent Thorne, forced her to become a part of Team Grendel- a group of highly trained ex-SEALs and former military types that worked for the mysterious Mr. Ballantine and "the company". Ballantine never explained who the company was, and all being former Special Operations, everyone knew not to ask too many questions.

So, it was the new Kinsey that manhandled Dr. Gunnar Peterson that morning. And Gunnar was less than happy about it.

"Kins? Kins! Knock it off!" Gunnar shouted. "What the hell? What time is it?"

"Time to get your ass up," Kinsey said. "What time did you get in last night?"

Gunnar kicked at Kinsey until she finally let him go and allowed him to stand up. He looked down and realized he was naked then turned to the bed.

"He snuck out a couple hours ago," Kinsey smirked. "How was he?"

Gunnar rubbed at his head and frowned. "Not sure. I think I got a little drunk last night."

"No shit, Sherlock," Kinsey replied. "You two were louder than two raccoons. I was worried the neighbors would call the cops."

"It's a discrete condo complex," Gunnar said. "More than a couple celebrities have places here. No one calls the cops."

"Lucky you," Kinsey said and pointed to the bathroom. "Get showered and dressed. No way I'm handling my cousins on my own."

Gunnar Peterson was of Scandinavian descent and had blond/red hair with a strong build, but he was a John Hopkins trained physician, not a Navy trained killer. Trying to fight off Kinsey Thorne was like a kid fighting an angry parent: a couple good hits may happen, but in the end the kid goes where the parent wants. He walked into the bathroom and shut the door then looked into the mirror and frowned.

"Lookin' good," Gunnar laughed then started the shower.

Best friend to Kinsey's ex-husband Darren Chambers, Gunnar had known Kinsey and Darren since they were kids, growing up in the same San Diego military dominated neighborhood. While Darren and Kinsey had pursued a life in the military (Darren as a SEAL and Kinsey as a Marine before trying out and washing out of BUD/S), Gunnar had always been the intellectual. He got his medical degree, but when Darren came to him with a wild story of a giant whale he'd seen, Gunnar dropped medicine and got a second degree in marine biology.

The two men had embarked on a wild whale chase, and were ridiculed for it, until they found the thing. And so much more.

Part of Team Grendel also, Gunnar offered for Kinsey to live with him in his trust fund paid for condo. Sometimes Gunnar wondered if he hadn't been insane when he made the offer. But most of the time he loved having an anchor like Kinsey around. It connected him to his past and gave him history to hang onto when things got crazy. Which they always did.

Such was the life on a Team.

***

"Ricardo," McCarthy said, forcing the smile back on his face. The smile was lost again quickly as the man frowned at McCarthy. "Uh, Mr. Espanoza, I mean."

"Are they ready, James?" Ricardo Espanoza asked, his voice smooth and completely void of any accent. He sounded like an American, and with his light skin and blue eyes, could have passed for a beach boy in any Southern Californian city. "As promised?"

McCarthy looked at Dr. Morganton and she shook her head.

"Not yet," McCarthy responded. "We need maybe a day or two to go over the latest test results. If they look as good as we think they will then the subs will be ready for you to use immediately."

Espanoza cocked his head and stared at McCarthy. He looked the man up and down then shook his head.

"A promise is a promise," Espanoza said, pointing at one of the techs that were busy securing the subs to the docks.

An armed man walked over to the tech, raised his AK-47 sub-machine gun, and put three bullets in the tech's back. The tech screamed and fell forward, plunging into the water between two of the subs. The man fired again and again, peppering the floating body with bullets before it slowly sank below the surface.

"Let me ask again," Espanoza said, his face passive, the complete opposite of everyone else's faces in the marina hangar. "Are they ready as promised, James?"

McCarthy looked back at Dr. Morganton, his eyes pleading with her. She took a deep breath and finally nodded.

"Yeah, they're ready," McCarthy said. "We can deliver them to you tomorrow."

"No, I don't think so, James," Espanoza said. "I am in need of them today. You said ready today so I made plans for today."

He waved a hand and one of the men stepped forward and leaned in close as Espanoza whispered to him. After some brief instructions, the man hurried off out of the hangar while the other men remained where they stood, sub-machine guns at the ready.

"Jimmy?" John asked, taking a step closer to McCarthy. Guns were turned on him instantly. "What the fuck is going on? Who is this psycho asshole?"

There were intakes of breath from several of the armed men and they moved forward, but Espanoza held up his hand and they stopped in place.

"Ricardo Espanoza at your service, Mr. Sherman," Espanoza said, walking over and offering his hand. "You may call me Mr. Espanoza. I am not fond of being called asshole. However, I do not mind psycho. It has flair."

John looked at where the body had just sunk then at the armed men. He reluctantly shook Espanoza's hand.

"Okay, Mr. Espanoza, who the fuck are you?" John asked.

"John, not now," McCarthy warned. "Just hang tight, okay? I'll explain later."

"You keep your men in the dark?" Espanoza asked McCarthy. "Good practice, James. Never give out information unless you absolutely have to. Information is currency in this world."

A large cargo door began to roll up into the top of the hangar and a truck beeped shrilly as it backed into the space, headed for the dock everyone stood upon.

"But there are many types of currencies," Espanoza laughed. "Some more valuable than others."

The truck stopped and Espanoza snapped his fingers. Half his men hurried to the truck, lifting the back door to reveal several white bundles wrapped in heavy-duty plastic. Each bundle was the size of a large barrel and it took two men each to pull the bundles out of the truck and onto the dock. When they were finished, there were a total of sixty bundles waiting by the water.

"Jesus," Bart said. "Is that...?"

"It is," Espanoza smiled. "Never seen that much coca before, Mr. Stern?"

"How do you know my name?" Bart asked, looking over at McCarthy. "How does he know my name?"

"I know all of your names," Espanoza said. "Information as currency, remember?"

"But I don't know you," John said, his face scrunched up in anger. "How about you tell us who you are?"

"John!" McCarthy snapped. "Clam it!"

"No, no, no, that's fine, James," Espanoza said. "I have already said my name, but I assume you want to know what I do since that truly defines a man." With barely a movement, he had a 9mm pistol in his hand, pointed at a spot right between John's eyes. "I am the man in charge. There is no disputing that. And I am the man that holds your life in my hands. Would you like to live, Mr. Sherman?"

"Yeah, I would," John replied, not impressed with the pistol pointed at him. "But that's not up to me, is it?"

"No, it is not," Espanoza replied. "I am very glad you are realizing that. Do you need me to explain myself more, Mr.

Sherman? Or can you infer from what is happening around you what it is I really am?"

"I'm getting the picture," John said, his eyes glancing at the bales of wrapped cocaine kilos. "Loud and clear."

The 9mm was gone as quickly as it had appeared and Espanoza clapped his hands together.

"Have your people load the cargo," Espanoza said to McCarthy. "You have practiced the routes I gave you?"

"They have," McCarthy replied, looking at the three sub pilots. "They just finished a run a few minutes ago."

"Good," Espanoza nodded. "I would like the submarines to depart within the hour. There is a fishing vessel waiting within US waters, just off the coast of San Diego. They expect delivery by 5pm this evening."

McCarthy quickly checked his watch and blanched. "That's cutting it close."

"Is it a problem?" Espanoza asked.

"No," Dr. Morganton said, stepping up. "Let me make some adjustments and they can be ready for service."

"Dr. Morganton, right?" Espanoza asked.

"Yes, sir," Dr. Morganton replied.

Espanoza looked her up and down. "Your career is impressive. Why are you working with James? I'd think you'd have a better future elsewhere."

"Money provides whatever future I want it to," Dr. Morganton said. "Don't you think, sir?"

Espanoza laughed. "That it does, doctor!"

***

"Really?" Kinsey said, her phone to her ear as she talked to her cousin Max. "I thought you were coming here first?"

She looked down at the pancakes she was busy scorching, then over at the pile of pancakes that looked even less appetizing.

"There's breakfast, Max," she said.

"Yeah, sorry, Sis," Max replied over the phone. Not having a sister of their own, the Reynolds always called their cousin Sis. It was endearing, but unfortunately, it seemed to give them license to pester her like a little sister. "Wait...breakfast? It's like noon, dude. You gotta get a regular schedule, Sis."

"You saying you won't eat pancakes after a certain time?" Kinsey asked.

Gunnar walked into the kitchen, a towel wrapped around his waist, and squinted against the bright Southern California sun that streamed in through the many windows of the open floor condo. He watched as she mangled the food, shook his head, then went into the living room and turned on the TV.

"*-that officials are calling the most addictive form of cocaine they've ever seen,*" an anchorwoman reported. "*911 calls of overdoses and drug induced psychotic breaks have almost doubled in areas such as La Jolla, and other affluent areas, puzzling police-*"

"What was that, Max?" Kinsey asked then pulled the phone from her mouth. "Gun! Can you turn that off or turn that down?"

"Fine," Gunnar said as he switched off the TV and walked back to the kitchen.

"I said I have no time limit on pancakes, and could totally go for some now, but we're hitting the VA first," Max said. "Tell Gunnar we're sorry we missed his cooking."

"Gun didn't cook," Kinsey said. "I did. It's my new thing."

"Oh," Max said. "Uh...great?"

"Fuck you, cuz," Kinsey said.

Gunnar picked up a pancake from the plate of "done" ones, looked at the almost white side, flipped it over and stared at the pitch black side for a second before looking at Kinsey.

"Fuck you too, Gun," Kinsey snapped.

"Yeah, so I love you and will see you soon," Max said. "Totally stoked to hang with my cousin and her gay roommate."

"That's Dr. Gay Roommate, assmuncher," Gunnar said, leaning into the phone. Kinsey shoved him away. "You should really turn the volume down. Or just put it on speaker."

"Oh, shit!" Kinsey shouted as one of her pancakes burst into flames. "How the fuck is that even possible?"

Gunnar took the phone from her as a second pancake caught fire.

"Um, Kinsey is busy burning my condo down, can I take a message?" Gunnar laughed then winced as Kinsey grabbed the flaming pancakes with her bare hands and threw them into the sink. "Jesus, Kins…"

"How's the roomy sitch going, dude?" Max laughed. "Out of the honeymoon phase yet?"

"Oh, we left the honeymoon phase the first time Kins didn't shut the bathroom door to take a shit," Gunnar replied.

"Nice," Max laughed. "It'll be good to see you."

"You too, Max," Gunnar replied. "How's Shane?"

"He's about to go in and get his eyehole probed," Max said. "He's looking forward to it."

The voice of Shane saying, "Fuck that" could be heard easily.

"Sounds like it," Gunnar laughed. "Oh, shit! Kins! The drapes are on fire now!"

"You better go," Max said and hung up.

"Sorry," Kinsey said, hosing down the drapes with the kitchen sink's spray nozzle. "There. All fixed."

***

"You'll have to push the subs at speeds we haven't tested yet to make your deadline," McCarthy said.

"Do what you must," Espanoza said.

"What I must? How do you mean?" McCarthy asked, pointing at the subs. "You want delivery, here is delivery. Once these subs leave this hangar I've done my part."

"Oh, no, I am sorry for not being clear," Espanoza said. "Since I have not had time to train pilots, I will need yours to make the deliveries."

McCarthy blanched. "You can't be serious? My guys didn't sign up for this. They're here to test the subs only, not be a part of your drug trafficking."

"Their roles have changed," Espanoza replied. "They will be compensated, of course."

"I'm out," John said, throwing his hands in the air. "I didn't agree to run drugs for some cartel fuck!" He pointed a finger at

Espanoza. "You gonna shoot me? Then shoot me! I could give a fuck, asshole! At least I die with my honor!"

"Will Carli die with her honor, Mr. Sherman?" Espanoza asked. "Or what about little Jack? Will he die with honor too?"

John stumbled a bit at the mention of his children's names. He was able to keep his balance, but he didn't know for how long.

"What do you know about them?" John asked. He glared at McCarthy. "What did you tell him about my kids, Jimmy?"

"Nothing, John," McCarthy said. "The guy does his homework."

"Which will be something your eight year old daughter will never do again if you do not get into your submarine, Mr. Sherman," Espanoza smiled. "And little Jack is what? Five? He will never get to do homework at all. Not when my men are through with him."

***

"Shane Reynolds?" a nurse called as two double doors swung open.

"That's me," Shane said, jumping to his feet. He smiled at the nurse, looking her up and down. "And who are you?"

"Off limits," the nurse said. "And don't wink at me."

"I wasn't," Shane said. "I was blinking. Blinks look like winks when you only have one eye."

"Whatever," the nurse said. "Follow me."

Shane turned and gave his brother a thumbs up as the double doors closed behind him. Max laughed and looked about the waiting room, studying the others that sat, stood, paced, and grumbled.

A woman with her son and daughter in tow stood at the reception counter, her hands gesticulating. Max couldn't hear what she was saying since she was making a point of keeping her voice down, but it was obvious she wasn't happy. The boy turned around and caught Max watching them. Max gave the kid a wave, but the boy didn't respond, just kept staring.

The boy's sister turned around to see what caught her brother's attention. Max waved to her too, but received a glare in response instead of a blank stare.

"Nice kids," Max muttered, his hand going to the left side of his face and his missing ear and scars.

The woman's voice started to rise and the kids blanched at the scene their mother caused. Max didn't want to keep looking, but since everyone else now was he didn't turn away.

"He hasn't answered his phone in days!" the woman shouted. "All I need to know is if he came for his check up yesterday."

"Ma'am, I cannot tell you that," the receptionist stated. "As you have admitted yourself, he is your *ex*-husband, not your *current* husband. It is against the law for me to give you any information without his consent." The receptionist checked her computer monitor. "And I do not see that consent here in his file."

The woman grabbed the monitor and tried to turn it around so she could see, but the receptionist smacked her hand away.

"Hey!" the woman yelled. "You can't assault me like that!"

"I can and I will, ma'am," the receptionist said. "Do I need to have security escort you from the premises?"

"You're goddamn right you do!" the woman screamed. "Because I'm not leaving until you give me some information!" She grabbed her daughter's upper arm and shook it. "He hasn't paid child support in two months. You want my children to starve, is that it? Are you such a heartless bitch you would rather my kids not eat than risk violating my deadbeat ex's precious privacy? I was married to a SEAL for ten years; I am fucking sick of privacy!"

The mention of the SEALs got Max's attention and he stood up and walked slowly towards the counter. The boy saw him coming, reached back and grabbed his mother's hand, his eyes locked on Max's face.

"Not now, Jack," the woman spat.

"Ma'am, I'm calling security," the receptionist said, picking up her phone.

The woman grabbed the phone and yanked it from the receptionist's hand and was about to hit her with it when Max rushed forward and stopped her. The woman looked at the hand clamped around her wrist then up at Max's face. She blanched at the sight, but recovered quickly.

"Do you mind?" she snarled at him.

"Do I mind what?" Max asked, not letting go. "Watching a good looking lady like you get tossed out of here on her ass? Yeah, I mind. No one should treat a fox like you that way."

The woman sputtered and blinked, unsure of how to take the compliments from a stranger while the stranger also held her arm immobile.

"Mind you own business," the woman said finally, yanking her arm free.

"I was trying to," Max said, waving at the waiting room and the spectators. "But you kind of distracted me."

The woman looked about and a range of emotions crossed her face as she saw everyone staring at her. Her features finally settled on a mix of resigned embarrassment. Then her eyes went wide as two officers of the VA Police marched over to her.

"Hold on, boys," Max said, stepping between the woman and her children and them. "I got this. We were just leaving."

The police officers glanced at the receptionist. She in turn glanced at Max then back at the officers and shrugged.

"Then go," one of the officers said. "You are disturbing the other patients."

"On our way out," Max said, looking down at the children. "Ready, kids?"

"What the hell do you think you're doing?" the woman snapped.

"Keeping you out of the brig," Max said. He looked at the police officers. "You do use a brig, right?"

"We have a holding room," the other officer replied.

"Well, even though that's not as scary sounding, I'll bet it has the same piss smell as a brig," Max said. "Am I right?"

The officers just glared at Max.

"Right," Max said. "We're outta here."

He took the woman by the elbow and started walking her to the exit. She tried to resist at first, but as the police officers fell in line behind them, she stopped her struggles and let Max steer her and the kids outside.

Once the automatic doors slid shut, and they stood on the sidewalk out in the bright sunlight, she yanked her elbow free and whirled on Max.

"I don't know who you are, but I didn't need your help back there," she snapped.

"Yeah, you did, Mom," the girl said.

"Smart kid," Max said. "I'm Max Reynolds. I heard you say your ex was a frogman. Me too."

"You're a SEAL?" the boy, Jack, asked. "Does your face hurt?"

"Jack!" the woman snapped.

"It's fine. I was a SEAL," Max said. "I'm in private security now. And no, my scars don't hurt."

"Another frogman. Great," the woman said. "You skip out on your wife too?"

"Nope," Max said, holding up his hand to show his empty ring finger. "Never been married."

"Then the women of this country dodged a bullet."

"Ouch," Max said. "That's a sharp tongue you have there. Got a name to go with that tongue or should I call you Crazy Angry Ex-wife Lady?"

The woman started to respond then saw the amused look on Max's face and laughed.

"I'm sorry," she said, shaking her head. "It's been a shitty few months. I'm Helen Sherman."

"Good to meet you, Helen," Max said. He bent down in front of the kids. "And this guy is Jack, I heard. What's your name, pretty thing?"

"Carli," the girl replied.

"Hey, Carli," Max said.

He stood up and pulled out his phone then looked at Helen.

"What's your ex's name?" Max said as he hit the contact for his uncle.

"What?" Helen asked. "Why?"

Max held up a finger as Thorne answered.

"What, Max?" Thorne responded on the line.

"Hey, Uncle Vinny," Max said. "Good to hear you too."

"You in trouble?"

"No, just need some help with something," Max said as he pulled the phone away from his mouth a little and looked at Helen. "What's you ex's name?"

"John," Helen replied. "John Sherman."

"Hey, Vinny, could you make some calls and see what you can find out about a former frogman named John Sherman?" Max asked, putting the phone back to his mouth.

"Right now?" Thorne responded. "I was taking a nap."

"Good for you," Max said. "Keep that specter of Death off your back a little longer."

"Max, I love you, but fuck off."

Max smiled at Helen and the kids, walked a few feet away and lowered his voice.

"I'd really appreciate your help on this," Max said. "I'm at the VA with Shane and this woman came in with her kids. Sounds like her ex-husband has skipped out on her. I'm just trying to do the right thing."

"She's hot, isn't she?" Thorne asked, sighing.

Max turned back around and looked at Helen.

"Uh, yeah," he smiled at her. She smiled back. "Very."

"Fine, fine," Thorne said. "What was the guy's name again?"

"Sherman," Max replied. "John Sherman."

***

"Fuck," John said. "What kind of monster are you that would kill kids?"

"Oh, I'm just a businessman," Espanoza said. "*I'm* not the monster. I'm the man that hires monsters. Would you like to hear what those monsters will do to your children, Mr. Sherman? Would you?" John didn't reply. "Let me tell you anyway. First, your children will have to watch as my men rape your ex-wife in front of them. She will be violated in ways that I can't even imagine, not being a monster myself. Your girl and little boy will have their heads held and eyelids sliced off so they cannot look away. Shall I go on?"

"Mr. Espanoza, please…" McCarthy begged. "You don't need to do this."

"You cannot get your men under control, James, so I will," Espanoza said. "Where was I? Oh, yes, what happens next? Once the monsters are done raping your ex-wife, they will move on to young Carli then little Jack. Finished with their fun, my men will then systematically dismember each one, piece by piece, keeping them alive for hours on end. Finally, once their bodies can take no more, they will be mercifully killed by an ice pick to the back of the brain." Espanoza tapped the back of his own head. "Right here."

Bart and Mike gulped loudly and Espanoza turned his attention on them.

"Mr. Stern never married, but he does have a mother living in Yuma, Arizona that will get the same treatment," Espanoza said. "And Mr. Pearlman is a homosexual, both parents deceased."

Several of Espanoza's men spat on the dock at the word "homosexual".

Espanoza frowned at the actions, but didn't reprimand them. Instead, he just shook his head, looking over at Mike. "Forgive them, they come from another culture," Espanoza continued. "I, myself, have nothing against the gays. As long as they do as they are told like everyone else."

He turned to a man standing off to the side. Tall, thin, with a ragged scar across his throat, the man walked over to Espanoza, leaned in and whispered into his ear.

"Ah, thank you, Diego," Espanoza smiled. "I have been told we have a list of some of your former lovers, Mr. Pearlman. It wasn't easy since you did not come out as gay until after your president rescinded your country's Don't Ask, Don't Tell law. But, as I have said, I am a man that understands the importance of information. It only took a little digging to find your gay friends."

"Fuck you," Mike snarled.

"I hate to break it to you, Mr. Pearlman," Espanoza replied. "But I am not gay, so that will not be possible."

***

19

"Here are blankets and pillows," Gunnar said, dropping the stack of bedding on the couch. "They can fight over who gets the floor."

"Don't you have like an inflatable mattress or something?" Kinsey asked.

"No, Kins, I don't," Gunnar replied. "I have a guest room instead with a very comfortable bed. But it's occupied by a woman that figured out how to turn pancakes into flaming projectiles."

"You still pissed about the drapes?" Kinsey asked, planting her hands on her hips. "Or is that attitude about me staying with you? I've said a hundred times I'm ready to move out on my own again."

"No, no, sorry," Gunnar said. "I'm just still tired, okay? I don't want you to move out."

He went to her and wrapped his arms about her, kissing her on the cheek.

"Get off me," Kinsey said.

"Come on, don't be a poop," Gunnar said. "Who's my favorite junkie?"

"Fuck you, Gun," Kinsey replied, struggling not to smile.

"Come on, say it," Gunnar grinned, nuzzling his head against hers. "Who's my favorite junkie?"

"Kinsey Thorne," Kinsey said.

"Damn right," Gunnar said, pushing back and holding her by the shoulders. "We cool?"

"Yeah, we're cool," Kinsey said.

***

Espanoza turned and watched as the last bales of cocaine kilos were loaded into the subs. He smiled as the backs of the subs were sealed up tight, leaving not a trace of a cargo area, returning them to their almost perfect whale facsimiles.

"Remarkable," Espanoza said. "You have done an excellent job, Dr. Morganton."

"Thank you," Dr. Morganton replied quietly. "I have one more adjustment to make."

"No time, I'm afraid," Espanoza said. "Unless you want to argue the point?"

"No, that's fine," Dr. Morganton said as she looked at one of the subs. "They're set."

"James? Are your pilots ready?" Espanoza asked, turning to McCarthy. "There is a time schedule to keep."

McCarthy looked at John, Bart, and then Mike. The three men glared at him, but one by one they nodded. McCarthy gave them an apologetic nod in return.

"They're ready," McCarthy said. "But this is it. After they make the delivery, then we are out, got it?"

"Of course," Espanoza said. "I have paid you a great amount of money and I am sure you would like to spend it."

"I would," McCarthy said. "And so would my pilots."

Espanoza nodded and motioned towards the subs.

"Time to get to work, guys," McCarthy said. "Sorry about this."

"I'll make you pay for this, McCarthy," Mike said. "You hear me?"

"Yeah, I hear ya," McCarthy replied. "But nothing I can do about it, kid."

Dr. Morganton started shouting commands to the techs and the subs were prepped for departure as the three pilots shimmied their way into a sub each. Three techs hopped onto Wave Runners and pushed the subs out of the marine hangar until they had enough room to turn them around and pointed out to sea.

"Is there a lounge?" Espanoza asked as the subs submerged and were lost from sight. "I would like to sit down and enjoy refreshment while we wait."

Dr. Morganton looked at McCarthy, but he only shrugged and waved his hand to a side door in the bay.

"Yeah, there's an office here where we have the monitoring equipment set up," McCarthy said. "It's probably not as comfortable as you are used to, but there're folding chairs for everyone." He looked at the men with the sub-machine guns. "Well, almost everyone."

"They'll wait out here," Espanoza responded, nodding to Diego. "It will only be my associate and I." Espanoza tapped his temple. "I'd hate for too much information to get free."

"Right, of course," McCarthy nodded. "Follow me."

Dr. Morganton watched the men closely, her hand in her pocket as she frantically typed blindly at her phone.

***

The cockpit of the sub barely allowed John to shift his shoulders from side to side without nailing them on one of several control panels. There was some room when he backed away from the main controls, but not much. Like many subs, the controls were old school analog- switches and toggles, dials and levers. Except for the bank of video monitors that covered the entire front of the cockpit and wrapped around slightly for a "peripheral" view.

"Are you reading me, Dr. Morganton?" John asked through the headset he wore. "Am I coming through?"

"Loud and clear, Mr. Sherman," Dr. Morganton replied.

"I'm here too, John," McCarthy said. "Just maintain your heading like before. You'll follow the same route until you get across the maritime boundary and into US territorial waters. At that point you'll be given new coordinates."

"Looking forward to it," John responded.

"I am sure you are, Mr. Sherman," Espanoza said.

"Get that ass off the com," John replied. "I don't need him in my ear."

"Don't worry about it, John," McCarthy said. "We'll be losing contact in just a few minutes once you hit cruising depth."

"Thank God for small favors," John said.

"What's this?" Espanoza asked. "Lose contact? The subs are supposed to have state of the art communications systems."

"That is part of what still needs to be worked on," McCarthy replied. "They can speak to each other, and even if the Coast Guard is listening it will be encoded and sound like whale song."

"Yes, that is what you had told me," Espanoza growled. "But there will need to be communication with the subs once they are in US waters."

"They'll surface and then communication will be restored," McCarthy said. "We just won't be able to communicate with them until then. It's temporary for now, I assure you, Mr. Espanoza."

"Do you two mind?" John snapped. "We need to concentrate on piloting these things. Can you bicker off com?"

"Careful with your tone, Mr. Sherman," Espanoza warned.

John just sighed and focused on driving the sub.

The subs continued their progress through the warm waters just south of Salsipuedes Bay. The coastline was a barren stretch, unmarred by tourist villages and condos, which made it ideal for launching three covert submersibles. Changing his heading to north by northwest, John led the other two subs out away from the coast and into deeper waters.

He checked his sonar readings and once in the correct position, began to dive deeper until he was at 500 feet and following along the San Benito fault. The occasional chatter from Dr. Morganton and McCarthy died away until nothing but static was left. John waited for several minutes before radioing the other pilots.

"We clear?" John asked.

"I think so," Bart replied. "What the fuck are we going to do, man?"

"We're going to do as we're told," Mike said. "Then kill every last motherfucker once we reach those fishing boats."

"I got a family, Mike," John said. "You heard what that psycho fuck is going to do."

"What do you think he's going to do to us?" Mike asked. "Give us a pat on the shoulder and tell us we did a good job?"

"But my family!"

"Fuck your family!" Mike shouted. "I want to live!"

Behind the three subs, three shapes emerged from below, locked onto the machines that looked like young blue whales.

***

"Thanks, Uncle Vinny," Max said. "I owe you one."

"You owe me a lot more than that," Thorne replied. "And I never told you this, got it? McCarthy is an asshole of a frogman and he's going to be pissed if he finds out I've been snooping in his business."

"He recruited two others also?" Max asked. "Both amputees like Sherman?"

"That's the scuttlebutt," Thorne replied then changed the subject. "Am I going to see you two this weekend?"

"Sure are," Max said. "We're hanging until the end of the month."

"No hippies to train?" Thorne asked.

"Nope," Max said. "We're on hiatus. Training pot growers to be snipers and defend their crops isn't nearly as fun as working for Ballantine. But it's a lot safer, so we're trying to figure exactly which direction we want to focus on. And, speaking of Ballantine…"

"Just sit tight," Thorne said. "I told you I'd call as soon as he has another assignment. Enjoy the paycheck and vacation until then."

"Yeah, but there are more of those fucking freak sharks out there," Max said, lowering his voice so Helen and the kids couldn't hear. "We need to get Team Grendel back on the water and do some hunting."

"Ballantine said he'd call once he had a lead," Thorne replied.

"You hear from Ditcher lately?" Max asked, using the nickname he and his brother gave Darren Chambers when he walked out on their cousin Kinsey.

"He took some time off to deal with Bobby's death," Thorne replied. "But he's now back overseeing the outfitting of the new ship."

"New ship?" Max said. "Please don't tell me it's named what I think it will be."

"I don't care what it's named," Thorne said. "All I care about is that it can't be taken down by a mega shark."

"I hear that," Max said. He turned about and smiled at Helen. "Listen, I better go. Thanks for the info on the Sherman guy. It'll help ease his ex-wife's mind."

"Any time," Thorne said. "Just not while I'm napping next time, hear?"

"Got it. See ya," Max said and hung up. "Well, I have good news and bad news."

"What's the good news?" Helen asked.

"Your ex found a job," Max said. "One that needed his specific qualifications."

"Who needs a frogman without legs?" Helen laughed. "The circus?"

"Ouch," Max frowned, looking at the kids. Their faces told him they were used to their mother denigrating their father. "Want the bad news?"

"Sure, why not," Helen shrugged.

"The job is down in Mexico," Max said. "And could be a while."

"Of course," Helen snorted. "The jerk loses his legs, but still finds a way to get deployed."

"Want me to go back to the good news?" Max asked.

"Unless it's that I won the lotto then no," Helen snapped.

"Close," Max smiled. "If my uncle's intel is correct then the job pays some serious coin. Your ex should be able to get caught up on that child support as soon as he gets back."

"Whatever," Helen replied. "I've heard that before. That would be the responsible thing to do. And John's not so good at being responsible."

***

John was quiet for a minute as he thought about how he had helped recruit the other two men for McCarthy. John had known McCarthy from the SEAL community and when the man offered him a chance to get back into some action, he jumped for it. Maybe not literally jumped, but he was ready and willing to do whatever kept him active. McCarthy said he needed two more men and John knew just who to ask, having met Mike and Bart at the San Diego VA Medical Center while being fitted for prosthetics.

Former frogmen all, they bonded quickly and took McCarthy up on his very lucrative offer. Just sucked he had to keep it secret and couldn't let his ex-wife know where he was going or how long he'd be gone. He hoped to make that up to her and the kids.

The job had turned out as McCarthy said, as they worked on fine tuning the piloting controls of the subs under the supervision of Dr. Morganton. John never really trusted her since he couldn't get a straight answer from McCarthy on what her story was. He did learn she'd been a major researcher for a bioengineering company that specialized in advanced bio-alternative mechanics.

John didn't have the faintest idea what the hell that meant.

All he knew is that the whale-like subs were seriously futuristic SDVs, or SEAL Delivery Vehicles; basically mini-subs designed to move people or cargo. Although the cockpit only had room for one operator, the cargo hold, which was sealed and filled with breathable air, could hold a dozen or more men with gear. John was more than glad to work on a project that would help SEALs in the field.

But that wasn't to be, it appeared.

"Let's work through this," John said finally. "There has to be a way we can deliver the coke and get Esperanza to not kill us."

"Espanoza," Bart corrected.

"What the fuck ever!" John shouted. "I don't give a good goddamn what the man's name is, I just want my family to be safe and to get out of this alive!"

"What if we get lost?" Mike asked. "Just disappear and not show up at all. There's a lot of ocean between here and there."

"The man will think we've double crossed him and still kill my family," John replied.

"And my mom," Bart added.

"Then, what?" Mike asked.

But before the others could answer, proximity alarms rang out in each sub.

"What do you have?" John asked. "Anyone have visuals?"

"Three, right behind us," Bart said. "Please don't let them be whales coming to hump us. It is mating season for blue whales, right?"

"Fuck if I know," John replied. He played with a couple of dials and brought up the rear cameras. "Holy shit. Are you guys seeing this?"

"Yeah," Bart said. "Are those what I think they are?"

"Jesus," Mike replied. "Whoa! Where did they go?"

"They dove pretty fast," Bart said. "Think they figured out we aren't real?"

"Either that or they are going deeper so they can come at us from underneath," John said. "That's how sharks hunt."

***

Max lifted Jack into his car seat in the minivan while Helen helped Carli with her seatbelt.

"Thanks," Helen said as the van's doors slid shut. "You really didn't have to do any of this."

"Not a problem," Max said.

The two stood there awkwardly.

"So, I better go," Helen said.

"Can I get your number?" Max asked at the same time.

"My what?" Helen asked, completely surprised.

"Too soon, I get that," Max said. "Sorry. Forget I asked."

"No, no, that's cool," Helen grinned. "It's just, well…"

"You could do better," Max said, pointing to his scars. "No worries."

"Oh, God, no!" Helen exclaimed, her eyes involuntarily checking out Max's very tone body. "You don't look bad at all." She glanced at the van and the faces of her two children watching her. "I'm just not sure frogmen are good for me."

"Totally get that," Max said.

"Hey!" Shane shouted as he crossed the parking lot to the minivan. "You ditched me, dude!"

"Who's that?" Helen asked.

"My brother," Max said as Shane ran up to them. "Helen, this is Shane. Shane, this is Helen."

Helen looked back and forth between the two. "Are you twins?"

"Nah," Shane said. "Irish twins. Nine months apart."

"Reynolds is Scottish," Max said. "And we're obviously not twins since I'm the good looking one."

Helen smiled and took Max's hand. "Thank you."

"You bet," Max said. "Take care of those kids. And don't worry about John. He'll turn up and when he does I bet he'll have a nice, fat check for you."

Helen rolled her eyes and hopped in the van. Max and Shane stepped away as she backed out of the parking spot, waved and drove off.

"Now that's a MILF," Shane smiled. "You get her number?"

"Don't be a jerk," Max said. "She's nice. Her ex was a SEAL."

"Huh," Shane said. "Maybe that's why she has a tail."

"I said not to be a jerk," Max replied. "You don't have to talk about her ass."

"Not her ass, dumbshit," Shane said, nodding towards the black pickup truck that pulled out behind Helen's minivan. "I mean that right there. Tinted windows. No plates. She's being followed. And we both know who uses vehicles like that when they need to."

"Fuck," Max said. "Cartel."

"Cartel," Shane nodded. "Where's the Jeep? I think we have an adventure on our hands."

***

"No video?" Espanoza asked as he watched three blips on a GPS monitor. "Just red dots? That's not what was promised, James."

"There will be video and boosted audio communications," McCarthy said. "There hasn't been time to fine tune the communications systems yet, like I said."

"So until then we just watch these blips?" Espanoza frowned. "Bloop. Bloop. Bloop."

"For now," McCarthy nodded. "But once we do get the com systems dialed in you'll have HD video streaming right to your monitors."

A shrill noise sounded and Dr. Morganton leaned forward, her brows furrowing as one then a second of the blips on the monitor disappeared. She looked at McCarthy, panic in her eyes.

"What happened?" Espanoza asked. "Where did they go?"

"I...I don't know," McCarthy replied. "Their GPS transponders must have shorted or something."

"Or they disabled them," Diego Fernandez said, Espanoza's right hand. "Trying to make a run for it."

"With my product," Espanoza snarled.

"No, they wouldn't do that," McCarthy said. "They know what will happen to their families."

"What families?" Espanoza grinned, looking at Diego. "Send word. Kill them all."

Diego nodded and left the room.

Espanoza looked at the stricken faces of Dr. Morganton and McCarthy.

"What?" he asked, looking honestly perplexed. "They were warned."

Chapter Two: Submarino De La Muerte

Water streamed into the sub as John fought to regain control.

"Mayday!" John shouted into the com. "Mayday! I am taking on water and, well, uh…"

He looked at the two video monitors that still worked and shook his head.

"Uh…I'm under attack from a giant fucking shark!" he finished.

The video monitor showed the right side of the sub and the massive shark that gripped it in its jaws. The sub shook as the shark wrenched it back and forth, trying to saw through what it thought was a whale's body. Oil and hydraulic fluid leaked out around the shark's head, but it wasn't daunted as it dove, driving the sub deeper.

"John….me…teeth…," the faint voice of Bart said over the com.

"Bart! I can't hear you, man!" John yelled. "Are you alright? Talk to me!"

There was no response except for a loud burst of static. John ripped the headset off and threw it against the monitors. He tried to push more power to the propulsion system, but the sub was designed to look and act like a whale. The only way it moved was by its specially designed, undulating tail.

That wasn't going to fight off or outrun a shark the size of the one that had him.

John gripped the controls, his knuckles popping, and held on for the fast descent to the bottom as he heard the hull around him groan and warp.

***

"John!" Bart shouted. "John! Can you hear me?"

There was no response. The com was dead. And as Bart watched his cockpit fill with water he knew he was dead soon too.

Unless…

He let go of the controls as his eyes found the depth gauge.

"Shit," he muttered as he watched the depth increase from 500 feet to 550 feet to 600 feet rapidly. "I better do this now."

He popped open a small compartment in the floor, grabbed a rebreather and a pair of hand fins. Not having the bottom halves of his legs made flippers useless. He settled the rebreather over his head and onto his shoulders, strapping the apparatus around his chest and back.

650 feet, read the depth gauge.

"Fuck," Bart muttered as he put the mouthpiece in.

He tucked a hand fin into his belt then reached up and twisted four bolts in the cockpit hatch. He yanked hard on a lever then slammed it back home and the hatch exploded outward. Cold ocean water rushed in at Bart and he held himself steady until he was completely immersed.

Then he slipped on the other hand fin and pushed himself up and out of the sub.

He was an ex-SEAL, and trained to fight his fear, but his wet suit became suddenly warm as he pissed himself at the sight of the shark that had his sub gripped in its jaws and was steadily pushing it towards to bottom of the ocean.

The thing had to be over sixty feet long. It was an impossible creature.

Bart knew his sharks well enough to quickly see that the thing wasn't a great white. He had no idea what the hell it was.

He took a large breath from the rebreather, oriented himself towards the surface, and started to swim, glad for the strength the hand fins added. But they weren't the same as flippers on feet. In a minute, he was exhausted and had to struggle to control his breathing.

He slowed himself, very aware that if he surfaced too quickly he'd get the bends and nitrogen bubbles in his blood stream would end up in his brain. That would be bad. Deadly bad.

***

The sub, and monster shark, came to a crashing halt as it smashed into a formation of volcanic rock. Frustrated by the lack of blood from its prey, the shark thrashed its head back and forth, desperate to tear open the faux whale's belly.

But instead of the delicious red that it sought, out came a steady stream of white. The shark chomped over and over, crushing the subs cargo hold, releasing kilo after kilo of drugs into the Pacific Ocean. The white powder dissolved quickly in its new saline environment, mixing perfectly with the seawater.

The shark pulled back, alarmed by the strange substance that filtered through its massive gills. The drug raced through the creature's bloodstream and the shark whipped about, its senses heightened to a level that even science couldn't have imagined.

Sixty feet of drug fueled shark sped through the water, ready to eat every damn thing in sight.

***

Suddenly, Bart had other bubbles to worry about than just the nitrogen ones in his bloodstream. Huge air bubbles rose from below. They slammed into him, bursting around his body, and he was surprised to find that when they broke, the water became milky white.

The cocaine.

Bart figured the shark must have finally ripped through the sub's hull and into the cargo hold. All of those kilos of cocaine were now leaking into the Pacific Ocean. Bart stared as the bubbles kept coming, then grew even more alarmed because he suddenly realized the water was too murky for him to see.

That meant he wouldn't know if anything was coming at him.

He said fuck it to worrying about the bends and started to swim as fast as he could.

Digging deep, pulling from his training, he reached above with his hand fins and stroked over and over. He'd once been offered special flippers that could strap to his shortened legs, but he'd refused out of pride. He felt like an idiot for that decision as he could have used the extra speed right then. But that was a worry best left for when he got out of the water.

And Bart actually believed that was possible as he rose higher and higher, his arms screaming with exhaustion.

He spread his fingers as wide as possible in the hand fins, hoping for more lift, but it didn't matter, his muscles were nearly spent. The cocaine bubbles continued to burst around him and he almost wished he could get some, if just for the energy boost.

But none of that mattered, not the exhausted muscles or the fanciful coke wishes, because from his right side came a nightmare. He was so focused on swimming, and waiting for the attack from below, that he never even saw the shark that came at him from the side. The shark hit him at full speed and Bart felt his pelvis shatter, his ribs crack, his flesh tear from bone.

Water streamed into his lungs as the rebreather mouthpiece fell away from his lips and the bright red of his life drained quickly into the ocean, turning the cocaine clouds from white to pink.

***

"What the hell do the cartels want with a mom and her two little kids?" Max asked as he kept the Wrangler at a safe following distance from the black pickup.

"I don't know," Shane replied. "Kinda weird, though, that this John Sherman guy is recruited by another ex-SEAL and now a cartel hit squad is tailing his wife."

"Ex-wife," Max corrected.

"Yeah, you're counting on that, aren't you?" Shane smiled.

"Fuck you, bro, she was a nice lady," Max said.

"And she didn't freak at your horrid appearance?" Shane asked.

"Fuck you, Patchy McPatcherson," Max responded. "She did not."

Shane shrugged. "Yeah, she's probably seen worse. She was married to a SEAL who got his legs blown off. Makes your lack of an ear and melty skin kinda weak."

"Hey, my melty skin is plenty scary, dude," Max said. "Don't knock the fear factor my face has."

"Are you taking pride in your hideousness now?" Shane laughed.

"I am a unique human being," Max said. "I am beautiful because I exist."

"What the fuck is that?"

"Some self-help book Aunt Marsha sent me when I first got back from Afghanistan," Max replied. "It really helped me with those rough few nights."

"Dude, some fat bowls of Northern California Lime Haze is what got you through those nights," Shane countered.

"Oh, right," Max smiled. "Speaking of…"

"Got it right here," Shane said as he opened the glove compartment and grabbed a box of rifle cartridges.

He opened the box and picked out one of the cartridges. He unscrewed the "bullet" and tipped the cartridge. Out came a very thick joint. He flipped the joint to his mouth, catching it easily between his lips despite the wind that whipped into the open topped Wrangler, fished for a lighter in his pocket, then sparked the joint, drawing deeply.

"Nothing like following a cartel pickup while smoking a fatty," Shane said, smoke billowing from his nostrils.

Max reached for the joint, but Shane took another drag before handing it to him.

"Jesus, bro, you hogged half of this," Max said, looking at the joint before taking his own long drag. He coughed a little then let the smoke slowly escape from his mouth.

"It was a stressful morning," Shane said, tapping his eye patch. "Turns out you can't grow eyes back. Who fucking knew, right?"

"Fucking medical system," Max said, taking another drag. "Thanks, Obama."

"Damn liberals not being able to let me regenerate my eyeball," Shane said. "I blame all the pot they smoke."

"Damn skippy, dude," Max coughed.

"Whoa," Shane said. "Where are they going?"

"The freeway," Max replied. "Shit."

"Get up closer," Shane said. "Fuck being casual. If they are going to do more than just follow, they'll do it on the freeway so they can escape fast through the chaos."

"What we got back there?" Max asked, hooking a thumb over his shoulder at the covered and locked cargo area of the Wrangler.

"Oh, we got something deadly, I'm sure," Shane said as he undid his seat belt and crawled into the back.

***

The shark's jaws were so large that when it bit all the way down, Bart's body split in half, crushed by several tons of pressure per square inch. The monster shook its head a few times then opened wide and gulped Bart's top half down in one swallow. It worked its jaws a some more, just to make sure it got every bite, then turned its attention to the lower half. It dove as the truncated legs sunk quickly to the bottom.

The drugs that filled the water passed through its gills and the shark felt a surge of energy it couldn't even comprehend. With a massive thrash of its tail, it covered the distance to the sinking legs in a millisecond. The taste of the flesh was like nothing it had experienced. Every drop of blood, every ounce of meat, was like bliss as the drugs turned the shark's hunger up to eleven.

But it wasn't the only enhanced creature in the ocean.

So busy enjoying the new sensations the drugs brought to its brain, the shark didn't notice its brother in fins rushing toward it from below.

That shark, the one that crushed Bart's sub and first found the delights of drug-filled gills, saw only a meal before it, not a fellow member of its genetically cloned species.

The two behemoths met nose to nose in a cartilage crushing collision of teeth and drug fueled rage.

***

Shane casually assembled his .338 MacMillan sniper rifle as Max roared up the on ramp to I-5.

"Are we worried about police?" Max asked, tossing the roach out of the Wrangler as he glanced over at Shane and the large rifle in his lap.

"I don't know, are we?" Shane asked, twisting the barrel into place. He reached behind him and grabbed a full magazine, one of ten in a case on the backseat, and slapped it home. "Personally, I think we're good."

Max shrugged. "If you say so, bro."

"I do," Shane smiled, resting the rifle against the dashboard.

They passed a station wagon filled with kids and Shane waved. The kids saw his eye patch and the rifle and just stared.

"They're passing the minivan," Max stated. "They'll come along side and open fire."

"You think they have guys in the bed?" Shane asked. Two men with sub-machine guns popped up from the pickup's bed and turned their weapons on Helen's minivan as they got parallel with the vehicle. "That answers that."

Shane stood up and braced his legs and feet against the side door and his seat. He settled his rifle on the top of the Wrangler's windshield frame and sighted through the scope, placing the crosshairs directly on one of the shooters.

"Try to keep it steady," Shane said.

"Will do," Max said. He didn't bother trying to close the distance between the Jeep and the pickup, since the four compact cars in front of him didn't make a difference to Shane. With the scope he had, it would be like reaching out and lightly kissing the man in the crosshairs.

Shane gently squeezed the trigger and the break happened almost as a surprise like always. The man's head centered in his scope was vaporized.

"Oh, that was pretty," Max said then cringed as a mist of blood coated the windshield.

The cars in front of the Jeep, and directly behind the pickup, swerved and braked, causing Max to yank the wheel hard to the left.

"Hang on!" Max shouted.

"Hanging on!" Shane replied as he grabbed onto the windshield frame.

The other cartel shooter, his face streaked with his dead comrade's blood and brains, whipped his sub-machine gun around and opened fire, sending a spray of bullets into the midday traffic.

Max floored the Jeep and raced around the panicked drivers, dodging a Prius here, whipping around a BMW there. A convertible VW Beetle slammed on its brakes, blocking the brothers' way, and Max had a split second to make a decision.

"This isn't going to be fun!" Max shouted as he rammed the Jeep's reinforced front bumper into the back of the Beetle.

The smaller car crumpled like paper and was shoved up onto the concrete divider to its left. Max never took his foot off the gas, just kept driving until they pushed through.

"How's it look?" Max asked as the Wrangler got clear.

Shane, having been knocked down into his seat, stood back up and looked over the hood of the Jeep. "Thumbs up, dude. A little twisted, but then so are we."

He put the sniper rifle back to his shoulder, but this time he rested the forestock on his doorframe as the Wrangler came parallel with the cartel pickup. They were separated by two lanes of chaotic traffic, but Shane didn't really care. He sighted, let out a breath, and broke that bitch, placing a .338 caliber slug dead center in the second shooter's chest.

The man flew backwards, his gun firing up into the air, then tumbled over the side of the pickup. His body was crushed under a Volvo and as Shane looked away from his scope, he could see the driver screaming at the top of her lungs.

"This isn't going to work out well for us, is it?" Shane asked.

"You mean cops?" Max asked.

"I mean cops," Shane responded.

"No, we're pretty much fucked," Max said. "Despite our heroic rescue."

The driver side window of the pickup truck rolled down and a TEC-9 sub-machine gun was shoved out. Its barrel barked fire and lead. Shane ducked down behind his door, glad the brothers had modified the Wrangler's panels with armor.

Slugs whined off the Jeep and Max growled.

"They're fucking up my ride, bro," Max said.

"Our ride," Shane replied.

"More my ride since you can't drive worth shit with only one eye."

"That's because I'm still training my depth perception," Shane countered.

"More like training pussy excuses," Max laughed.

"Want me to pluck out your eye? Then we'll see how you drive."

More slugs hit the Jeep and Max pointed over at the pickup. "How about you fucking pluck out that asshole's eye?"

"Sure thing."

Shane waited until the gunfire stopped, then jumped up, secured his rifle, and squeezed the trigger. The pickup truck swerved back and forth then fishtailed out of control. It smashed into another pickup then got its rear bumper tagged by a semi that tried to speed past it. The pickup flipped up into the air, rolling side over side, then came down with a brutal crash of metal and plastic.

"I think we won," Shane said. "But I don't see your girlfriend's minivan back there."

"She probably took the first exit," Max replied. "Hopefully."

"If she's heading home then she's driving right into another ambush," Shane said as he sat down and pulled out his phone. "I'm calling Uncle Vinny. He can get her address."

"Shit, hold on," Max shouted as he swerved around a car that had come to a screeching halt. "All good."

"I hate you boys," Thorne said when he answered his phone. "Part of being retired is I get to nap in the middle of the day. It becomes hard to accomplish that napping when my nephews keep calling and waking me up!"

Shane looked over at Max. "Did you already call him today?"

"Yeah. Is he pissed you woke him up?"

"Like really pissed."

"Say you're sorry."

"Hey, Uncle Vinny," Shane said. "Sorry to wake you up again, but we kinda need some help."

"With what?" Thorne asked.

"Just need an address for-" Shane looked at Max and raised his eyebrows.

"Helen Sherman," Max said. "Ex-wife of the SEAL I called him about earlier."

"Helen Sherman," Shane said into the phone. "The ex-wife of the SEAL Max-"

"I know who she fucking is," Thorne snapped. "I just talked to your brother like a half an hour ago. I'm trying to take a nap, not recover from amnesia."

"Sorry," Shane said.

"Do you need it right this second?" Thorne asked. "Or can I take a shit first?"

"Uh, well, we're sorta in a hurry," Shane responded.

"Of course you are," Thorne sighed.

A news helicopter flew over the freeway and Max nodded his chin towards it. "Tell him to turn on the TV. That should hurry his old man ass up."

"Uh, yeah, you may want to turn on the TV and put it to the local news," Shane said. He pulled the mouthpiece away and looked at Max. "He's turning on the TV."

"Thanks for the play by play."

There was a loud groan in Shane's ear then, "Boys, what the fuck have you done?"

***

The cockpit of the sub was completely filled with seawater and John had to fight the urge to take a breath. His lungs were desperate for oxygen, but his training overrode nature, keeping his lips firmly sealed until he was able to finally wrestle the rebreather free of the small compartment it was stuck in. He gratefully put the mouthpiece between his lips and exhaled his stale air then took an almost ecstatic breath. Stale air had never tasted so good in his life.

After getting the rebreather secured over his shoulders and around his chest, John found an emergency pack and snapped a couple of glow sticks, then tried to see what systems still worked in the sub. It took all of three seconds to realize none of them did except for a few gauges that didn't rely on power to work.

One of those gauges was the depth meter. Steady at 675 feet.

So why did the sub still feel like it was moving?

John braced himself as the sub shuddered and shook as impact after impact began to cave in the hull. He watched in horror as the cockpit started to shrink around him and the right side buckled before his eyes. Scrambling to the main hatch, John was only able to get two bolts in position before the hull was breached and a nightmare of teeth tried to chew its way inside.

The water in the cockpit clouded immediately and John looked about him as the seawater took on a milky green hue from the glow sticks. The teeth worked at the metal of the hull, gnawing continuously, determined to widen the hole. John shoved himself as far away as possible, but the cockpit was barely bigger than himself, so there was nowhere to go.

He compartmentalized the terror that threatened to overtake him and looked up at the main hatch again. It was his only shot.

He flattened himself against the side of the cockpit and reached up, turning the third bolt into place then the fourth while his eyes stayed glued on the beast. When the fourth bolt clicked home he looked up and found the handle, pulled it down, then shoved it back in place.

The explosive bolts only sent the hatch about a foot and a half away from the sub before it crashed to a stop. John realized the sub must have gotten wedged under a large outcropping or some rock. The space wasn't big enough for him to get through with the rebreather on. He took a deep breath then worked the apparatus up over his head and shoulders.

John squeezed his body through the hatch, one hand still holding the rebreather. He was able to wiggle all the way out and found he was indeed crammed under a rocky outcropping, but he couldn't get the rebreather out also. He didn't have the leverage to twist it correctly and the back kept getting hung up on the hatch. He tried and tried, but he was quickly running out of air.

He pulled the mouthpiece to his lips and sucked hard, filling his lungs with usable air once more. But that was the last breath he was able to take as the shark ripped into the cockpit and the teeth tore the rebreather from him.

John kept the panic at bay and hurried out from under the outcropping and away from the sub. His eyes went wide as he saw the rest of the shark's massive body sticking out from the sub, its head wedged firmly into the hole in the cockpit. White bubbles billowed out of the cargo hold and John realized the cocaine kilos had torn and were mixing their contents with the ocean.

No hand fins, no flippers, just skin and muscle, John swam as far and fast as he could, angling his body upwards. It was dark at the depth he was at and the surface was only a faint glow above. His chest started to burn and he knew he didn't stand a chance of making it to the surface alive.

So he dove back to the sub.

He reached the cargo hold, and shoved his arms through the breach, yanking out kilo after kilo of cocaine until he found a couple still intact. Spots formed in front of his eyes and he knew he only had seconds left as he swam the few feet to the thrashing shark. The monster's jaws, and most of its head were still wedged into the cockpit, but it thrashed so hard that John knew it would be free soon.

He couldn't let that happen.

Getting right next to it, John jammed the kilos of drugs into one of the shark's gill slits. He reached to his belt and pulled the short dive knife he kept strapped there then jammed the blade into the plastic-bagged drugs. The skin on his bare arms was rubbed raw as he brushed against the shark's hide, but he ignored the pain and kept stabbing the bags, allowing them to open directly into the shark's gills. His hope was to OD the massive thing.

Surely, a couple of kilos of pure Columbian cocaine could kill the beast?

The monster bucked and heaved then tore free from the sub. It whipped its head at John and he suddenly found himself without his right arm. And most of his torso.

No longer in control of himself, his mouth opened wide and his lungs filled with ocean water.

The last sight he saw was the shark's own mouth opening wide.

The last thought he had was of his children and his ex-wife.

The last prayer he had was that none of what he'd done would blow back on them.

Then it was over in one final chomp.

***

"Can you text the address to us?" Shane asked.

"Yeah," Thorne replied over the phone. "But with the way the police scanners are screaming, you won't make it to the woman's house before San Diego PD catches you."

"Uncle Vinny thinks SDPD will take us before we get to your girlfriend's house," Shane said to his brother,

"Challenge accepted," Max smiled as the Wrangler screamed down the I-5 off ramp and onto Clairemont Drive. Cars and trucks honked their horns as they threw on their brakes to avoid the Jeep. "Where are we going?"

"Linda Vista," Shane replied. "She has a townhouse there."

"Oh, I know right where that is," Max said. "Remember Tatiana? That exotic dancer I was trying to get with?"

"That was a man, dude," Shane said.

"It was not," Max protested. "Did you see the tits on her?"

"Did you see the bulge below?" Shane replied, shaking his head. "I can't believe you never figured that out."

"My tongue was in her mouth," Max replied. "I can't undo that."

"Good kisser?" Shane asked.

"BOYS!" Thorne roared into the phone. "Shut the fuck up and pay attention!"

"Sorry, Uncle Vinny," Shane responded. "I'll hang up now."

"No, wait!" Max shouted. "The other guys!"

"Hold on," Shane said. "Don't hang up yet."

"What now?" Thorne asked. "I need to get off the phone and make some calls. I have a feeling I'm going to cash in every favor I'm owed to keep you two from going to prison."

"The two other guys that McCarthy recruited," Max said. "If they have families then they'll be in danger too, right?"

"Good catch," Shane said. "Hey, Uncle Vinny? You'll need to use a couple of those favors to get some police to the other two recruits' families. If this shit is all connected then the cartel will hit them as well."

"Fuck," Thorne replied. "Fine. Can I go now?"

"Sure thing," Shane said. "Talk to you later if we aren't dead."

"Jesus...," Thorne swore. "Try not to get killed, please?"

"We can try," Shane said, bracing himself as Max whipped around a corner onto a one way street. "But Max is driving so no promises."

***

Mike kept the sub at 500 feet and pushed it as hard as the thing would move. Adolescent blue whales top out at twenty miles per hour, but the sub could only manage fifteen. Mike didn't care, as long as he was moving away from the hell behind him.

He couldn't get the image of what he saw in the monitors out of his mind. Sharks. Really fucking big sharks.

He'd lost com with Bart and John a while back, but at that point he was more concerned with himself than the other two sub pilots. Either they made it or they didn't. SEAL brotherhood was strong, but so was the instinct to stay alive. Which brought a very critical thought to mind.

Did he still try to rendezvous with the cartel's fishing vessel or not?

All of his systems still worked and he watched his navigation system specifically as he piloted the sub into US waters, passing the international boundary without a problem. Certainly a lot faster and easier than the land crossing in Tijuana. After a mile, a beep sounded and his GPS showed a small dot about thirty miles out to sea.

The fishing boat.

But he also realized he was only fifteen miles from a place he knew well. A hidden place. A place he could call for help.

A debate raged in his head as he looked at the GPS map and the small dot then at the San Diego coastline and the other possible destination.

If he took the sub to San Diego, would he be able to get it where he needed? And could he get help before the cartel found him?

He stared at the screen for a few seconds more then made his decision.

***

"Are you seeing this?" Kinsey asked, sitting cross legged in front of Gunnar's huge flat screen TV. "Some psychos started shooting up I-5."

"They what?" Gunnar asked, looking up from the sandwiches he was throwing together for them both since the pancakes didn't work out so well. He sliced the two sandwiches, placed them on plates and hurried into the living room. "Where?"

"Here," Kinsey replied, seeing the sandwiches. "Hand me mine, will ya?"

"No," Gunnar said, setting the plates on the coffee table as he sat down on the couch. "You'll come eat over here so you don't get crumbs all over the carpet." He took a big bite of his sandwich and kept talking around the food. "And you're sitting too close. You'll ruin your eyes."

"I used to blow random guys for smack cash," Kinsey said, as she stood up, unwinding gracefully from the floor. "Ruining my eyesight doesn't even register as one of my worries."

"Well, it should," Gunnar said. "You need strong eyes if you want to stay on Team Grendel."

She sat down next to Gunnar, bumping him over with her hip, and picked up half a sandwich. She took a bite bigger than Gunnar's and focused back on the TV.

"They think it's drug related," Gunnar said.

"Yeah, I can read the ticker on the bottom," Kinsey said. "Turn it up."

Gunnar looked for the remote, but when he couldn't find it he stood up and searched the couch.

"You're sitting on the remote," he snapped, yanking it out from under Kinsey's ass. He was about to turn up the volume when the doorbell rang. "That must be the boys."

"Come in!" Kinsey yelled.

"It's my condo," Gunnar said as he turned up the volume too much. "COME IN!"

The news reporter's voice blared from the TV and Gunnar turned it down as the two of them watched a helicopter view of the carnage on I-5.

"Ooooh, looks like they found one of the cars," Gunnar said, pointing to the TV as the view changed from the freeway to residential neighborhoods close by. "Don't the boys have a Jeep like that?"

The doorbell rang again.

"COME IN!" Kinsey yelled. She nodded at Gunnar and watched the footage. "Yeah, they have a Wrangler. Silver, I think."

"That's funny because that one is silver," Gunnar said. "Probably a popular color."

The doorbell rang a third time.

"Oh, for fuck's sake!" Kinsey snapped and stood up quickly. "I left the door unlocked so they could just come in. I'm not going to be their butler while they are here."

"No, I'd hate for you to suffer that indignity," Gunnar smirked, waggling his sandwich at her.

"Shut up," Kinsey said as she wiped her hands on her jeans and walked towards the small entryway and front door.

Gunnar kept watching the footage as he took another bite. The helicopter camera zoomed in on the speeding Jeep, showing the distinctive paint job, and the bite lodged in Gunnar's throat. He turned towards the front door and started to yell, but only a choking sound came out.

Kinsey stopped and looked back at him. "You okay, Gun?" she asked then saw him choking and pointing at the TV. "Jesus, chew before you swallow."

Gunnar coughed out the piece of sandwich and Kinsey actually jumped as it flew from his mouth and splattered against the TV screen. Her eyes saw the smear of grease and mustard then focused past as the camera zoomed in closer and closer on the Jeep that was dodging between cars and running streetlights.

"Is that...?" she asked. "No..."

"That's what I was trying to tell you!" Gunnar said. "That's the-"

The rest of his words were drowned out as automatic gunfire turned the front door into splinters.

***

"Dude! Only a few blocks away!" Shane yelled. "Take a right here!"

Max yanked the wheel to the right then immediately to the left, taking the Wrangler up onto someone's front lawn as he avoided the two police cars that sped towards them.

"Fence!" Shane yelled as the Jeep ripped through the wooden slats like they were paper.

"Got it," Max grinned.

"Pool!" Shane shouted.

"I see it!" Max shouted back. "I have both of *my* eyes!"

"Uncool," Shane snapped.

Sirens filled the air as Max swerved to avoid the backyard pool and continued through the back fence, into an alleyway behind. He turned right and floored it, taking out several plastic trashcans and recycling bins, sending empty milk cartons and fat free Greek yogurt containers flying into the air.

They nearly made it to the end of the alley when the exit was blocked by four San Diego PD cruisers screeching to a halt. Max growled as he hit the brakes then slammed the Wrangler into reverse. Shane stood and started firing at the cruisers. He made sure the rounds only hit the dirt in front of the cars, not wanting to injure the officers, just keep them inside their cruisers.

"Fuck!" Max snapped as cruisers came at them from behind.

"Fence," Shane pointed.

"Fence," Max replied.

He put the Jeep back into drive and turned the wheel to the left, sending the Wrangler through yet another residential fence. No pool in the backyard that time meant he didn't have to slow

46

down as he took out the front gate and thumped across the lawn onto the next street. He didn't bother turning straight onto the road, but instead just kept going forward.

"How close?" Max asked as one more fence met a splintery end.

"Just another block over," Shane said, pointing ahead. "Actually keep going and we'll just run right into the place."

Max bumped up over the curb and sent the Jeep across another yard, thankfully a fenceless one. But the yard behind was fenced and it wasn't made of wood.

"Shit," Max said as he stopped the Wrangler in front of the wrought iron bars. "Is this it?"

"Right there," Shane said as he jumped from the Jeep, pointing at the back of the row of townhouses in front of them. "She's number seven."

Max reached under his seat and pulled out a .45 pistol, racked the slide and hopped from the Jeep also. The sirens grew louder and he knew they had maybe two minutes before the police were there. If they were wrong, and there weren't any cartel soldiers ready to ambush Helen and her kids, then the brothers were going to have a very hard time explaining their actions.

Not that it would be easy in any way, shape or form.

But that worry was quickly put to rest as bullets peppered the ground close to the Jeep.

***

The first man through the door met Kinsey's fist to his face as he raced into the condo. She spun him about, turning him back towards the other men that charged inside, and yanked the AK-47 from him with one hand while snapping his neck with her other.

The second man through the door ended up with his intestines spilling everywhere as Kinsey opened fire.

"Get back to my room!" Kinsey screamed at Gunnar as she held the trigger down, sending lead flying into the bodies of the cartel soldiers as they tried to get to her. "Lock the fucking door and get a gun!"

"I don't have a gun!" Gunnar shouted as he sprinted into the kitchen. "And I'm not leaving you!"

The AK clicked empty and Kinsey jumped onto the pile of men and flipped the rifle around, smashing it into the face of the next soldier that came through the door. He staggered and fell against the jamb, allowing the man behind him to get a clear shot.

Almost.

Bullets ripped through the man's side and into the wall next to Kinsey as she dove away from the door, rolled, and came up running, heading for the hall.

"What are you doing?" she shouted as she passed the kitchen and saw Gunnar yanking open drawers. "Come on!"

She reached in and grabbed his arm, pulling him out of the kitchen and back towards the bedrooms. More gunfire erupted and the corner of the wall exploded in a shower of plaster and drywall. Kinsey ducked and shoved Gunnar forward, but he didn't keep running, instead he turned and threw what was in his hand, just missing Kinsey by an inch.

The knife flew end over end then embedded itself in the shooter's throat. The man squeezed off a few wild rounds as he fell to his knees, choking on his own blood. He was shoved out of the way by more cartel soldiers and this time Gunnar didn't pause as Kinsey lowered her shoulder into his chest and pushed him down the hall.

They rushed into Kinsey's bedroom and slammed the door shut, then grabbed the long dresser and braced it between the door and the bed. The top of the door became riddled with bullet holes and Kinsey yanked Gunnar to the floor. She reached under the bed and pulled out a long black case. Hurrying through the combo on the locks, she clicked the case open and grabbed the M-4 carbine inside.

"Got any blades?" Gunnar shouted over the gunfire.

"There!" Kinsey yelled, pointing to the bedside table. "Plenty!"

Gunnar crawled over and opened the drawer. Several knives of various sizes and shapes were piled inside. He jerked the drawer out of the table and set it next to him as he stayed to the side of the bed while Kinsey slapped a magazine into her carbine.

"I only have the one!" she said to him. "Thirty rounds and we're done!"

Gunnar picked up a basic MK 3 MOD O knife typical of what the US Navy used, felt the weight in his hand, flipped it around his fingers quickly then looked at Kinsey.

"Then don't miss," he smiled.

"Are you enjoying this?" she snapped. "You better not be enjoying this!"

"I never get to be in the shit!" he replied.

"That's a fucking good thing, asshole!" Kinsey yelled as she chambered a round and put the carbine to her shoulder.

"Well, try being the gay scientist on a Team of ex-SEALS and see how you like it!" Gunnar yelled.

The top of the door was completely obliterated and one of the attackers shoved his rifle barrel through. Kinsey squeezed off three shots and the man screamed and fell away. He was immediately replaced by another man who met the same fate. Then another. And another. The men finally stopped trying to get through and stood back away from the door.

"Can we get out the window?" Kinsey asked, her eyes never leaving the doorway.

"No," Gunnar said. "No fire escape on this side."

***

The Reynolds boys were busy hiding behind the Wrangler when the first cruisers came up over the yard behind them. They tried to wave the police off, but they just kept coming. Right into the automatic rifle fire the boys were taking cover from.

The cruisers' windshields were puckered with bullet holes, the men inside jerking and shaking as they were ripped apart by heavy caliber slugs.

"Motherfuckers!" Max shouted.

The machine gun fire stopped and Shane rolled over onto his stomach, his rifle to his shoulder, one eye to his scope.

"Second floor, third window in," Shane said then rolled back just as the gunfire started up again. "I can take him."

"You suck," Max said. "You want your brother to die?"

49

"What?" Shane asked flinching as dirt kicked up into his face by a dozen bullets.

"You'll need a distraction so you can have time to set the shot," Max said. "And I'm the only distraction."

"Not quite," Shane said and nodded back to the police cruisers.

More came from the street and sped through the yard towards them. The trajectory of the gunfire changed and the cruisers screeched to a halt, then sped in reverse to avoid the dozens of slugs that rained down on them.

Shane took that second to roll back out and set his shot He squeezed the trigger then rolled back to Max.

The automatic fire stopped.

There was silence for a few seconds and Shane ducked his head out from behind the Wrangler. A shot hit the earth two feet in front of him.

"Pistol," Shane said, ducking back.

"9mm," Max said. "They must have only sent two here thinking the road crew would get the job done."

"WEAPONS DOWN! HANDS IN THE AIR!"

A SWAT team came running from the other side of the house the brothers faced, their rifles up and aimed at the two men.

"There's still a shooter!" Max yelled as he set his pistol on the ground.

"I got the other one, thank you!" Shane shouted as he laid his rifle carefully on the grass.

"On your faces! Hands laced behind your heads!"

More shots rang out and the SWAT team turned their attention to the townhouses. They scrambled for cover, which was the shot up cruisers behind the Jeep, and all hit the deck.

"Told ya there was another shooter!" Max said.

"I said to get face down with hands behind your head!" the SWAT commander yelled. "Do it! NOW!"

"Asshole," Max grumbled as he and Shane complied.

"I can take him out," Shane said. "See the big gun I have? That's called a sniper rifle. It shoots bad guys."

"Shut up!"

"Fuck you!" Max said. "We'll be here all day and there is a woman and her children that need our help!"

"I said shut up!"

"Fucking asshole," Max said. He looked over at his brother. "What now?"

They both heard the squawking of radios and looked towards the SWAT team.

"State your names!"

"Max Reynolds!"

"Shane Reynolds!"

There was more radio noise. Then hushed voices followed by, "Take the shot."

"Uh…what?" Shane replied.

"If you can take the shot then take the shot!"

"Cool," Max smiled.

"I'll need some cover," Shane said.

Three SWAT members leaned out from the cruisers and started firing towards the townhouse. Shane took his opportunity, grabbed his rifle, rolled away from the Jeep and took aim.

The shooter wasn't in the same window as the other one, but Shane quickly found him two windows down. The man ducked back as the SWAT members fired on him then leaned out quickly to return fire. He never got to duck back again as Shane took the shot.

Everyone waited for a couple minutes.

"Move in!" the SWAT commander ordered and the team rushed forward to the townhouses. "You two! Stay put!"

"Not moving an inch," Shane said as he got to his knees, his rifle held above his head.

The SWAT commander stomped over to them, his face pinched with rage.

"I don't know who the fuck you yahoos are, but you're lucky you have friends in high places."

"We're the Reynolds," Shane smiled.

"We have friends in high places?" Max asked.

***

"Fuck this," Kinsey said and stood up, her M-4 barking as she put several rounds through the walls on each side of the doorway.

Men screamed and bodies fell then there was silence.

"Fuck, Kins!" Gunnar yelled as he crawled to her and pulled her back down on the ground. "What the fuck? They could have shot you!"

"You hear anything?" Kinsey asked. "Because I don't."

She stood back up and grabbed a shirt off the floor with the barrel of her carbine. She inched forward and stuck it just barely out the door. It was ripped apart by gunfire.

"How many?" Gunnar asked.

"No clue," Kinsey said. "At least one. Maybe more."

"That's good math, Kins," Gunnar frowned.

"I'm not fucking psychic, dickhead," Kinsey snapped.

There was a crash outside the room then a gunshot followed by two more.

"Kinsey? Gunnar?" a woman's rough, gravelly voice shouted. "Talk to me."

"Darby?" Kinsey yelled. "That you?"

"It's me," Darby replied. "It's clear. Come on out."

Kinsey scrambled over the dresser, M-4 still in hand. At the end of the hall, standing over three bodies, was Darby, Ballantine's bodyguard and member of Team Grendel. Barely five feet tall, but muscular and looking like business was all she meant, Darby held a Beretta 92Fs pistol in each hand. She locked eyes with Kinsey and nodded.

"Good to see you," Darby said, her voice harsh from nearly being choked to death by a Somali pirate almost a year earlier. "Where's Gunnar?"

"Here," Gunnar said, peeking his head out of the bedroom.

"Good," Darby said. "We need to go."

"Go? Go where?" Kinsey asked.

"First, to pick up your cousins," Ballantine said, walking from the living room into the hallway behind Darby. Middle-aged, but fit, tan and built like he could handle himself, Ballantine stood there looking like a golf pro in his khakis and polo shirt. But Kinsey and Gunnar knew he was nothing so mundane. "We have a job. A big one. And not much time. Pieces have already started shifting on the board and we are a few moves behind."

"What about my dad?" Kinsey asked. "And the rest of Team Grendel?"

"All taken care of," Ballantine said, leading them outside.

Down in the parking lot was a MH-65F Dolphin helicopter. Primarily used by the Coast Guard's HITRON (Helicopter Interdiction Tactical Squadron) unit to take down possible terrorist threats to the US, which included drug smuggling, the Dolphin was fast, maneuverable, and in the hands of the right pilot and gunner, a deadly bird of prey.

"Wyrm II?" Gunnar asked as he saw the name stenciled on the side. Several of his neighbors were staring at the helo and Gunnar waved at them weakly. "Still holding onto that Anglo-Saxon poetry theme?"

"Oh, I wouldn't call it a theme," Ballantine grinned as he placed a pair of aviator sunglasses on. "More of an obsession, really."

***

The two teenagers sat on the decrepit dock, their arms around each other, the smell of pot and beer wafting off them. The boy leaned the girl back onto the boards, his hands fumbling about her shirt until she swatted them away.

"Come on," he whispered in her ear. "No one's around."

She pushed him back and shook her head. Even with a good buzz on, she knew she didn't want to do it there on a dock that was missing more boards than it had.

"No," she said. "We can do other things. But not that. Not yet."

"Okay, okay, that's cool," the boy said. "Want another beer?"

The girl frowned. "I'm not going to change my mind just because you get me even more…drunk…"

Her eyes went wide and her hand went to her mouth. The boy turned in the direction she was looking and his jaw dropped.

"Is that a whale?" he asked.

The whale moved up close to the old dock and then stopped. Forty feet of massive, blue mammal just floated there and the teens couldn't believe their eyes. It was even more unbelievable when part of the whale's back split and a hatch opened.

"Hey, either of you have a cell phone I could use?" Mike asked as he took a deep breath of the fresh San Diego air. "Hey! Do you have a cell phone?"

The girl fished around in her pocket and held out the phone.

"Can you toss it me?" Mike asked, pulling himself all the way out of the sub. "Kinda hard for me to climb up there right now."

"Dude," the boy said, leaning into the girl. "Was that pot laced with something? Because I think I'm seeing a legless guy crawling out of a fucking whale."

Chapter Three- Just One Fix

Chip left the white sands of the Baja Mexico coastline behind him as he raced through the Pacific Ocean swells on the rented Wave Runner. He laughed heartily, his body fueled by tequila and too much sun, as he hopped wave after wave, pushing the machine to its limits.

Behind him on his own Wave Runner, and not having near as much fun, was his friend Luther, a young man anxious to get out of the water and back to the cabanas of Playas Rosarito so he could drink a few pina coladas and just chill.

Luther was not a fan of the open ocean. He was also not a fan of sweating, working hard, or water on his face. Baja was not Luther's idea.

"Chip!" he shouted as ocean spray whipped him in the face, irritating him with every drop. "CHIP! Come on, man!"

Chip couldn't hear his buddy over the racing machine beneath him. He probably wouldn't have cared even if he had. Luther was there because he had a car and he had a sister with a rockin' bod. Oh, and the money to pay for a trip south of the border. Otherwise, Chip could do without the doughy mama's boy.

He hit a wave at a steep angle and soared into the air, twisting the handlebars to the side so the back end of the Wave Runner kicked out, sending a stream of water out behind him. He came down hard and didn't quite have the coordination, or experience, to stick the landing. Chip found himself flung from the Wave Runner and into the bright blue of the Pacific.

"Chip!" Luther yelled, gunning his Wave Runner as fast as he was comfortable with, which wasn't very fast, and aimed towards where his friend went under. "Chip!"

Other watercrafts and pleasure boats dotted the water all around them and several less than sober eyes were turned towards the young man with the too tight wet suit. Luther ignored the stares as he raced to the abandoned Wave Runner that bobbed along in the waves. Once there, he reached back and grabbed a towline then tossed it around Chip's Wave Runner.

"Chip!" Luther shouted.

"Right here, dork," Chip laughed as he slapped the back of Luther's machine. "That was awesome! Did you see that?"

"Yeah, I saw it," Luther said, glad he didn't have to call Chip's parents to tell them he was dead. "Can we go back in now? This wet suit chafes."

"That's because you need to lose a few, dude," Chip said. "I ain't saying you're fat, just that you need to work on your core, bra."

"Screw you," Luther said, shaking his head. "I'm going back."

"Ah, come on, I was just fucking with you," Chip laughed. "Chill out."

Chip swam over to his Wave Runner and struggled to get back up on it. Every time he tried to hook a leg onto the running board, he just slipped back into the water, too drunk to get a good grip. Luther shook his head some more and reeled in the rope so the Wave Runners bumped up against each other.

"I'll hold it while you get on," Luther said. "Then we go back to the beach. I'm hot and thirsty."

"You know who's hot and thirsty?" Chip said, still failing to get on. "Your sister, dude."

"Shut the fuck up," Luther said. "And stop fucking around. Get on the damn thing."

Chip slipped again, this time going all the way under the water. He came up spluttering, his eyes wide with fear.

"Holy fuck!" he cried. "There's something down-"

Luther didn't hear the rest as Chip disappeared under the water once again.

"Ha ha, asshole," he said. "I'm sick of your shit, Chip! Get up on the Wave Runner!"

Chip's response was to burst from the water thirty yards away, his arms flailing and mouth coughing blood.

"Fuck!" Luther yelled and turned his Wave Runner towards his screaming friend.

Blood spewed from Chip's mouth like a fountain of red. Then he was gone, taken back under. Luther stopped the Wave Runner and looked at the shoreline. He had seen what had a hold of Chip's bottom half. He wanted nothing to do with that.

It didn't take him long to decide between his loyalty to an asshole or his desire to stay alive. Luther let go of the towrope and gunned his Wave Runner towards the beach. He slammed across wave after wave, praying he was fast enough to outrun whatever it was he saw.

His Wave Runner launched into the air and Luther at first thought he must have hit a wave just right. But when he looked down and saw he was still going higher and higher, not because he launched off a wave, but because he was clutched in the jaws of the largest shark he'd ever seen, Luther shat himself.

The shark crunched down and the huge teeth ripped into the Wave Runner, and Luther's legs, before crashing back into the waves.

Luther screamed as he was dragged under. He thrashed about, trying to reach the shark so he could punch it in the nose like all the nature shows said to do, but his body wouldn't obey; the pain was too much. Water filled his lungs as the shark bit all the way through the Wave Runner, taking Luther's legs completely off at the thighs.

Choking, drowning, dying, Luther tried to use what faculties he had left to swim to the surface, but he no longer knew which way was up. All around him he was surrounded by his own blood; the water was clouded and dark with it. He gasped one last time, topping off his already water filled lungs, blinked, then began to sink to the bottom. He twisted and could see the sand below him.

There were crabs. He liked crabs.

Then it was all gone.

***

The girls screamed as they watched the shark fall back into the water. The man piloting the speedboat thought they were just having fun as he zipped and zoomed across the blue water. He always knew having a boat would be they way to get the gringas to pay attention to him. Seeing their tight American bodies crammed into those tiny bikinis was worth the night shifts and weekend hours he had to work to pay for the boat.

Hands started slapping at his shoulders and he turned, his sunglass-shaded eyes looking the blonde up and down.

"What's up, chica?" Hector grinned. "Having fun?"

"There's a shark!" the blonde screamed. "It just ate a guy!"

Hector frowned at her and slowed the boat. "A shark? I don't think so. I haven't seen a shark in these waters in years."

"There!" one of the other girls screeched. "Oh, God! It has someone else!"

Hector looked where the panicked girl pointed and ripped his sunglasses off his face so he could get a better look. Only fifty yards away a boy was being shoved through the water, half his body swallowed inside the massive jaws of a shark that defied logic.

"Ay dios mio," Hector whispered.

"Get us out of here!" another girl screamed. "Take us back! TAKE US BACK!"

"Yeah, yeah, no problem," Hector nodded and turned back to the wheel.

He gunned the throttle and spun the boat back towards the Playas Rosarito pier. It took all his strength not to concentrate on the water in front of him and not the water behind. If he looked back and saw that shark again, he was certain he'd freeze up. How'd that look in front of the pretty gringas?

"It's coming!" the blonde screamed, her hand pounding his back. "Hurry!"

"I am!" he shouted, swatting back at her. "Stop it!"

The blonde, in shock and scared for her life, didn't stop, just kept pounding on Hector and screaming at him to go faster. He was fine until she grabbed his arm, causing him to swerve violently.

"Knock it off!" he shouted, shoving her away.

And right off the boat.

The girls screamed for him to stop, but Hector had no intention of doing that.

***

As the boat sped away from Vanessa, she couldn't believe it was all happening. She'd saved up all year to go on the summer trip to Baja with her friends. It was her last fling before senior year at UCLA.

But all of her dreams, hopes, aspirations, disappeared in one chomp as the shark came at her from below, taking her entire body into its mouth before falling back to the water. Vanessa's blood actually spurted from the shark's gills as water rushed back through them.

***

Hector heard Vanessa's scream, even over the roar of the boat motor and the shouts of the other girls, but he didn't slow down. He kept the throttle pushed and aimed the boat for the closest pier.

But his path was quickly blocked as a fifteen foot wide mouth opened before his precious boat. He swerved to the side, sending two girls flying right at the shark. The shark's mouth clamped down as the girls flew inside. Blood was everywhere and Hector tried not to throw up, but the vomit wouldn't be held back.

He puked all over himself as he changed directions and hit the throttle again. Yet the boat started to slow, not speed up and Hector slammed his hand against the throttle over and over. The motors whined and then he smelled smoke. He whipped his head around and screamed as he saw the shark that had its jaws clamped onto the dive ledge.

Hector cut the motors and looked around for something to use as a weapon. One girl was still onboard, and when he couldn't find anything large enough to hit the shark with, he decided to distract it.

"WHAT ARE YOU DOING?" the girl screamed as Hector picked her up and threw her over the side.

She screamed her head off. Then her head actually came off as the rest of her was swallowed whole. Hector shrieked as the head popped up into the air, spinning over and over until it landed right next to him. He tried to kick it away, but lost his footing.

And fell into the water.

Blood. That was all he could see. Blood.

It was so thick he never saw what came at him from the side, killing him instantly as it crushed his body like he was hit by a Mack truck.

***

The other vacationers on the water started slamming into each other as they panicked and tried to get their watercrafts back to the shore as fast as possible. Hunks of fiberglass filled the water along with terrified tourists that splashed and screamed as they were pulled under one by one, sometimes two by two, by chemically driven eating machines.

The monster sharks gorged themselves, oblivious to the plastic taste of sunblock and silicone implants.

***

Gunnar looked at his phone and shook his head.

"Same number?" Kinsey asked, shouting over the roar of the helo's rotors. "Who the hell is it?"

"I don't know," Gunnar replied as he adjusted the microphone on his headset. "I don't recognize the number."

"We're here," Darby said from the pilot's seat. She brought the helo around in a tight circle then slowly lowered it to the street below. "Five minutes."

"Thank you, Darby," Ballantine said from the co-pilot's seat. "We won't be long. Kinsey?"

"Yeah, what?" Kinsey snapped. Ballantine raised his eyebrows at her tone. "Sorry. Shitty day."

"I can imagine," Ballantine nodded. "It would have been considerably more shitty if I hadn't arrived with Darby, don't you think?"

"Yes, thanks," Gunnar said.

"Right," Kinsey nodded. "Thanks."

"Care to join me so we can fetch your cousins?" Ballantine asked, looking at Kinsey.

"Sure," Kinsey replied as she yanked open the door and jumped down from the helo.

"Sis!" Shane yelled.

"Kinsey, my binsey!" Max shouted as the two brothers casually leaned against a SWAT van, several angry looking police officers glaring at them.

"My binsey? What the fuck is that?" Kinsey asked as she shoved through the police officers and hugged Max then Shane.

"Fuck if I know," Max grinned. "Rhymes with Kinsey."

"It's not a word, dude," Shane said. "You can't just rhyme shit. You have to use actual words."

"Fuck those rules, snules," Max said.

"It's good to see you two," Kinsey smiled.

"It is," Ballantine said. He looked around at the chaos of the scene and shook his head. "I'm looking forward to the story that goes with this mess."

"Oh, it's a story," Shane said. He frowned at the helo. "Nice ride. Wyrm II? Really?"

"Your services are needed," Ballantine said, ignoring Shane's comment. "Or, Team Grendel's services are needed, to be more precise."

"About fucking time," Max said. "It's been almost a year. You don't call. You don't write. We were beginning to think our time with you meant nothing, Ballantine."

"It hurt, man. It hurt," Shane added. "Use us, abuse us, and toss us aside."

"There have been logistical issues to work out with the company," Ballantine said.

"You talked to Ditcher?" Max asked Kinsey.

"We will be meeting Captain Chambers shortly," Ballantine said, gesturing to the helo. "So, if you don't mind, we are in a hurry."

"Whoa, whoa, whoa," Max said. "What about the Wrangler?"

"Can't make us leave his baby here all by herself," Shane said.

"Your Jeep will be taken to the San Diego PD impound lot," Ballantine said. "It is part of a police investigation."

"So are these two assholes!" a man snarled as he stomped up to Ballantine. "And they have quite a few more questions to answer before they are released!"

"I think not," Ballantine said, looking at the man's nametag. "Sergeant Velasco, is it? You'll want to speak to your captain. I am sure she will explain everything to you."

"She has," Velasco snapped. "And I don't care. These jokers shot up a pickup truck on I-5!"

"It had it coming," Max said.

"Shouldn't have let those bad guys ride in it," Shane added.

"Sure, pickups get mixed up with the wrong people, we get that," Max said.

"But that's no excuse," Shane continued. "It should know better. Those guys were obviously cartel."

"Stupid pickup," Max said, shaking his head.

"What the hell is wrong with these guys?" Velasco asked, looking from one brother to the other then at Ballantine.

"It's a mystery of science," Ballantine smiled. "I'll take them off your hands now. Thank you for babysitting."

"He wanted to have his boyfriend over, but we said we'd tell Mom and Dad," Max said, pointing at Velasco.

"And we didn't get our snack," Shane frowned. "Shittiest babysitter ever."

Velasco just stood there, eyes wide, mouth hanging open.

"Right," Ballantine said, clapping the brothers on their shoulders. "Shall we? Thank you, Sergeant, for your cooperation. The service you do for our citizens does not get enough credit."

They left the sergeant with his men as they hurried into the helo.

"Darby!" Shane shouted as she started the rotors back up. "How the fuck are you, killer?"

Darby gave him a thumbs up then looked back at Max.

"Maxwell," she croaked, her voice even more throaty as it was filtered through the headsets.

"Maxwell?" Shane asked, looking at his brother. "Is there something I don't know?"

"Nope," Max said, winking at Darby. Her upper lip twisted with the small hint of a smile as she took the helo up.

"Wow," Shane said. "My brother Max is the player today."

"How'd you find us?" Max asked Ballantine.

"Same way I found your cousin and Gunnar," Ballantine said. "Vincent Thorne."

"Right," Shane said. "That's how he got the info to us so fast."

"He called you," Max said. "Good thinking."

"It was," Ballantine said.

"So where to now, boss man?" Max asked.

"We fetch your uncle," Ballantine said. "Then rendezvous with the rest of the Team and crew."

"Crew?" Kinsey asked. "You mean the Beowulf crew?"

"Precisely," Ballantine said. "I do apologize for the limbo I have put you in, but I needed to make sure the Beowulf III was perfected before I could even consider placing any of your lives in danger again."

"Perfected?" Kinsey asked. "Does that mean shark proof?"

"It does, Kinsey," Ballantine said. "I have spent a lot of political capital over the last few months to turn the Beowulf III into the greatest shark hunting vessel in history."

"Does it have a water slide?" Shane asked. "Because if it doesn't have a water slide then you have failed, Mr. Ballantine."

"Lay off," Max said. "This isn't funny. This is serious."

"Thank you, Max," Ballantine nodded.

"A water slide would take up the space needed for the Jacuzzi," Max said. "And it would stick out like a sore thumb. Duh."

"Right. My bad," Shane nodded.

"I have missed you gentlemen," Ballantine said. "It's never boring with you two around."

Gunnar's phone rang again and he shook his head.

"Answer it," Kinsey said.

Gunnar pointed to the roof of the helo. "Too loud. Whoever it is finally left a message. I'll check when we land to get your dad."

"Five minutes," Darby said, banking the helo sharply.

"Not the weekend we expected, huh?" Max said to Kinsey.

"Still good to see you guys," Shane added, smiling at Gunnar.

"You too," Gunnar nodded as his phone rang one more time. "Jesus!"

Darby banked the helo the other way then circled an apartment complex for a minute before setting down in the large parking lot where Vincent Thorne stood waiting.

"Convenient that a helicopter can land in your parking lot," Ballantine said, shaking the man's hand as he climbed into the helo.

"Not so much convenience as just good planning," Thorne said.

Max and Shane shook their uncle's hand and then looked over at Kinsey.

"Hey, Daddy," Kinsey said, leaning across them to hug her father.

"Hey, baby," Thorne said. "Been too long."

"I did invite you for dinner last month," Gunnar said.

"True, you did," Thorne responded.

Gunnar's phone rang again.

"Dammit!" he snapped. "Who the hell is it?"

Ballantine tossed him an audio cord. "Plug it directly into your headset. You'll be able to listen to the voice message that way. Must be important if they won't stop calling."

Gunnar plugged his phone into the headset jack and played the first message. Everyone watched him as he listened, his eyes growing wider and wider.

"I appear to be right," Ballantine smiled when Gunnar unplugged the phone. "Care to let us in on the mystery?"

"We need to make a detour," Gunnar said. "There's someone we have to meet."

"That's not going to happen," Ballantine said. "We have a very strict timetable to keep."

"Monster sharks?" Shane asked.

"Monster sharks?" Max echoed.

"We need to make this detour," Gunnar replied.

"Michael Pearlman?" Thorne asked, looking at Ballantine. "Is that who called?"

"Yeah, how did you know?" Gunnar asked.

"How do you think we knew to come rescue you?" Ballantine said. "Commander Thorne contacted me as soon as the Reynolds needed help. One branch of the trail led to Mr. Pearlman, which led to you, Gunnar. As a former lover of Mr. Pearlman you were on a short list of possible targets by this cartel that has caused so much trouble today."

"He didn't say much, but I know where he is," Gunnar said. "He says he's in a lot of trouble and needs my help."

"Considering the day so far, I am sure he does," Ballantine said. "But first we get to the Beowulf III. Mr. Pearlman got himself into his situation and he'll have to hang tight for just a while longer." He held up a finger before Gunnar could protest. "If he is involved with what I think he is then we'll want the full Team as well as the resources the Beowulf III can provide."

"B3," Max said.

"Way shorter," Shane said.

Ballantine looked over at Darby and she shrugged.

"B3 it is then," Ballantine smiled. "Settle in, we'll be at the B3 in just a few minutes."

***

Chief Officer Martin Lake -mid-thirties, tight cropped black hair, brown eyes, a perpetual no nonsense look in those eyes-watched as the helo landed on one of the three helipads built into the upper deck of the Beowulf III. He made a quick announcement over the PA to the entire ship and 20 person crew that the Wyrm II had landed safely. About twenty meters longer and ten feet wider than the Beowulf II, the B3 could accommodate three helos at once, as well as four full sized enclosed lifeboats, four zodiacs, and two mini-subs. It was more equipment than Lake thought was needed, but Darren Chambers was the captain of the B3, and between him and Ballantine, there was no stopping the overkill.

"Wow," Chief Engineer Morgan "Cougher" Colfer said as he stood next to Lake on the bridge and watched the helo power down. His long, stringy black hair flopped in his face and he brushed it aside. Average height, he looked like he would be more at ease at a comic book convention instead of on a research vessel outfitted for Special Forces Operations. Only his suntanned skin and calloused hands betrayed the fact he was used to working hard on a ship and not sitting at a desk writing code all day. "We're really getting back in the shit, huh?"

"Yep," Lake said.

"You cool with this?" Cougher asked. "It didn't turn out so great last time."

"Last time we thought we were hunting Darren's whale," Lake said. "And ended up getting hunted by giant sharks. This time we're doing *all* of the hunting. We know what to expect."

"Yeah, right," Cougher laughed then honked a namesake cough into the crook of his elbow. "When it comes to that Ballantine guy I don't think we ever know what to expect."

Lake just shrugged as he looked down on the deck, watching as Captain Darren Chambers hurried up to the helo pad.

***

Late twenties, dirty blond hair, bright blue eyes, Captain Darren Chambers looked more like a GQ model than an ex-SEAL and Captain of the Beowulf III. The black t-shirt he wore hugged his muscles and stretched tight as he ran up the steps to the helipad.

"Hey!" he shouted as the helo's doors slid open and everyone piled out. "Welcome aboard the Beowulf III!"

"B3," Max said, shaking Darren's hand.

"There was an executive decision," Shane said, shaking Darren's hand next.

"Captain Chambers," Ballantine smiled. "I'll be in the briefing room."

"Howdy to you too, Ballantine," Darren said. "Darby."

"Captain," Darby nodded and followed Ballantine down to the deck and then up a set of stairs to the glass window enclosed briefing room just past the bridge.

"Hey there, son," Thorne said. "Good to see you."

"You too, Vinny," Darren said, shaking the man's hand and clasping him on the shoulder.

"Hey, man," Gunnar said and gave Darren a big hug. "Miss me?"

"You know it," Darren said. "Still a little pissed you didn't want to help design the lab on the Beowulf III."

"B3," Kinsey said, smiling at Darren. "Didn't you hear the boys?"

"Hey, 'Sey," Darren smiled back.

"Hey, 'Ren," Kinsey said.

"Oh, just hug it out, you two," Gunnar sighed. "You used to be married, for fuck's sake."

Kinsey and Darren hugged, each taking a deep breath and glad, in their own way, to be back in each other's arms.

"Okay, okay, I didn't mean all day," Gunnar said. "Can we get this meeting on with?"

"You bet," Darren said, letting go of Kinsey and gesturing to the stairs. "Lake has our course set for Baja. We'll be where we need to be in an hour."

"We're making a detour," Gunnar said. "I'll let Lake know and meet you two in the briefing room." He took off running to the bridge before Darren could respond.

"What the hell?" Darren shouted after him. "Only the captain gets to change course!"

"Whatever!" Gunnar shouted back.

Darren shook his head and looked over at Kinsey. "How you been? You look great. Healthy."

"Thanks," Kinsey said. "Gunnar has been a big help keeping me clean. I think that's why he didn't come help set up the lab. Didn't want to leave the junkie alone."

"Ex-junkie," Darren said.

"No, 'Ren," Kinsey said. "I'll always be a junkie. I went too deep to ever have 'ex' in front of my name."

"That include ex-wife?" Darren smiled.

"That happened before I started shooting, snorting, drinking, and swallowing anything I could get my hands on," Kinsey said. "That ex is grandfathered in on that one."

"Move ass, you two!" Max shouted from the briefing room door. "We got shit to kill and Gunnar's butt buddy to pick up first!"

"Dude!" Gunnar yelled as he stepped out of the bridge. "What the fuck? Bigot much?"

"Dude!" Max yelled back. "You know I'm kidding! Can't take a joke from a friend much?"

Gunnar flipped him off and went back into the bridge.

Kinsey laughed as she and Darren walked up the steps to the briefing room. She glanced into the bridge and Lake smiled at her.

"I'll come say hello once I get us turned around," Lake said.

"Hey, Kinsey," Cougher smiled.

"Hey, Cougher," Kinsey replied. "Popeye and Beau on board?"

"Yep," Cougher nodded. "Popeye's hobbling around aft and Beau is below deck."

"Cool," Kinsey said. "Talk to ya soon."

Darren showed her into the briefing room and Kinsey stared at the state of the art monitors that dropped from the ceiling, showing various videos and pictures of a bloody nightmare. The room looked more like a corporate boardroom, with expensive wood paneling and a conference table in the middle made from teak. The open side of the room was nothing but sliding glass doors that everyone filtered in through. The view out the doors was amazing and Kinsey marveled at the Pacific Ocean, glad to be on a ship again.

"Holy shit," Kinsey said. "This looks great."

"You can say that again," Lucy Durning said, getting up and hugging Kinsey. "But you're the one that looks great."

"Thanks," Kinsey responded. "You too."

Nearly six feet tall, wide at the shoulder, with a head of shockingly red hair, Lucy was an ex-shooter for the HITRON division of the US Coast Guard. But issues of improper advances by a superior forced her to leave. Not as trained in hand to hand fighting as the ex-SEALs, or small arms as Kinsey, Lucy was a sniper with skills that rivaled even the Reynolds brothers, and everyone knew she could hold her own in combat.

"Well, the gang's all here," Ballantine said, clapping his hands together. "Welcome back, Team Grendel."

"Are Darby and Ditcher included in that?" Max asked.

"Yeah, are they? Or is Darby still your girl Friday and Ditcher just our humble captain?" Shane asked.

"We need clarification," Max added.

"For peace of mind," Shane continued.

"Boys, shut up," Thorne said. "You're exhausting me and I've only been around you for twenty minutes."

"I'm no one's girl," Darby said, fixing her eyes on Max.

"He said it," Max responded, hooking a thumb at his brother.

"Dude, I think she was giving you a signal," Shane said, whispering loudly.

Darby just sighed and shook her head.

"Well, this has been plenty of fun so far," Ballantine said, pointing at the monitors. "But, out of the fire and into the frying pan."

"You got that backwards," Max said.

"Does it really matter?" Ballantine asked, his eyes cold steel.

"Uh, no?" Max replied.

"Exactly," Ballantine said. "Earlier today two very, very large sharks decided to feast on some tourists down off the coast of Baja Mexico." He stepped to the largest monitor and swiped his hand across the screen. A new image came up and everyone in the briefing room gasped. "They went on a bit of a feeding frenzy rampage, to say the least."

"Those the same sharks as we dealt with off Somalia?" Max asked, looking at Gunnar.

"The images are shaky and hard to make out, but I'd say yes," Gunnar replied.

"I agree with Dr. Peterson," Ballantine said. "And the intel I have gotten through back channels tells me they are the very sharks we are looking for, the clones of *C. Megalodon*."

"No sign of the pseudo *Livyatan Melville* in the area this time," Darren said.

"Oh, God, Ditcher," Shane said. "The whale? Again? Let it go, bro. No one cares about your Moby Dick when there're people-eating sharks getting all feedy with American tourists."

"As captain, I can have you thrown overboard," Darren frowned. "And don't call it Moby Dick."

"Why are we turning back to San Diego?" Lucy asked.

"I got a call from an old friend," Gunnar said. "He's in trouble and since his name came up with the whole cartel trying to kill us thing, I thought we should go see him before we get to Mexico."

"Normally, I'd argue that saving lives is more important," Ballantine said. "But the word from the company is that the two incidents may be related."

"The company going to stay out of our shit this time?" Thorne asked. "Or are they sending more observers to betray us just like last time?"

"Yes, that was unfortunate," Ballantine replied. "In more ways than you know, Commander. But I have been assured I have full autonomy with Team Grendel from here on out."

"Good," Thorne said.

"Where're we picking up your bud?" Shane asked Gunnar.

"Remember that old private marina we used to hang out at in high school?" Gunnar asked. "I took him there a few times when we were seeing each other. He said that's where we'd find him."

"And while we are making our way there," Ballantine said. "I think we should use our time to brush up on our megalodon trivia. Dr. Peterson, would you do the honors?"

"Me? Why me?" Gunnar asked.

"You are the marine biologist here," Ballantine said. "And I know you have been studying every ounce of data we've collected on these creatures."

"Been checking up on me?"

"I get an alert anytime someone logs into the company mainframe and accesses certain information," Ballantine replied. "It's a precaution. In your case, it's a nice surprise. I'm glad Kinsey hasn't taken up all of your attention."

"What does that mean?" Kinsey asked.

"Just that helping someone with recovery from substance dependence is not an easy task," Ballantine said. "It can also be a time consuming task since diligence is of the utmost importance. Wouldn't you agree, Ms. Thorne?"

"The sharks we are looking for are exact clones of a *C. Megalodon* fossil found in the Mariana Trench," Gunnar said, moving the conversation away from the conflict that was about to erupt as he saw Kinsey's face start to turn red with anger. "However, according to Mr. Ballantine, the outfit that did the cloning also messed with the shark's genetics. There was supposed to be only one, but the specimen escaped and turned out to be pregnant. We have no idea how many are out there currently."

"There are at least two off the coast of Baja at the moment," Ballantine said. "Possibly a third." He paused then shrugged. "Maybe a fourth."

"How do you know that?" Thorne asked. "Witnesses?"

"I haven't been idle while we've been apart," Ballantine replied. "Let's say there are more cogs in the machine than what you see here."

"But we don't get to know about those cogs, do we?" Thorne asked.

"Safer that way," Ballantine nodded. "And not everything is as black and white as I know you like, Commander. Let's just leave it at that."

"Anyway, as I was saying," Gunnar said. "If the rampaging sharks are like the ones we dealt with in Somalia, then they were created to be hunter/killers. They will attack without regard for their own safety. So I hope the B3 is up for this mission."

"It is," Darren grinned. "Titanium triple hull with anti-shark defenses."

"That's a thing?" Max asked.

"It is now," Darren replied.

"Cool."

"Yes, very," Ballantine said. "Dr. Peterson, please continue."

"As far as we know, megalodons didn't grow much longer than sixty or seventy feet," Gunnar continued. "But we all saw in Somalia that these cloned bastards can get a shit ton longer than that."

"That big mofo we took down was closer to 100 plus," Shane said.

"Yeah, it was," Gunnar agreed. "But that was the 'mother' clone. These should be 'adolescent' clones birthed by the 'mother' and not fully mature, so closer to sixty feet."

"Oh, just sixty? No problem," Max said.

"Scared, Reynolds?" Lucy smirked.

"Uh, no, shut up," Max said. "Are you?"

"Fuck yeah," Lucy said. "I still wake up screaming sometimes."

Everyone looked at her for a second, a little taken aback by the honesty, but one by one, they nodded in agreement.

"Okay, we all went through hell," Thorne said. "We had almost a year to get over it and pull it together. Now we suck it up and put it behind us. Anyone think they need more time can head down to the galley and help Beau peel potatoes."

"Don't do that," Lucy said. "The guy is still pissed he got ditched last time. I'd stay away from the mess and galley, if you can."

"What is for dinner?" Shane asked, ignoring Lucy's warning. "I haven't eaten in fucking forever." The look he received from his uncle shut him up quickly. "Never mind. I'm good."

"We don't know what all the genetic modifications to the sharks are since the company will not divulge that information," Gunnar said, looking at Ballantine to move along the conversation.

"My hands are tied on that one, Gunnar," he replied. "Sorry. Even an outfit like the company has to sign non-disclosure agreements. I have tried to get all the details, but even I have limitations." He smiled slightly. "But you know me and limitations."

"Dear God," Lucy whispered as she watched one of the monitors. It showed a shaky cell phone video of a woman being bitten in half by one of the sharks. The beast disappeared from view, but whoever held the phone, focused in on the severed torso bobbing in the water. "Please tell me this hasn't been uploaded to YouTube."

"I wish I could," Ballantine said. "But there was no way to contain it. The videos are all over social media. The lid is off the box and the Mexican government is not happy. They are our new client."

"Say what?" Max said.

"The company is a multinational conglomerate with a wide and varied client list," Ballantine said. "This wouldn't be the first time I've interacted with the Mexican government in my capacity as a company representative."

"We're almost there," Lake's voice sounded over the PA in the briefing room. "But the B3 is too big to get into the marina. You'll need to take a Zodiac in."

"Thanks, Marty," Darren said, standing up. "We done with school time?"

"Dick," Gunnar said.

Darren gave him a big grin and turned to leave the briefing room.

***

As the Zodiac sped across the water with Darren, Gunnar, Max, and Kinsey, with Shane driving, Mike sat on the edge of the old dock and waved to them, glad to know someone was coming to get him out of the shit he'd found himself in. The teens had long since bailed, and although reluctant to give it back, Mike had let them leave with the cell phone so he really had no idea if Gunnar was going to show or not. He was beyond grateful to see the man wave back.

The Zodiac reached the dock and everyone proceeded to ignore the man missing the bottom half of his legs; they were too busy staring at what floated in the water next to the dock.

"Hey, Ditcher, there's your whale," Max smiled.

"I'd tell you to fuck off, Max, but I don't really care enough to do it," Darren said. "What I care about is finding out what the fuck that thing is."

"I thought it was going to be an SDV," Mike said from above them. "But turned out to be a mule."

"That's a SEAL Delivery Vehicle?" Shane asked. "Uh, kinda dressed up, isn't it?"

"To sonar, radar, and pretty much to the eye, it looks like a blue whale," Mike said. "Which is why the cartels want it."

"Cartels?" Kinsey asked. "Which one, exactly?"

"Don't know," Mike said. "There's some guy named Espanoza running it. He's the one that sent us out in the subs with his coke."

"Coke?" Darren said. "There's coke in that?"

"Yeah," Mike replied, pulling his way over to the side of the dock where the whale was. "I'll show you."

He deftly pushed himself off the dock and onto the back of the sub, grabbing onto the cockpit hatch to keep from sliding off. He was lost from sight for a minute, then the cargo hold doors started to open on the back of the sub. Mike pulled himself back out and rested, pointing to the cargo hold.

"How much you think that is?" he asked.

Shane brought the Zodiac about and Darren climbed up onto the sub.

"Shit, that's got to be over a hundred kilos, maybe two," Darren said.

"Lookout," Max said as he climbed up also. "Dude, you don't know shit about eyeballing quantity. You're staring at almost a thousand kilos."

"Bullshit," Darren said.

"No, that'd be about right with how much weight this sub can carry," Mike said. "And that cargo hold isn't even full."

"Shit," Darren said.

"Not to be a dick, Mike, since it is good to see you," Gunnar said. "But what the fuck did you get yourself mixed up in?"

"Sorry," Mike said. "The guy said he wouldn't hurt our friends or family if we made the run. We agreed and were doing fine. Then it all went to shit fast."

"We? Who's we?" Darren asked.

"Let me guess," Max said. "John Sherman was one of the other guys?"

"Yeah," Mike nodded. "How'd you know that?"

"We saved his ex-wife and kids' lives today," Shane said. "Ruined some cartel thugs' plans."

"What went to shit?" Gunnar asked. "Where are the other subs?"

"I don't know where they are," Mike said. "I got the fuck out of there too fast to see what happened to them."

"Dude, you're gonna have to just come out with it," Shane said.

"You won't believe me," Mike said, looking at Gunnar. "I barely believe it."

"You called me for a reason, Mike," Gunnar responded. "Why? Because we were together a while back? Because you thought they'd come after me? Why?"

"Because I knew you were connected," Mike said. "And because you're a doctor of marine biology. If I tell you what I saw you'd know if it actually happened or if I'm crazy."

"Tell us," Gunnar pushed. "Now."

"Sharks, man," Mike said. "Giant fucking sharks. They came out of nowhere and I just kept going. Didn't look back."

Mike laughed and rubbed his face.

"I know, I know, what fucking shark could take down a sub this size, right?" he sighed. "A great white could hurt a whale like this, but this isn't a whale, it's a sub. I must just be crazy." He smacked his forehead. "And when I ran, Espanoza must have given the order to kill John's family and to go after my old boyfriends."

"Boyfriends?" Gunnar asked. "Are others in danger?"

"Probably," Mike said.

"On it," Darren said. He activated his com. "Ballantine? We have a problem. Mike Pearlman says there may be others that are in danger."

"Not to worry, Darren," Ballantine replied over the com. "The company has them under watch as well as Mr. Stern's mother. I'm nothing if not thorough."

"Good. Thanks," Darren said. "Oh, and have Popeye get one of the specimen bays ready. We'll need it."

"Already done," Ballantine said.

"Seriously? Okay," Darren said. "Chambers out." He looked at the cockpit hatch then Mike. "How many people can fit in there?"

"Just one in the cockpit," Mike said. "And only if you're like me. It's not designed for people with their whole legs. Something about hydraulics configuration. They needed the space by the cockpit in order for the body to swim right and actually look like a whale. One of you guys would barely be able to move in this thing."

"Fine," Darren nodded. "Then you get in there and pilot that thing to my ship. Does it have to submerge to move?"

"Yeah," Mike replied. "Otherwise the tail just splashes everywhere."

"Hmmm. Then this is going to be tricky," Darren said, activating his com again. "Hey, Marty?"

"What's up?"

"Gonna need divers to help get a whale into the specimen bay," Darren said. "But it's not really a whale, it's a sub."

"Why do I even ask what's up?" Lake sighed. "I'll have Popeye get the best divers from the crew down there. How much time do we have?"

"Like none," Darren said. "We're on our way back now."

***

It took six divers to help maneuver the sub into Specimen Bay #1, a fifty meter space close to the keel of the ship. On the other side of the keel was Specimen Bay #2. Darren had learned his lesson about where to put big, giant sea creatures after losing a shark and a whale in Somalia.

Once the sub was all the way in, the bay sealed up and the water was pumped back into the ocean. Mike popped the cockpit hatch and pulled himself out as the six divers took off their gear.

"Holy shite and shaboodle," Popeye said, looking down from a catwalk that ran the length of the bay. "That ain't something you see every day."

Boatswain Trevor "Popeye" De Bruhl looked just like the cartoon character he was nicknamed after. Short, thin, bald, with massive forearms that were covered in tattoos. All he needed was the corncob pipe. And a right leg. That he lost to a hunk of metal in the Indian Ocean. In its place was a segmented titanium rod that ended in a splayed piece of heavy-duty rubber. It was his new school, old school peg leg and he was quite proud of it.

The hatch at the end of the catwalk opened and Ballantine walked in with Darren.

"You weren't kidding," Ballantine said as he looked at the sub. "You must be Michael Pearlman."

"Call me Mike," Mike replied. "And could I get some help? Left my wheels back in Baja."

"I'll bet," Ballantine replied. "And you lost your legs in the Hindu Kush region of Afghanistan."

"How'd you know that?" Darren asked. "Did you already do your homework on him?"

"I always do my homework," Ballantine replied. "Especially when dealing with a headache like today. And seeing this submarine means my headache just got considerably larger."

Ballantine studied the sub for a long time from the catwalk as Mike was helped down and offered a wheelchair that Popeye was able to find in the infirmary.

"Was Dr. Lisa Morganton there with you, Mike?" Ballantine asked.

"Morganton? Yeah, she was," Mike replied as he was pushed to a hatch in the wall by the bay floor. "She invented these things."

Ballantine snorted and chuckled lightly. "Is that what she said? She invented the subs? Conniving cunt."

"Whoa," Popeye said, looking at Ballantine. "Don't think I've ever heard you say that, boss guy. You must really hate that broad."

"I only hate three people in this world, Popeye," Ballantine replied. "Dr. Morganton is not one of them. However, with the amount of hell she has put me through over the years, I would say the name 'cunt' is being kind."

"Oh," Popeye said. "Wouldn't want to be her when you two finally get face to face."

"No, you wouldn't," Ballantine said. "Please make sure Mr. Pearlman gets nowhere near the briefing room until I speak to him, will you, Popeye? I would appreciate that."

"Thorne wants him there right away," Darren said. "Since he has intel on the sharks."

"Commander Thorne is going to be disappointed," Ballantine said. "The man doesn't get near the briefing room until after I speak to him."

With that, Ballantine stormed out of the bay, the hatch slamming behind him.

"Damn," Popeye said. "Company man is ticked off."

"No shit, Pop."

***

Mike stared at Ballantine. Ballantine stared at Mike. The two men, one in a wheelchair, the other seated behind an ornate wooden desk, refused to yield and speak first. Darby was the one to break the silence.

"They are expecting us," Darby said. "You are wasting time."

Ballantine sighed. "What do you know about Dr. Morganton and the program she was working on?"

"Not much," Mike said.

"Then tell me the much you do know," Ballantine ordered.

"Just that she developed the subs so they mimicked blue whales and could get past anywhere without detection," Mike said. "Or at least, if they were detected, they looked like whales."

"She succeeded in that," Ballantine nodded.

"Yeah, no shit," Mike said. "They look so real they were attacked by sharks."

"It appears that way," Ballantine said. "Now, tell me about the cocaine. I've read your file. You aren't the type of guy that would get in bed with the cartels. This is out of character for you."

"Didn't have much choice," Mike said. "If we didn't, then they would kill our family and friends. We had to do what they asked or else."

"And who did the asking?"

"Um, some guy named Espanoza," Mike said. "He was scary as hell."

"Ricardo Espanoza?"

"Yeah, that's him," Mike said. "He kinda looked familiar, but I don't know why."

"I do," Ballantine said. He looked over at Darby and sighed. "It's time. Go get prepped."

Darby nodded and left the office quickly. Mike watched her go then turned back to Ballantine.

"Who is Espanoza?" Mike asked.

"A complication," Ballantine replied. "And someone you will not mention to anyone. Not to my Team, not to the crew, and not to Gunnar Peterson. Do you understand me?"

"Why do I have the feeling I'm back in an 'or else' situation?" Mike sighed.

"Because you are," Ballantine said. He stood up, walked around the desk to Mike, and took hold of the man's wheelchair. "Now, I am going to take you up to the briefing room where you will answer questions with generic answers only."

"Or you kill me," Mike said. "I get it."

Ballantine pushed Mike towards the office hatch. "No, Mr. Pearlman, I'm not that person. I just need your cooperation so others don't die. This is so much bigger than you. Can you help me with that?"

"Yeah, sure," Mike said as they left the office. "I just want to be done with all this shit."

"Soon you will be," Ballantine said. "And if I can hold things together, then maybe we all will be."

***

"This ship is huge. Has to be at least 130 meters," Mike said, sounding as casual as possible as Ballantine wheeled him into the briefing room. "What's it name again?"

"Beowulf III," Ballantine said as he parked Mike next to the conference table and then took his own seat. "And it's 125 meters."

"What happened to the Beowulf II?" Mike asked.

"We don't talk about that," Max and Shane said at the same time then high fived.

"Guys, shut up," Darren said then looked around. "Where's Darby?"

"She is handling some company business," Ballantine said. "Don't worry about her."

Darren and Thorne shared a look, not happy about one of the members of Team Grendel absent from the briefing.

"Ugh! This is going to break my brain!" Gunnar shouted. "I'm seeing something here, but I don't know what. There's a pattern of behavior with these attacks, but no matter how I analyze it, it's completely random."

"I've had the company run them through every possible scenario," Ballantine said. "The report came back as chaos. No true pattern, just frenzied attack after frenzied attack."

"Doesn't make sense," Gunnar said. "Sharks hunt, they don't go berserk. They are cold and calculating."

"If they are our monster sharks then they are different," Thorne said. "Something triggered them to act this way."

"What can you tell us about the subs?" Gunnar asked, looking at Mike. "Is there anything that the sharks could have come in contact with that would make them freak out?"

"I don't know anything about sharks," Mike replied.

"Yes, but you know about the subs," Gunnar pressed. "What are they made out of? What is that skin? It looks so real. Could it be such a good analog that that is what attracted the sharks? Maybe there's a compound in there that is pushing the sharks' aggression centers of their brains."

"Gunnar, I don't know," Mike said.

"There was," Kinsey laughed.

"How do you mean?" Gunnar asked.

"The two subs that were lost, were they running coke too?" Kinsey asked Mike.

Mike looked at Ballantine briefly before answering. "Uh, yeah, they were. I don't know if it was the same amount, but it was at least as much as was in mine."

Gunnar looked at Kinsey then over at Darren then turned and looked back at Mike.

"How'd you get mixed up in all of this, Mike?" Gunnar asked.

Another glance at Ballantine. "Long story," Mike replied. "We were just pilots. We thought we were testing some secret project. Not running coke. Honestly, I had no idea this would all happen."

"Shit," Gunnar said then let out a sad laugh. He glanced at Kinsey. "You don't actually think...?"

"I don't know," Kinsey said as she stepped closer to the monitors.

She studied the gory images for a couple minutes. Every time someone tried to talk, she snapped her fingers and growled. The briefing room remained quiet for a while.

"No fucking way," Kinsey finally said, laughing and looking at Gunnar. "I'm right."

"Right?" Ballantine asked. "Fill us in, please."

"The behavior has no pattern because there isn't one," Gunnar said. "It is chaos at its most basic. Except for the obvious pattern of behavior."

"Dude," Shane said. "Contradict yourself much?"

"How can there be a pattern and not be a pattern?" Max asked.

"Because they're fucking high," Kinsey said, stepping away from the monitors. "I'd know that behavior anywhere. Used to be an apartment of tweakers below me that would just run out into the street and terrorize cars. The fuckers just went nuts. Classic methamphetamine psychosis."

"This is cocaine, though," Max replied.

"Oh, right, my bad," Kinsey laughed. "Then I'm totally wrong. You know, since everyone here is an expert on coked out mega sharks, right?"

"Good point," Max frowned.

"There is nothing good about this, people," Gunnar said. "If the sharks attacked the subs, and ruptured the hulls, which we know they have the power to do, then they probably broke open that coke. It mixed with the water and they breathed it through their gills."

"What the fuck does cocaine do to sharks?" Shane asked.

"That, apparently," Max said, pointing to the monitors. "They go loco."

"Say hello to my little fin," Shane replied in his best Al Pacino as Tony Montoya voice.

"Gold, bro. Solid gold," Max said. "That was like spot on." The brothers high fived again.

"Boys?" Thorne asked.

"Yeah, Uncle Vinny?" Max responded.

"Shut the fuck up."

"Right. Sorry," Shane said.

Ballantine turned his attention to Mike. "And you don't know where the cocaine came from?"

"No, no," Mike replied. "Not a clue. All of a sudden we were told we had to move it north or bad things would happen."

Ballantine took a deep breath. "This twist complicates things. Lord knows what those beasts are capable of while stimulated."

"Darren?" Lake asked over the com. "You and Ballantine busy?"

"Define busy?" Darren responded.

"We're about to leave US waters and there are two Mexican patrol vessels steaming towards us on the other side of the boundary. Each has a Panther with rotors active," Lake replied. "I'd feel better if one or both of you was up here on the bridge with me. The boats are coming in fast."

"I bet they are," Ballantine said. He stood up, looked at Thorne, and pointed at Mike. "Get him below. Hide his ass. If any Mexican nationals board the B3, I don't want them finding him. Are we understood, Commander?"

"Not really, but I'll make sure he isn't found," Thorne said. "I know this boat pretty well."

"Take him to my lab," Gunnar said. "We can lock it down tight. No one can get in there if I don't want them to."

"What do you mean by you know this boat pretty well?" Kinsey asked her father. "When have you been on the ship?"

"Unlike you, I haven't been on rehab vacation, Kins," Thorne said harshly. "I've been working all this time since Somalia."

She watched as her father wheeled Mike out of the briefing room.

"You okay, 'Sey?" Darren asked, seeing the stricken look on Kinsey's face.

"Fine," Kinsey said through gritted teeth. "The asshole just can't help being…"

"An asshole?" Max finished.

"That's our uncle, dude," Shane said, punching him in the shoulder.

"And her dad, dude," Max replied.

Kinsey gave them a weak smile and walked out of the briefing room.

"Guys? Try to be a little more sensitive, okay?" Darren asked. "She's been through a lot."

He exited the room also and Max and Shane were left with Ballantine. The man shook his head and gave the brothers a big grin.

"It can be hard being the one that isn't batshit insane," Ballantine said, clapping them on the shoulders as he exited as well.

"Dude, did Ballantine just put us in the non-batshit category with him?" Shane asked.

"Yeah, I think he did," Max said.

"This place is so fucked."

"That it is, bro," Max replied. "Want to get the guns, climb into the crow's nest, smoke a fatty, and watch it all play out from on high?"

"You know I do," Shane grinned.

Chapter Four- Conflicts Of Interests

The two Mexican Navy patrol ships flanked the Beowulf III, each taking a side so the "research" vessel was boxed in.

Ballantine could see the impressive figure of Ricardo Espanoza standing on deck of the port side patrol boat, clad in black and dark grey camo fatigues.

"The coke isn't all that's going to complicate things," Darren said from Ballantine's side. "That guy is Mexican Fuerzas Especiales- Mexican Navy Special Forces. How do we play this?"

"Like always, Captain," Ballantine smiled big then waved at Espanoza. "Cool. With our fingers on the triggers"

"It would be handy to know where Darby is," Darren said. "What company business is she handling?"

"Business you don't need to worry about," Ballantine said. "So let it go."

"Fine," Darren said. "Whatever you say." He looked over at the other ship. "Are we going to get on with this and do our job? Or is this a game to see who blinks first?"

"It's always a game of who blinks first, Darren," Ballantine responded. "That's what life is. But, to answer your question, we are here to do our job. That job is to kill, or potentially capture, two, maybe three, possibly four, monster sharks. The most expedient way to do that is invite the commander onto the B3. Get everyone on the same page."

"Fine," Darren nodded. "I'll have Lake hail- Wait, a fucking minute!" Ballantine smiled as Darren finally heard what he just

MEGA 2

said. "Capture? Are you out of your fucking mind? We both know what those fucking things can do sober!"

"You realize you just referred to sharks and sobriety in the same sentence, right Darren?" Ballantine smiled wider. He reached out and gripped Darren's shoulder. Darren tried to pull away, but Ballantine was having none of that and pulled Darren in closer. "Don't you just love this job?"

Darren tried to be angry, tried to protest, tried all kinds of emotional indignation, but he just couldn't. When it came down to it, Darren did love his job.

"Nobody gets killed this time," Darren said. "We err on the side of caution."

"Of course," Ballantine said. "That's why there's Team Grendel."

***

Kinsey watched from the bridge, Gunnar by her side, her father on the other side, as Lake piloted the B3 as close to Espanoza's ship as possible.

"Anyone else have a bad feeling?" Lake asked.

"I always have a bad feeling," Thorne said. "That's why we're a shoot first kind of Team."

"Not today," Lake said. "You shoot first and those patrol ships will open up on us. The B3 will be ripped apart in seconds."

"Maybe," Thorne said. "Maybe not."

"You do see the 76mm on the bow of that ship, right? How about the M2 turrets?" Kinsey said. "Not impressed? Maybe that 30mm cannon on the stern will change your mind. There's no maybe not about what those guns can do."

"If they do fire, they better be lucky," Thorne replied. "Because this ship won't go down easily."

"What do you know that I don't?" Lake asked, obviously annoyed with Thorne's attitude.

"Just that I never plan on being on a sinking ship again," Thorne said. "And I made sure Ballantine knew that."

Gunnar looked from the commander to the CO and then at Kinsey. "Shouldn't you guys gear up or something?"

85

Thorne turned and frowned. "Shouldn't you be in that fancy lab of yours below deck with your boyfriend?"

"Right," Gunnar glared. "I probably should. Thanks for reminding me, Commander."

He gave Kinsey a pissed off frown then turned and left the bridge.

"What the hell is wrong with you?" Kinsey snapped.

"Nope, not gonna happen," Lake said, pointing to the hatchway. "No family drama on the bridge while I pilot between two Mexican naval patrol ships. New rule."

Kinsey stomped to the hatch and gestured for Thorne to follow. He didn't budge.

"We're going to have a chat," Kinsey said. "Now. Not negotiable."

Thorne focused on her, his eyes cold and blank. "Fine."

"Yeah, it's fucking fine," Kinsey said as Thorne stepped past her and out into the warm sea air. "Let's chat."

Kinsey walked to the aft observation deck and made sure no one was watching then whirled on her father, her fist coming up fast. Thorne took the shot to the jaw and stumbled back a bit. He shook his head, rubbed his jaw, and then smiled.

"This how we're going to chat?" Thorne asked.

"If it it'll get through to you, then yeah," Kinsey said.

"Okay," Thorne said as he rolled his head on his neck, the sound of vertebrae cracking like gunshots. He put his hands out, fists clenched. "You want to fight then we'll fight."

"I don't want to fight!" Kinsey shouted. "I want to know why you're being such a dickhead!"

Thorne watched her for a moment then lowered his hands. "You really don't know?"

"No!"

"It's too soon, Kins," Thorne replied. "Too soon for you to be out."

"Too soon?" Kinsey asked, puzzled. "Too soon how?"

"Your recovery," Thorne said. "You aren't ready for the field yet."

"How do you know what I'm ready for?" Kinsey asked, her hands on her hips, jaw stuck out defiantly.

"Because I'm Team leader of Grendel and it's my job to know," Thorne said.

"Daddy, I'm not a delicate fucking tea cup," Kinsey said. "I won't break. Not this time."

Thorne rubbed his face and his whole body seemed to deflate.

"You have no idea how many people in recovery say that," Thorne said. "You never trust a junkie to diagnose their own readiness."

"So when *do* you trust a junkie?" Kinsey asked.

"Never," Thorne replied. "But you learn to deal with that."

"Bullshit!" Kinsey shouted. "I'm not some horny sailor that got strung out on smack by a Thai whore! I'm not a fucking SEAL that came home to find his wife banging the neighbor and decided to dive into a bottle! I'm-"

"Different?" Thorne interrupted. "Every junkie thinks they're different, Kins. Every single one. That's what makes them exactly the same. You know why I've been cold and haven't talked with you for a while? Because I could have written this conversation down word for word. It's never different. Ever. At one point, I thought it would be, I thought giving you a job would get your head straight. But it's been time away from the life that's gotten your head straight. I don't want to mess that up."

"But it is messed up," Kinsey said, getting her father's face. "I act like it's all good, but it's not. Know what could help make it good? If instead of distancing yourself, you actually got involved. I could have used my father these past few months. I could have used your support, your friendship, your love. Instead, I got the 'busy with work, we'll talk soon' emails and texts. You were too chicken shit to be there. You decided to just lump me together with all the other junkies and write me off."

"I never wrote you off," Thorne growled. "Not ever. You of all people should know that."

"Oh, because you resigned when my blood work came back positive for amphetamines?" Kinsey asked, her head cocked, defiant. "This again? You resigned to save your own reputation, not to save mine."

"You think that's it?" Thorne asked. "It's all of this! I brought you into Team Grendel to get you clean, to get you thinking straight. Then it all went to shit. We all nearly died. I couldn't protect you."

"I didn't need you to. Risk of death is part of the job," Kinsey said. "You shouldn't have brought me in if you didn't want me to be at risk."

"It's not that," Thorne said. "It's when we got home. When I dropped you off at Gunnar's that last time…"

Kinsey watched her father for a minute then took his hand. He flinched at first, but relaxed into Kinsey's grip.

"What is it, Daddy?"

"I dropped you off, drove two blocks, and watched a drug deal happen right there in the open," Thorne snorted. "On a street corner in La Jolla. The *good* part of town."

"It's SoCal, Daddy," Kinsey laughed. "There is no good part."

"Yeah, I realized that," Thorne said. "It just all hit me so hard. I'd lived in the insulated world of the Navy for my entire adult life. Drugs happened, people fell apart, but it was the Navy. There was structure; rules and regulations in place to handle everything. But there is none of that in the real world."

"Okay, you aren't wrong there," Kinsey said. "I wish you would have just told me, instead of bailing. But it is what it is. However, that doesn't explain the sudden assholeitis you came down with today."

"We're back in the routine," Thorne replied. "Back with Team Grendel. And even though it is crazy, it still should have some of that structure. But it doesn't. Even out here, even chasing monster sharks, there're still drugs. I can't shield you from them in real life or in our work life."

"Oh, Daddy," Kinsey laughed, hugging him tight. "You don't have to worry about me. You want a deterrent from doing coke? Watch some of those videos down there. Ballantine should have the company sell that shit to the networks. Have kids watch that and they'll stay off drugs forever."

"So, I'm just being a stupid old man, is that it?" Thorne grumbled.

"No," Kinsey said, pushing back so she could look him in the eye. "You're just being a father worried for his daughter. Probably the most natural thing in the world." She stuck a finger under his nose. "So don't go AWOL on me again, got it? No more of that bullshit, frogman."

"No more of that bullshit," Thorne nodded then sighed. "I should probably apologize to Gunnar, huh?"

"Probably," Kinsey said. "But later. Gun does some of his best work when he thinks people are mad at him."

"He does?"

"That's what Darren has always said," Kinsey smiled.

They hugged again and then Thorne turned and hustled to the lower deck, ready to join Ballantine and Darren.

***

Max and Shane passed the joint back and forth as they sat in the crow's nest, their sniper rifles resting across their laps.

"Gets ya right there," Max said, pounding his chest, his eyes on Kinsey below.

"No shit, bro," Shane replied after a long drag. "Those two, man. Too much love, too much pride."

"That's why we never argue," Max said. "I hate you and have zero pride in myself."

"Me too," Shane said. "You are the bane of my existence." He held up the joint. "And I try to cover my own self-loathing in a haze of the pot."

"You two are idiots," Lucy said as she climbed the ladder to them. She handed her .50 caliber rifle to Shane then punched him in the leg. "A father and daughter have a touching moment and you make fun of them? Jerks, both of you."

"Oh, please, shooter," Max said. "Those two have been practicing that dance our whole lives."

"Longer," Shane said, taking another drag. "If you consider the possibility of reincarnation."

"I don't," Max said. "I'm a firm believer of one and done."

Lucy sighed and smacked Max on the leg. "Shut up and move over."

The brothers made space for her in the crow's nest. Shane offered her the joint after he gave her rifle back, but she waved it off.

"I'm not as experienced as you two," she said. "One toke and I'd be asleep. Or talking about reincarnation. Low tolerance."

"You actually have a higher tolerance when you start out," Max said.

"True fucking story," Shane nodded, handing the joint to his brother. "Pot doesn't act like other drugs. You can train your mind to use it, not abuse it."

Lucy nodded down at Kinsey who stood by the railing and stared out at the transport vessel. "Try telling her that."

"Sis? No, no, she was deep into the heavy shit. Heroin, meth, pills," Shane said. "We don't touch that. Barely drink."

"Except for a good beer or glass of wine," Max said. "Organic preferably."

"And we keep this away from her," Shane said, taking the joint back from Max. "Only smoke if we're up here in the crow's nest."

"Yeah, we could totally hotbox the whole ship if we lit up below deck," Max said.

"Which would be an interesting thing to try," Shane added.

"Are you two hippies or SEALs?" Lucy laughed.

"We are complex men with complex tastes," Max smiled as he licked his thumb and forefinger and put out the joint then tucked it into his pocket.

"Speaking of complex," Shane said. "Looks like things are about to get going.'"

***

The ships steamed to a stop and all dropped anchors. Darren watched as Ballantine and Espanoza faced off across the waters.

"He doesn't look happy," Darren said.

"He never looks happy," Ballantine replied. "But he's tolerable."

"Wait? You know him?" Darren asked. "Who is this guy?"

"He's corrupt, ruthless, and lacks compassion for anyone or anything," Ballantine said. "He'll slice your belly open in front of a crowd of people without batting an eyelash. And no one will question him for it."

"Jesus," Darren said. "That's just great."

"What's great?" Thorne asked, walking up next to them.

"Ballantine was just informing me that the commander over there is basically a Mexican wolverine," Darren said.

"Will he piss on everything he has just to make sure no one else will take it?" Thorne asked.

"Without hesitation," Ballantine replied.

"Good," Thorne said. "Those are the easy ones to deal with."

Ballantine kept his eyes on Espanoza while Darren turned to look at Thorne.

"What was all that shit up there?" Darren asked. "You and Kinsey okay?"

"We are," Thorne said.

"Not going to implode while we need you two to bring your A games, are you?"

"Have you ever seen me without my A game, Darren?" Thorne asked.

"No, I haven't," Darren said. "But there's a first for everything." He looked at the observation deck. "She going to be alright with all that coke down below deck? That's quite a temptation."

"I think she'll be just fine," Thorne replied.

"I never wanted her on this Team, remember?" Darren said. "You insisted."

"I know," Thorne said in a voice that stated the conversation was done.

"Well, this has been fun, but how about we get down to business?" Ballantine said, cupping his hands to his mouth. "Hello! Shall I come over there or would you prefer to meet on my ship?"

"*My* ship," Darren said.

"Shut up," Ballantine replied. "Captain."

"We shall meet aboard your ship, Mr. Ballantine," Espanoza shouted back. "I am looking forward to a brief tour."

"As am I, senor," Ballantine smiled then turned to Darren. "Lock the decks down. He only sees the briefing room."

"He going to be okay with that?" Darren asked. "He did say he wanted a tour."

"Then he'll have to be disappointed," Ballantine said.

***

Espanoza watched the videos of the shark attacks off the coast of Playas Rosarito. He nodded and sighed then turned to Ballantine who was seated at the conference table.

"I have seen all of these," Espanoza said. "Why waste my time?"

"Because we believe the sharks may be on a cocaine binge," Ballantine said. "Crazy, I know, but then I work for a company that specializes in crazy."

"Cocaine?" Espanoza frowned. "You must be joking?"

"I enjoy a good ribbing as much as the next man, but not today," Ballantine said. "People are dying. That is not funny to me."

"How in the name of God could sharks be high on cocaine?" Espanoza laughed. "Are *you* high on cocaine?"

"If I was, I wouldn't tell you," Ballantine said. "But I'm not." He pointed at the monitors. "Those things are. You wouldn't happen to know how that could be possible, would you?"

"The cartels have smugglers running up and down Baja," Espanoza shrugged. "Perhaps the sharks found a sunken narco sub? Perhaps they each ate a tourist that had coca inserted in their rectums? There are many possibilities. None of them matter because the idea that sharks are high on cocaine is absurd, Ballantine. You are wasting more of my time with this fantasy."

"Do you have a better explanation?" Ballantine asked.

"If I did then I wouldn't be here, would I?" Espanoza glared.

"Neither would I," Ballantine said. He gestured towards Thorne and Darren who were seated at the conference table. "Please tell us what has already been done to get the situation under control. And how we can help before we get down to what we do best."

"We have evacuated the beaches and the waters along the coast," Espanoza said. "No more people will die today. So there really is no need for your assistance."

"Except that's not up to either of us, is it, Ricardo?" Ballantine said.

"Commander," Espanoza replied. "That is my rank."

"I can see that by your pretty epaulets," Ballantine grinned as he stood up. "Congratulations on your promotion. Never thought that would happen."

"Ballantine…," Espanoza warned, looking at his officers that stood by the wall of the briefing room. "Please show respect."

"Look, Ricardo," Ballantine said as he took Espanzoa by the shoulder. "The company has told me to cooperate with you. Your government has told you to cooperate with me. We both know what a farce this is, right? Let's not pretend anymore. We do our jobs and go our separate ways when it's all over, okay?"

"Yes, of course," Espanoza said. "That is what I would like. Our separate ways."

"Good," Ballantine said as he let go of Espanoza and clapped his hands together. "Tell me more about this cocaine that could be up some tourists' butts."

"I don't know what you are talking about," Espanoza replied. "I am here to deal with sharks. Sharks that a client of yours created." He smiled at the brief look of surprise on Ballantine's face. "It's a small world, Ballantine. News travels fast in the naval circles. A private group takes out pirates and blows up a monster shark and you expect it to stay quiet? Not when that same group is then called in to be a thorn in my side."

"A man can hope," Ballantine said. "And I don't think Commander Thorne here appreciated your use of that analogy."

"Leave me out of this," Thorne said, his arms crossed.

"I wish I could, Commander," Espanoza responded, turning back to the videos on the monitors. "But while one man wishes, other men act."

"So we can proceed to Playas Rosarito?" Ballantine asked. "Unmolested and unimpeded?"

"Why, of course," Espanoza said. "Today we are allies."

"Aren't we always allies?" Darren whispered to Thorne.

"Great," Ballantine said, looking over at Darren. "Captain? Please inform Chief Officer Lake to steam us down the coast."

"We will accompany you the entire way," Espanoza said. "As support."

"We invite all the support we can get," Ballantine said. "Isn't that right, Commander?'

"Yeah," Thorne said. "We invite it."

"Anything you'd like to add?" Ballantine said, looking from Thorne to Darren. "Before we get going?"

"I'm good," Darren said.

"I wouldn't mind that tour now," Espanoza said. "I have heard of the many special modifications made to your ship. It would be a privilege to see them first hand."

"And you believe they are still there?" Ballantine asked. "The sharks?"

"I know they are still there," Espanoza replied. "I have made sure of it."

"You have?" Ballantine asked. "How have you managed that?"

"We are feeding them," Espanoza said. "They are fond of cattle."

"You're feeding them?" Thorne exclaimed. "Are you insane?"

Espanoza bristled at the insult, but took a breath and let it slide.

"We are launching a carcass into the water every thirty minutes to see if the sharks have left the area. They have not. In fact, they seem to be staying put for now. Both of them."

"Well, yeah, sharks will do that if you feed them," Darren said.

"Just two?" Ballantine asked.

"Just two," Espanoza replied. Ballantine frowned.

"Then why not blow them out of the water yourself?" Thorne asked.

"I have been instructed not to," Espanoza said, glaring at Ballantine.

"We all have our orders," Ballantine said.

"In some ways," Espanoza said then nodded and left.

The Mexican officers followed Espanoza from the briefing room as Ballantine returned to the table and took a seat. He watched them go then turned his attention to Darren and Thorne.

"That was a little enigmatic. I wonder what that could mean," Ballantine said. "In some ways…"

"Don't know," Darren said as he stood up. "I'll let you two worry about that. I'll be on the bridge with Lake."

Darren left and Thorne looked at Ballantine then at the video monitors.

"We better be going to kill these fuckers, Ballantine," Thorne said. "Not capture them. You hear me? Darren told me of your less than assuring chat. We blow these fuckers out of the water. I'm not putting my Team through Hell again."

"Life is Hell, Commander," Ballantine replied. "Sometime we get to choose which part we live in and sometimes we don't."

"Cut the fatalistic poetry," Thorne snapped. "The techs have our gear ready?"

"They do," Ballantine said. "I made sure of that before picking you up. Right now, though, I have them focusing on our little secret below."

***

"Not that one!" Carlos yelled.

Short, squat, with a thin, black Mohawk, Carlos slammed his hand against the hull of the whale sub as he peered inside the cockpit. He wore a ratty t-shirt that once had the X-Men logo on it, but was so faded it was hard to make out. A roll of fat folded over the waist of his jeans and he absentmindedly tugged at the hem of his t-shirt to cover it.

"Stop," Ingrid said, shoving Carlos out of the way. "Don't yell at Moshi."

The opposite of Carlos in many ways, Ingrid was tall, skinny, and had long, bright green pigtails that were braided up around the back of her head. She wore a bright yellow jumpsuit that fit her perfectly. Her white blue eyes glared at Carlos then looked down into the cockpit.

Below was the ever silent Moshi. Black hair in a bowl cut; short, but not squat like Carlos, with dexterous fingers that flew across the controls of the sub. Moshi shrugged off the annoyances above and focused solely on the task before her.

"I wasn't yelling," Carlos said. "I was telling her not to turn a dial that obviously has to do with the bilge system of the submarine. If she turns the dial while the sub is dry docked then that could harm the pumps! And since we know nothing about the construction of this vessel we could end up rendering it non-operational!"

"Now you're yelling at *me*," Ingrid said. "Stop that."

"I am not yelling at anyone!" Carlos yelled.

"Problem?" Ballantine asked from the catwalk above. "Trouble with my elves?"

"WE ARE NOT ELVES!" Carlos roared. "You refer to me as an elf again, or as the armory as the 'Toyshop', and I will quit immediately!"

"We both know you can't do that, Carlos," Ballantine said. "So stop threatening it."

"Whatever," Carlos fumed.

"Any progress?" Ballantine asked.

"Some," Ingrid replied. "Moshi seems to be figuring it all out. It would be easier if we could all get down there, but Moshi is the only one small enough to fit and still move."

"Have you cracked the navigation system yet?" Ballantine asked.

"Have we?" Ingrid asked, looking down at Moshi. The timid woman shook her head. "No. Not yet."

"Let me know when you have," Ballantine said. "We need to be able to backtrack the sub's passage and find out where it originated from."

Ingrid gave him a thumbs up.

"Are we in Mexican waters yet?" Carlos asked.

"We are," Ballantine responded. "We'll be to the site in less than an hour. Is the equipment ready?"

"Yes, the equipment is ready," Carlos snapped. "Had it ready the moment you told me what we were doing and where we were going."

"Excellent," Ballantine nodded. "I'll expect you to show the operators what they will be using when the time comes."

"Ugh," Carlos said. "Can't Ingrid do it?"

"I'd love to," Ingrid said enthusiastically.

"No, I'd prefer you did, Carlos. You are such a better people person," Ballantine said. He looked down and noticed the cargo hold was open and the cocaine was removed. "Uh, might I ask where the hell the drugs have gone?"

"Gunnar," Carlos said. "He wanted to run tests. I told him to knock himself out."

"He took it all?" Ballantine asked. "Why would he take it all?"

"Sampling," Ingrid said. "He wanted to test each and every kilo for consistency."

"Oh," Ballantine nodded, not looking happy. "Well, I better see what he has found."

***

"You're pissed," Mike stated as he sat in the wheelchair, out of the way of Gunnar.

"Maybe," Gunnar said as he grabbed another kilo from the pallet resting in the corner of his lab. "I don't have time to really think about it. I have work to do."

"It's not like we were serious, right?" Mike asked. "We had a good thing, but it was casual."

Gunnar snorted.

"What? It was," Mike insisted. "You had your whale thing with Chambers and I had the SEALs. Neither of us could commit."

"If that's what you want to tell yourself," Gunnar said as he dropped a spoonful of cocaine into a test tube. He capped it, shook it, then set it into a centrifuge. "Whatever gets you through life."

"Oh, good one," Mike said. "Throw my words back at me."

Gunnar turned on him. "Listen, this *us* shit will have to wait, okay? You can sit there and be quiet or you can get the fuck out of my lab. But we aren't doing this right now."

"Just once I'd like to walk into a room on this ship, or on deck, or into a bay, and not have to listen to drama," Ballantine sighed. "Is that so much to ask from a group of people that are supposed to be professionals? Do you hear me airing my dirty laundry every five minutes? No, you do not."

Ballantine looked over at the pallet of coke.

"I would also like to be advised when a ton of drugs is moved about on my ship."

"It's Darren's ship," Gunnar said. "He's captain."

Ballantine sighed again and walked over to counter where Gunnar was working. "Debatable, as always. What do you have for me?"

"Nothing yet," Gunnar said. "Every sample I test shows up the same. This is pure cocaine. Uncut, unadulterated. You have any idea what this is worth?"

"Probably more than you do," Ballantine said. "But my knowledge of its market value is not what I'm interested in. Can this cocaine cause the sharks to act the way they are? That's what I *am* interested in."

"Sure," Gunnar said. "Why not? People lose their shit on this stuff all the time."

"But we aren't dealing with people," Ballantine said. "We're dealing with genetically altered sea life." He looked over at Mike. "I suggest you keep that information to yourself."

"Not a problem," Mike said. "I'm used to keeping secrets."

"Even taking into account the sharks' altered genetics," Gunnar said. "My opinion is still that this cocaine is causing the erratic behavior of the sharks. We need to hunt the creatures down as fast as possible. Considering how deadly they are when not high, these monsters could end up eating everything in the ocean."

"No need to hunt them down," Ballantine said. "Apparently they are staying right where they are."

Gunnar stopped what he was doing and looked at Ballantine. "How? Sharks this size would have scared off all food sources in minutes. They could be anywhere now."

"They're being baited," Ballantine said. "With cows."

"Cows?" Gunnar asked. "They're just dumping cows into the ocean?"

"That is what I have been told," Ballantine shrugged.

"Okay," Gunnar said, turning and leaning against the counter. "This is good. Keeping them fed could slow them down while they digest. It may also counteract some of the stimulant effects of the cocaine. Tell the Mexican navy to keep it up. How often are they feeding them?"

"Every thirty minutes," Ballantine replied.

"Thirty? No, no, that won't do," Gunnar said. "They have to constantly chum the water. Keep the sharks engaged. Thirty minutes gives them way too much time to swim off to other feeding grounds." Gunnar paused, lost in thought for a second.

"Gunnar?" Ballantine asked. "What are you thinking?"

"That even feeding them cows shouldn't hold them in that area," Gunnar said. "There has to be another reason."

"Well, you're the expert, you would know," Ballantine said and waved at the cocaine samples. "Save this work for later."

"I'll keep working until you need me," Gunnar said. "How's that?"

"That is fine," Ballantine said. He nodded to Gunnar then Mike. "Gentlemen."

Mike waited for him to be gone before speaking. "That guy is kinda messed up, isn't he?"

"Yep," Gunnar said. "But it's a messed up job."

"What if you're wrong?" Mike asked. "About the sharks? These sharks are different."

"True," Gunnar replied. "They are *way* different. But for right now I have to go with what I know."

***

"Hey, bro, take a look at this," Max said, his eye to his scope as he watched Espanoza's ship turn about and lead them further into Mexican waters.

"What am I looking at?" Shane asked, looking through his own scope. "Spot me."

"Just outside the bridge," Max said. "See the guy standing there?"

"I see a few guys standing there," Shane said. "All wearing the same uniform. You're gonna have to be more specific."

"The tall one, thin as a rail," Max said. He pulled back from his rifle and looked at his brother. "Nasty scar across his throat."

"Scar across...?" Shane echoed then gasped when he saw him. "Fuck no! No, no, no! Not good!"

He pulled back from his rifle and the brothers stared at each other for a second. Then both scrambled down from the crow's nest, leaving Lucy behind.

"What the fuck, guys?" Lucy asked. "Where are you going?"

"To talk to Ditcher!" Shane yelled back. "We have a problem!"

***

Darren stared at the Reynolds, looked over at Lake, then back at the brothers.

"Are you 100% sure?" Darren asked. "You guys are pretty high."

"Fuck that," Shane said. "You know us, man. This isn't high. This is focused."

"It's him, dude," Max said.

"Can't be," Darren said as he started to pace the bridge. "It isn't possible."

"Afraid so, man," Shane said. "It was him. No doubt about it."

"We wouldn't just throw this on you if we weren't for sure on this shit," Max added. "This is going to be a problem."

"Someone want to clue me in?" Lake asked. "Or am I just the guy that drives the boat?"

"There's a man on that ship that should be dead," Darren said. "Because I killed him. I slit his throat from ear to ear and tossed him off a cliff."

"Maybe he has a brother," Lake said. "You know, one that looks just like him even though they aren't twins?"

"Ha ha," Max said, turning back to Darren. "It's him, dude."

"We saw all the wanted posters too," Shane said. "Hell, our Team was sent to track him once in Columbia, but came up empty. We know that face."

"Who is this guy?" Lake asked.

"One of the most ruthless killers in Mexico," Darren said. "And a top lieutenant in the Colende cartel. Or was. Maybe still is. If it's him." Darren narrowed his eyes. "I have to speak with Ballantine. Where the fuck is he?"

***

"I'm sorry to do this to you," Ballantine said as he looked into the Wiglaf II at Darby.

The mini-sub was locked into its short bay at the stern of the B3.

"If she is still alive then it has to be done," Darby replied as she went over her instrument check for a third time. "It's my responsibility, anyway. I lost track of her. We got lucky she surfaced."

"It happens," Ballantine said. "We're all human."

"I'm not paid to be human," Darby said. "I save that for my vacations."

"You never take a vacation," Ballantine smiled.

"Maybe I will after this," Darby said. "If I live."

Ballantine frowned. "Don't say that. You know if there was any other way, I'd take it."

"There isn't," Darby responded, finally looking up at Ballantine. "We both know this is likely the only opportunity we're going to get."

"I know, I know," Ballantine nodded. "You understand exactly what needs to be done?"

"I do," Darby replied. "I just wish we weren't so hurried. We were supposed to be contacted in a few months, not now."

"Again, I know," Ballantine said. "That's why I'm sending you. Once we get in the thick of things, you launch. Hopefully there will be enough chaos that no one will notice."

"Hopefully," Darby said. "And hopefully you keep those sharks occupied so I can slip past."

"Hopefully," Ballantine nodded. "You need anything?"

"That vacation," Darby smirked.

"Trying out an uncomfortable sense of humor," Ballantine smiled. "You're growing, Darby. I approve."

"Close the hatch," she said. "I'm going to take a nap until we get there. Anyone looking for me?"

"Captain Chambers keeps asking," Ballantine said.

"No one else?"

Ballantine cocked his head. "Who else would there be? Thorne?"

"Never mind," Darby said. "Shut your hatch."

"You mean shut *the* hatch."

"I know what I said."

***

"There you are!" Darren yelled as he stomped down the passageway towards Ballantine. "Where the hell have you been?"

"Around," Ballantine replied.

"Around?" Darren laughed. "Why am I not surprised I'm getting an evasive answer?"

"What's on your mind? Darren?" Ballantine asked. "Must be fairly important to keep you from the bridge."

"What's really going on, Ballantine?" Darren asked. "Who the hell is this Commander Ricardo Espanoza?"

"You said it yourself, Captain," Ballantine responded. "He's part of Mexican Special Forces."

"Bullshit," Darren snapped. "If that were all then why is he with Diego Fernandez?"

"Who is Diego Fernandez?"

"El Serpiente," Darren replied. "But I know you fucking know that."

"The Serpent is dead, Darren," Ballantine answered. "You killed him with your own blade."

"The boys saw him," Darren said. "On Espanoza's ship."

"They were high, I'm sure," Ballantine said.

"Yeah, I tried that excuse too. We know they can smoke half of Jamaica and still not lose their edge. If anything they gain an even better edge."

Ballantine struggled with several excuses, but finally just let out a huge puff of air.

"Espanoza is the head of the Colende cartel," Ballantine said. "He built it up from scratch, absorbed other outfits, and has worked his way deep into the Mexican government. He's not untouchable, but it would take some hard evidence to root him out."

"Fuck," Darren said. "He's done a good job keeping his real life hidden. Has Fernandez always worked for him?"

"They're half brothers," Ballantine replied.

"Makes sense with the way the cartels run. Trust family first," Darren nodded. "Then what do we do? How can we work with these assholes?"

"We don't," Ballantine replied. "We work around them. Let them think they have us snowed. Let them think we are here to chase our sharks. Once we handle that then we take them down."

"How?"

"I'm working on that," Ballantine said. "Let me put a few more pieces into place first, alright? Then I'll let you and Thorne in on everything and Team Grendel can do what they do best."

Darren studied Ballantine for a minute then nodded. "Okay, but the second it goes south we turn guns on the Mexicans."

"That would be a big mistake," Ballantine said. "We may be private, but they are not. We attack those ships in any way and we could start an international incident even the company can't get us out of."

Darren growled and glared.

"I know, it's frustrating," Ballantine said, taking Darren by the shoulder and walking him in the direction of the bridge. "Imagine how I feel? I actually *know* what's going on."

Chapter Five- Uno

"So, since we do expect you muscle heads to end up in the water with the sharks," Carlos said, standing in front of the armory cage, which everyone except Carlos called the Toyshop, as he showed Team Grendel a mesh wetsuit. "This will keep you from being chomped in half."

"Chainmail," Max said. "Whoopty shit, dude. So the shark can't cut through me. Have you seen these fuckers? One bite and my insides will be mush."

"Squish goes Max," Shane nodded.

"Ingrid," Carlos barked. "A demonstration."

Ingrid walked from out of the Toyshop with an oversized bear trap. She set it on the ground, and with Carlos's help, was able to pry it open and set the spring.

"The zucchini!" Carlos shouted.

"I'm standing right here," Ingrid sighed. "You don't have to yell."

She went back into the Toyshop and came out with a large zucchini.

"The pole!" Carlos yelled.

"Dude!" Shane snapped. "Stop yelling!"

"You're the one yelling," Carlos sneered.

"Carlos," Ballantine said coolly.

Ingrid handed Carlos a large metal pole.

"Why do you have a bear trap on a ship?" Lucy asked.

"In case of bears," Carlos replied, completely serious. He slid the zucchini into one of the legs of the wetsuit then dramatically held his arm out across Ingrid. "Stand back!"

Everyone was not impressed. Until Carlos pressed the pole on the trigger mechanism and the bear trap snapped shut on the wetsuit. They all stared as the mesh seemed to solidify under the teeth of the bear trap. Carlos struggled to get the trap open.

"A little help, Ingrid," Carlos ordered.

"Dude," Shane said as he stepped up and yanked the trap open then let it snap shut after the suit was removed. "A few push-ups, maybe some curls, and you can get those arms into shape."

Carlos just glared as he pulled the zucchini free of the wetsuit. There were some marks and bruising where the trap closed on it, but other than that the vegetable was unharmed.

"How?" Max asked, dumbfounded.

"That is propriety information," Carlos said, a smug look on his face. "Isn't that right, Mr. Ballantine?"

"It's magic. That's all you need to know," Ballantine said. "Move it along, Carlos."

"Ingrid!" Carlos shouted.

"Shut up!" Ingrid shouted back as she walked out of the Toyshop with a large rifle in her hands. "Yell at me again and I'll demonstrate this on your balls."

Shane and Max politely clapped.

"Well said, well said," Max said in a bad British accent.

"Nicely done, love," Shane added.

"I am not going to be abused like this," Carlos said. "I am a genius and deserve-"

"Can I shoot him?" Thorne asked, pulling his pistol and holding it against his leg.

"No, please don't," Ballantine said. "At least wait until he has shown you the equipment."

"Funny," Carlos replied then gulped as Ballantine glared at him. "Okay, this is a Maechter 459k compression rifle. It shoots the equivalent of .50 caliber rounds, but without gunpowder or a firing pin."

"So it's a gas gun?" Kinsey asked.

"No, no, no," Carlos replied. "Well, yes, but not like any gas gun you have used. Ingrid, the target, please."

The gate around the armory lifted and rolled into the ceiling. Several shelves moved out of place and a container flipped up with a paper target inside. Carlos turned, put the gun to his shoulder and fired. The paper target flapped about, but showed no signs of being penetrated by the round.

"That was really impressive," Max said. "Can it make a farting noise too?"

"Ingrid," Carlos said as he sneered at Max. "The tank, please."

A long tank of water lifted up from the floor and connected to the target container. The container sealed itself and filled with water rapidly.

"As you can now see, the target is fully submerged," Carlos said. "Now, we'll see who wants a farting noise."

"I do," Shane said.

"Me too," Lucy agreed.

"I've changed my mind," Max said. "I'd prefer more of a raspberry sound, not a full on fart noise."

Carlos lowered the rifle into the tank and fired. This time the target was ripped to shreds as the round exploded on contact; pieces of paper slowly floated about the water-filled container.

"How the hell?" Max and Shane said at the same time as they stepped forward.

"Explosive rounds that only activate when submerged," Carlos said. "Don't ask me why because I'm not at liberty to say. It's what was developed for a different client that didn't-"

"That's enough, Carlos," Ballantine said.

"Right, yes," Carlos nodded.

He pulled the rifle out of the tank, shook off some of the water, then ejected the magazine. He slid his thumb along one of the rounds and popped it free.

"See the channels?" Carlos asked, showing the round to each of the Team members. "It's similar to the rifling in a rifle barrel, but reversed. This time the rifling is on the round itself. The round will actually pick up speed as it flies through water. The farther the target, the more damage it will do. It actually means you have more stopping power from longer distances."

"That's not physically possible," Darren said. "Has Gunnar seen this? He'd back me up. It's not physically possible."

"Yet you saw it happen," Carlos said. "Ingrid?"

"There are also pistols," she said and set out eight large pistols on the Toyshop counter as the tank and container withdrew and the armory cage rolled back into place. "But we have limited rounds. Which doesn't matter since the weapons can only hold a gas charge for a single magazine."

"Always a catch," Max said.

"So when the magazine is empty so is the gas?" Shane asked.

"Exactly," Ingrid said. "You would have to bring it back to the Toyshop to be recharged. Do not try it yourself! We don't use compressed air!"

"What do you use?" Kinsey asked.

"Proprietary information," Carlos smiled.

"He smiled," Max whispered to Shane. "I'm scared."

"Boys," Thorne snapped. "Knock off the bullshit." He turned to Carlos. "How about above water? Anything new?"

"Nope," Carlos said. "You all have your weapons of preference. Far be it for me to get in the way of an operator and his, or her, guns. Right, Ballantine?"

"Carlos is subtly saying that he had some ideas, but I nixed them because I wanted him to focus on the channel guns."

"Channel guns?" Kinsey asked.

"That is what I call the submersible, pre-rifled round firing weapons," Ballantine said. "Channel guns. Because of the channels in the rounds."

"Stupid name," Carlos muttered then cringed under Ballantine's glare.

"I like it," Kinsey said. "Easy to understand. Rolls off the tongue."

"Thank you, Kinsey," Ballantine said.

"Kiss ass," Max coughed.

"Brown noser," Shane coughed also.

"Boys, for the love of God shut the fuck up," Thorne said. "What else do you have for us?"

"The suits and guns aren't enough?" Carlos asked.

"Are they?" Thorne countered.

"The rebreathers?" Ballantine suggested. "Are they operational?"

"They are, yes…," Carlos replied. "But untested."

"We already have rebreathers," Max said. "What's special about these?"

Carlos sighed. "Ingrid. Will you fetch the-"

"Mustaches!" Ingrid squealed. "I love these!"

"I hate that name as well," Carlos muttered. "Channel guns and mustaches..."

Ingrid hurried deep into the Toyshop's shelves then came running back with two large, black cases. She flipped the catches and opened the cases, spinning them around so the operators could see what was inside.

"Try them on! Try them on!" she squealed some more. "I'm going to get a mirror!"

Max and Shane were first as they each grabbed a matte black hunk of plastic and metal about the size of a small banana connected to some seriously strange looking goggles.

"Huh," Max said. "Where's the rest?"

"That's it," Carlos said as Ingrid came back with a mirror. "Is that really needed? Seriously?"

Ingrid grabbed one up and placed it under her nose and over her eyes.

"Now, these can work in water and out. It doesn't matter," she explained. On her face, the part under her nose made her look like an old time villain with a thick mustache. She pulled a tab on each end.

The tabs became small chords which she wrapped around to the back of her head. She gave a quick turn and showed the Team how the chords fused together snuggly then cinched themselves up so the rebreather was secured to her face.

"Now, you'll panic slightly at first," Ingrid laughed. "I did. Kinda peed my jumpsuit. Freaky."

"You really know how to sell it," Shane said.

Ingrid smiled at him and pressed two buttons simultaneously that sat right by her nostrils. Two black tubes extended from the top and snaked their way up inside Ingrid's nostrils. After a second, she choked and gagged a bit them seemed to relax. She took several deep breaths through her nose then tapped her ears.

"I'm activating the com system," Carlos said. "Didn't want you to freak out and shoot me or anything."

"Dude, if we wanted to shoot you it would be at night and up on deck," Max said.

"That way we could just push you overboard and no one would know," Shane added.

"I hate SEALs," Carlos replied.

"Hi guys!" Ingrid's voice rang through the com. But her lips didn't move. In fact, her mouth was wide open. "Isn't this cool?"

"Explain it to them, Carlos," Ballantine ordered. "We don't have much time."

"The tubes extend up the nostrils, through the sinuses, and down into the trachea," Carlos said. "The rebreather actually seals off your airways from your mouth. You can swallow all the water you want, but it will just make your stomach bloated. It is impossible to drown with one of these operational."

"How are we hearing her?" Kinsey asked.

"The tubes also work as conductors from the larynx," Carlos explained. "Speak normally, just with your lips closed, and you will be able to hear each other over the com just like a regular mic. There are processors that clean up the diction and any distortion the placement of the tubes might create."

"What happens if the rebreather is damaged?" Thorne asked.

"Then don't breathe seawater," Carlos nodded. "Or you drown."

Ingrid pressed the buttons again and the tubes withdrew back into the mustache. She coughed a few times and smiled at everyone. "It's a little rough, but you'll be fine."

Carlos pointed at the cases. "The goggles are set for multiple spectrums. Just tap the button up by the temples, either side, doesn't matter, and you can switch between everything from infrared to night vision."

"Night vision?" Max asked.

"It can get dark in the water," Carlos said.

"Yes, it can," Max nodded. "Thanks."

Darren walked forward and picked up a "mustache" from a case. He looked it over them threw it on the ground and stomped on it. Carlos shrieked, his eyes going from Darren to the mustache and back to Darren.

"Why…why? Why would you do that?" Carlos sputtered.

Darren bent down and picked up the mustache and handed it to Carlos.

"Did I break it?" Darren asked, grinning.

Carlos snatched the mustache from him and quickly looked it over. He stared at it for a second then looked at Darren.

"Uh, no, it's fine," Carlos responded.

"I want one," Max said.

"Me too," Shane added.

"We all get one," Thorne said as he pointed to the gear. "Get your shit together people. Meeting on deck in twenty."

***

"Holy shit," Darren said as he stepped onto the bridge on his way to the Team meeting. He stopped next to Lake and stared out at the water. "That's a blockade."

They looked out of the bridge at the dozen Mexican naval vessels that formed a rough, half mile long semi-circle in the ocean just off the coast of Playas Rosarito.

"I didn't know Mexico had that many ships," Lake said. "And even if they did, how'd they get them here so fast? Shouldn't some be out on exercises?"

"I gave up trying to figure out governments a long time ago," Darren said. "I have to meet with the Team. You got this?"

"I've always had this," Lake replied. "It's why I'm here. So someone does."

"Thanks," Darren said. "Just keep steaming through. We're going to park it in the middle."

"Right where the sharks are?" Lake asked. "Great. What could go wrong?"

"The B3 can handle the sharks," Darren said as he walked out of the hatch. "Trust me."

"Right," Lake said. "Because that's gone so well in the past."

Lake popped open a small compartment and pulled out a Desert Eagle. He ejected the magazine, made sure it was full, then slapped it back into the pistol. He racked the slide and set the gun by the wheel.

***

"Where should you be?" Ballantine asked Carlos.

"In the bay with Moshi," Carlos frowned. "Working on the sub."

"Exactly," Ballantine said. "You had your fun showing off your new toys, now get back to work."

Carlos glared, but didn't argue. He grabbed up a tool bag from the counter and stomped out of the armory.

"Why are you so hard on him?" Ingrid asked as she gathered her own tools. "He idolizes you."

"Does he?" Ballantine replied. "I didn't think he idolized anyone but himself."

"Please," Ingrid laughed. "He hates himself. That's why he's such a jerk. He knows what happened and I don't think he'll ever live it down."

"He shouldn't," Ballantine said.

Ingrid frowned and punched Ballantine in the shoulder. Hard.

"Ow!" Ballantine exclaimed. "What the hell do you think you're doing?"

"What happened to the first Beowulf wasn't his fault," Ingrid said. "You know that so stop acting like it was."

"He could have done more," Ballantine replied, rubbing his shoulder.

"Coulda, shoulda, woulda," Ingrid said as she walked out of the armory. "Like you haven't ever fucked up."

***

Gunnar slammed his fist down on the lab counter, his face scrunched up in frustration.

"What?" Mike asked. "What's wrong?"

"The exact same results," Gunnar said. "Every single sample of cocaine yields the exact same results."

"And that's a bad thing?" Mike asked.

"Yes," Gunnar said. "Because kilos shouldn't be identical."

"But it's all the same coke, right? So why wouldn't the samples be the same from kilo to kilo?"

"Because they aren't the same," Gunnar said. "Sure, two samples from the same kilo can be identical, but not from different kilos. Difference in handling, packaging, atmosphere when packaged, possible contaminants in the bags themselves. All kinds of variations should show up. They'd be minuscule, but I'm running tests to pick up minuscule!"

Gunnar slammed his fists down on the counter again and again.

"Whoa, chill, Gun," Mike said, wheeling over to him. "So run them again. This time look for the opposite of what you were looking for before."

Gunnar turned and raised his eyebrows. "What the hell are you talking about?"

"You were looking for difference and couldn't find them. So look for the sames this time."

"The sames isn't exactly a scientific term," Gunnar frowned.

"That's why I'm a SEAL and not an egghead," Mike replied. "Or was a SEAL. Just a sad, broken man now."

"Boo hoo," Gunnar laughed. "Cry me a river, frogman."

He looked over at the pallet of cocaine kilos and narrowed his eyes.

"Okay, let's try this again," he said. "Look for the sames."

***

Darby sat in the Wiglaf II, her legs crossed beneath her as she relaxed in front of the controls, ready and waiting for Ballantine's signal. She took several deep, cleansing breaths then closed her eyes. Just as Ballantine called over the com.

"Be ready," he said.

"I am," Darby replied.

"When you drop in the water, you'll have only minutes, maybe seconds, to clear the blockade and get away from the area," Ballantine said.

Darby's eyes shot open. "Blockade?"

"Espanoza has pulled out all the stops," Ballantine said. "Half the Mexican navy is here."

"How'd he manage that without raising suspicions?" Darby asked.

"He used us," Ballantine said. "He used the company's influence as a smokescreen. He has an agenda."

"Feels like he's scrambling," Darby said.

"That's when he's at his most dangerous," Ballantine said. "You get to the launch site of the subs and complete the mission. That's all I need you to do. We'll be close behind."

"You hope," Darby replied.

Ballantine sighed. "I do."

***

Thorne watched from the bow as the B3 steamed past two Mexican ships and into the secured area of ocean. He turned around and faced the mesh wetsuit clad Team Grendel. Max, Shane, Lucy, Kinsey, and Darren waited for him to speak as he looked each one in the eye.

"Who thinks this is all bullshit and there's something else going on?" Thorne asked.

Everyone raised their hands.

"Excellent," he grinned, but there was no warmth in the smile. "Good to know I don't have idiots on my Team. Darren? Would you care to tell us what you know?"

Everyone looked at the captain and waited for him to respond. It was obvious the internal struggle that was waged inside him.

"Spill it, Ditcher," Max said.

"We know part," Shane said. "Want us to start?"

"Fernandez," Darren said. "El Serpiente."

Thorne's eyebrows raised. "You killed him."

"Nope," Max said. "Gave him a nice scar though."

"El Serpiente?" Lucy gasped. "What does this have to do with that monster?"

"He's on the ship with Espanoza," Darren said. "They're half brothers. Espanoza is head of the Colende cartel."

"The coke," Kinsey said, shaking her head. ""This is about the coke, not the sharks, right?"

"No," Thorne said. "You all saw the footage. This is about the sharks. For us, at least. For those fucks?" He pointed back at Espanoza's ship as it took its place in the blockade, letting the B3 continue on. "I don't know what their fucking agenda is, but I can guarantee it isn't the same as ours."

"So what's the plan, Commander?" Max asked, all joking lost. "We focus on the sharks and let Ballantine sort the rest out?"

"Yes," Thorne said. "We focus on the sharks. After we kill those fuckers then we deal with Espanoza."

"Sharks first," Darren reiterated. He screwed up his face. "I wish Ballantine would tell us where the fuck Darby is. We could use the air cover."

"Yes, we could," Thorne said.

"Not to worry, operators," Ballantine said as he walked from a hatch and out onto the deck. "I'll handle the Wyrm II."

Team Grendel turned as one and gaped at him.

"You can fly a helo?" Max asked.

"And we are just finding this out now?" Shane added.

"Never show your cards unless you have to," Ballantine said. "I'll go prep. Let me know where and when you need me."

Thorne glared. "I was under the distinct impression you could not pilot a helo. Why would I be under that impression?"

"Because I told you I couldn't?" Ballantine grinned.

"That would be why," Thorne growled. "Where the hell is Darby?"

"Around," Ballantine replied. "I'll be in the Wyrm II if anyone needs me."

"Hold on, meeting isn't done. Lucy, you're with Ballantine," Thorne ordered. "I want that bird in the air and circling the area the second I stop talking here. Your job is to put .50 caliber rounds in any large shadow you see. I don't give a fuck if it's a goddamn manatee. You shoot the fucking thing."

"Manatees are off Florida and Africa," Lucy said. "Not Mexico."

"Don't. Fucking. Care," Thorne said. "Shoot it."

"Got it," Lucy nodded. "I will shoot the fucking manatee."

"We're taking the Zodiacs out," Thorne said. "This is a direct assault. We're getting in the water with the sharks."

"We what?" Kinsey asked. "Love you, Daddy, but have you lost your mind?"

"No, I haven't," Thorne said. "We take the fight to them. If these suits work like they are supposed to then we have an advantage."

"Really? What's that?" Shane asked.

"Maneuverability," Thorne said. "They are too big to turn and swim like we can."

"They don't need to if they chomp us in half," Max said.

"Which is why we have the suits," Thorne replied. "At some point we have to trust the equipment. Otherwise we should just be back on land drinking beer an a goddamn recliner."

"Can we?" Shane asked. "I totally volunteer."

"Two Zodiacs," Thorne glared. "Kinsey and Max are with me. Darren and Shane are in the second one. I want the shooters to stay in the boats while we dive. You two will man the motors and keep your rifles ready. Same orders as Lucy. Shoot any shadow you see."

"Any shadow that doesn't look like a person," Darren said. "Just to clarify."

"Do I need to clarify that, boys?" Thorne asked.

"No, sir," the Reynolds replied in unison.

"Good," Thorne said. "We drop in five minutes."

"Uh, sir?" Max asked, looking at his rifle. "Last time we dealt with these sharks we needed rockets to kill them. You think our guns will really be enough?"

"Have you been studying shark anatomy as you were ordered to during your leave time?" Thorne asked.

"Yes, sir," Max replied.

"So you know where the brain is?"

"Yes, sir."

"Do you need a rocket to hit that brain or are you a fucking SEAL sniper, son?"

"I'm a fucking SEAL sniper!" Max shouted.

"And did you or did you not see what these rounds can do?"

"I did, sir," Max stated.

"And didn't I just say we have to trust the equipment?"

"You did, sir," Max nodded.

"Does that answer your question?" Thorne asked.

"Yes, sir," Max replied.

Thorne focused his gaze on Ballantine. "Do you have a problem with us killing these sharks?"

Ballantine weighed his answer for several seconds. "Personally? No. But the company wouldn't mind if they could be captured alive. Our client would prefer that."

"Do I look like I have a Team that captures?" Thorne asked.

"No, Commander, you do not," Ballantine replied, smiling.

"Will we have a problem if my Team comes back with nothing but shark steaks?" Thorne asked.

"No, Commander, we will not," Ballantine smiled. "It's your Team. All I can do is pass on what the company wants. If things get crazy in the heat of battle then steaks happen."

"Good," Thorne said. "Welcome to the Team, Ballantine. This is a provisional assignment for you. You do what I say when I say it. Understood?"

"Wouldn't want it any other way," Ballantine grinned. "Can I be dismissed to perform my duties as helo pilot now?"

"You are all dismissed," Thorne said looking at everyone. "Get your asses to work!"

"I wonder if coke tenderizes shark steaks?" Max asked Shane.

"Let's find out," Shane smiled.

***

"Sir?" Carlos asked over the com. "We have it."

Ballantine smiled over at Lucy as the two of them hurried across the deck and onto the helipad. They hopped into the Wyrm II and got strapped in.

116

"Good," Ballantine said as he sat in the pilot's seat and started up the rotors. He put on his headset and switched to Carlos's channel. "Send the coordinates to Darby. Then get your ass down to the mini-sub bay and make sure her launch is fast and trouble free. There is no margin for error with this. Once the shooting starts she needs to use that cover to get away."

"I understand," Carlos replied. "I am on it."

***

"Ready?" Popeye asked from the side of the B3, his eyes focused on the Zodiac with Thorne, Kinsey, and Max in it. Behind that Zodiac was the one with Darren and Shane. Two of Popeye's deckhands waited for his signal.

"Ready," Thorne said. "Put us in the water."

Popeye lowered the Zodiac to the ocean below and waited for Max to release the cables before giving the deckhands a thumbs up. The second Zodiac was released and Team Grendel was in the water.

***

Kinsey placed the mustache under her nose and pressed the buttons. She gagged and choked and had to fight every instinct not to rip the thing from her face. But in seconds the rebreather was secure and working.

"Can you hear me?" Kinsey asked.

"I can hear you," Thorne said.

"We all can," Lake replied over the com from the bridge. "It's an open channel, by the way."

"Good to know," Thorne said as he put his mustache on. He hesitated and Kinsey laughed.

"It's not that bad," she said.

Thorne pressed the buttons then went through the same choking and gagging as Kinsey. His eyes drilled daggers into her.

"Not that bad?" he snapped once he found his voice. "Are you kidding?"

"I've had worse things up my nose," Kinsey smirked.

Thorne just shook his head and pointed at Max. "Your turn."

"But I'm staying in the boat," Max argued.

"For how long, do you think?" Thorne asked. "We all know how these things hunt."

Max looked at the Zodiac then into the water as he sped the boat across the small whitecaps created by a strong, warm breeze.

"Right," Max said as he donned his mustache as well.

***

"You look ridiculous," Shane said, shouting over the motor as he secured his mustache. "How do I look?"

"Probably as bad as I do," Darren replied. "You ready for this?"

"Always," Shane said.

Darren lifted his channel gun, checked the magazine, slammed it home, then turned his attention to the blue water surrounding them. His eyes scanned the surface, hoping to catch a glimpse of something, but only sunlight reflected back at him.

"Another twenty meters should do it!" Shane announced.

Darren kicked his feet together, making sure his flippers were on tight, then scooted his ass up onto the side of the Zodiac.

"Shit goes bad and you follow me in, got it?" Darren said. "Leave your .338 and grab your channel gun."

Shane gave a thumbs up and took a deep breath, surprised at how fresh it felt even through the mustache. He cut the motor and let the Zodiac drift into position.

***

"How do they look?" Ballantine asked as he circled the Wyrm II far above the Zodiacs. "Any sign?"

"Nothing," Lucy said. "Team Grendel is good to go. Stay safe, people."

There were several inappropriate words said in response and Lucy laughed.

***

Thorne and Kinsey flipped backwards into the water, sank a few feet, then oriented themselves, their channel guns gripped firmly in place.

"See anything?" Thorne asked as he tapped at his goggles, testing the different spectrum views.

"No," Kinsey said. "You?"

"Nothing," Thorne replied. "Darren? You in the water?"

"I'm in," Darren said. "I see nothing here."

"There's nothing on the sonar," Lake said over the com. "Not a single fucking fish anywhere. I bet if I dial it in I'll see that the crabs have even bailed."

"I would't blame them," Darren replied.

"Ten meters down," Thorne ordered. "Then wait. If we see nothing then we keep going. If there's still nothing then we make our way back up to the Zodiacs, move, and start again."

"We're aren't going to grid it?" Kinsey asked.

"No," Thorne said. "No need. If the sharks are still here then they'll find us."

***

The sub rocked back and forth as the shark tore into its cargo hold, puncturing more kilos of the drug. Clouds of white water puffed around its head as it thrashed, frustrated it couldn't get all the way inside and to the cargo all at once.

It wanted more. It needed more. It craved more.

Then its senses detected the dying sounds of motors. It didn't care. It didn't want what the motors brought; it wanted what was in front of it.

The giant shark pulled back then rammed the sub over and over, desperate to dislodge its contents. More white streamed from the hold, but the frame wouldn't budge despite the force of the shark's attacks.

Its rage grew.

***

"Ten meters," Thorne said. "Report."

Kinsey was a ways off from her father as she searched the water, looking for any sign of the sharks. Her channel gun was firmly against her shoulder and she sighted down the barrel, her goggles on a motion detecting setting. She had no idea what would happen when the goggles detected motion, but she was pretty sure she wouldn't have to guess.

"I still don't see anything," Kinsey said.

"Darren?" Thorne asked.

"Nope," Darren replied.

"Keep going," Thorne said. "Drop another ten meters."

***

Not too far off, a second shark struggled with the same issue. It hit the sub, tore at the faux skin, thrashed against it with its tail as it flipped about, swimming up and down the length of the sub.

It heard the motors too and could care less as well.

All it wanted was what was in the sub.

Then a new smell hit its heightened senses. Something fresh, something alive, something not dead cow. The shark had grown bored with dead cow. At first the taste, and abundance, had kept the shark occupied, kept it going back to the surface for more.

But it didn't want that taste again; that was old taste. It wanted the new taste.

It slammed itself into the sub once again, producing a huge plume of white from the cargo hold. It swam back and forth, breathing it in, letting the drug infuse its power into every cell of the its body.

Alive, and hungry for the new taste, the shark whipped about and rocketed towards the surface.

***

"Anything?" Ballantine asked Lucy. "Tell me what you see."

"A lot of blue water," Lucy replied. "And two boats bobbing up and down. No shadows. Nothing."

"Maybe I should have the Mexicans launch another cow," Ballantine said.

"I doubt that would help," Lucy said. "If the things aren't reacting to our people in the water then a dead cow won't do anything."

"Not sure what you are basing your theory on," Ballantine replied. "But you could be right. From the insanity on those videos, I would have expected an attack right away."

***

"I got movement!" Lake said as he watched the large mass moving quickly from the bottom of the ocean. "Holy shit! This thing has to be doing fifty miles an hour or more! Get the fuck out of there!"

"Not our job to get out of here!" Thorne replied. "Give me a location!"

Lake studied the image on the sonar. "It's coming for Darren! Looks like about a twenty-five degree angle, man! Turn east and get ready!"

***

Darren twisted around in the direction Lake had indicated. He scanned the dark waters with his goggles, but didn't see anything. He didn't want to run out of ammo, but he took a risk and fired the channel gun. The round sped out of the barrel, large bubbles of gas flowing out from behind it. He tried to follow the round's progress, but it was lost from sight quickly.

Then an explosion lit up the water below him.

And he saw the shark, its mouth open wide, illuminated by the dying light of the explosion under it.

Darren didn't know what he hit, but it wasn't the shark. He could see that clearly.

***

"'REN!" Kinsey yelled as she swam towards Darren.

She was a good hundred meters away when her goggles started to chirp and a small window popped up in the bottom of the left lens. It showed the shark, magnified to a close up, its mouth wide, racing up at Darren.

The small image was distracting so Kinsey tapped it away and decided to rely on her naked eyes alone. She kicked her legs as hard as she could, pushing her body through the water, and propelled herself towards Darren.

The shark raced towards Darren and it wasn't until the thing was only three meters below him that Kinsey realized she wouldn't get there in time. She slowed and brought her own channel gun up. She was only able to get one shot off before the shark hit Darren dead on.

***

"CONTACT!" Thorne yelled into the com. "Darren has been hit!"

"He's still alive," Ingrid said over the com. "Heart rate is dangerously elevated, but he isn't dead. The suit worked."

"What?" Thorne asked. "How the fuck do you know that he isn't dead?"

"The wetsuit monitors all vital signs," Ingrid replied. "And I'm back in the Toyshop, monitoring the wetsuits. Didn't we mention that?"

"No, you fucking didn't mention that!" Thorne shouted. "Darren! Darren, can you hear me!"

There was nothing.

"The impact may have damaged the com," Ingrid said. "Or dislodged the rebreather. That could be why he isn't responding."

"If that happened then he'll drown," Thorne said.

Instead of swimming towards Darren like Kinsey was, Thorne maintained his position, watching the waters around and underneath him for the second shark.

"He's not drowning," Ingrid said. "His vitals are weak, but not getting weaker. He's still breathing."

"Can you tell what the impact did?" Thorne asked. "Broken bones? Internal bleeding? Anything?"

"Well, no," Ingrid replied. "Those would be cool features to add later."

"There is nothing cool about this," Thorne snapped.

"Right, sorry," Ingrid apologized.

"Lake? Talk to me," Thorne ordered. "What do you see?"

"Just the one shark, so far," Lake said. "And it's diving fast!"

"The wetsuit will help with decompression," Ingrid said. "So if he gets free, he can swim to the surface without worrying about the bends, no matter how deep the shark takes him."

"Is that another feature you forgot to mention?" Thorne snapped.

"I guess so," Ingrid replied. "I'm no good at giving a demonstration. I blame Carlos. He just gets me so flustered."

***

"Coordinates are locked into your navigation system," Carlos said to Darby as he crawled out of the Wiglaf II and looked back down inside the mini-sub. "Head straight for them and you'll be there in thirty minutes."

"Still no sign of the second shark?" Darby asked.

"Not from what I hear," Carlos said. "I'm going to flood the bay right now. As soon as they say they've engaged the second shark then I'll launch you from the B3."

"Launch me anyway," Darby said.

"But, Ballantine wanted you to wait-"

"I'm tired of waiting," Darby said. "I should be out there fighting. If I can't do that, then I want to get on the way. Flood the bay and launch me. Now."

Carlos could see the look in Darby's eyes meant there was no arguing with her. He nodded, closed and secured the hatch, then made his way across the plank to the edge of the deck. Glancing back at the mini-sub, Carlos shook his head; he couldn't imagine having the guts Darby had. He much preferred the safety of the Toyshop.

"Armory," he said aloud, smacking his forehead for even thinking the name "Toyshop."

He left the launch bay, sealed the hatch, and opened a panel on the wall.

"You sure?" he asked over the direct com as he pressed a button in the panel.

"Don't piss me off, Carlos," Darby said.

"No, no, I won't," Carlos replied. "In three, two, one."

He pressed his palm against a flat, red button and a siren rang out as the launch bay began to fill with water. In less than two minutes, the Wiglaf II was completely submerged and Carlos opened the bay doors, letting the mini-sub drive off into the deep.

***

"Sir," an ensign said, turning from a monitor to look at Espanoza who had taken the captain's chair on the bridge of the ship even though he wasn't technically the captain. "A mini-sub just launched from the Beowulf. Did they say they were going to employ that tactic?"

"No, they did not," Espanoza said. "Keep an eye on it."

He watched as the Wyrm II circled in the air above the two Zodiacs in the ocean below.

"The men are ready," Diego said as he stepped onto the bridge. "Loaded into the boats and awaiting your orders."

"Good," Espanoza said. "Once I see all of those Americans in the water then you are free to launch."

Diego nodded and left the bridge.

"What is the mini-sub's heading?" Espanoza asked. "Is it diving towards the bottom? I want to know if it goes anywhere near my subs."

"No, sir," the ensign replied. "It's leveled out and is heading away from us. Due south."

"Due south?" Espanoza asked.

"Yes, sir."

"Why would it go south?" Espanoza wondered.

***

Darren felt like he was being crushed from the inside, even though the massive jaws that gripped him were obviously crushing him from the outside.

Maybe this is what a banana in its peel feels like when you step on it, Darren thought.

It was a crazy thought, but still a thought. Which meant he was alive enough to think.

Think. Think, think, think.

Darren assessed his situation.

He was clutched in the jaws of a genetically cloned, sixty foot monster shark, being dragged deeper and deeper into the Pacific by the second. And his arms were pinned to his sides by teeth the size of small dinner plates.

It was a short assessment.

His body grew colder as he felt the compression of the Shark's jaws increase. Darren had no idea how long the wetsuit could hold off the inevitable, but he knew he couldn't take much more. Sure, he wasn't chomped in half, but that didn't mean it didn't hurt like fucking hell.

Darren concentrated on his body, trying to figure out how long he had before he lost consciousness. Or his spleen exploded.

He realized that he still held his channel gun in his right hand. Which was inside the shark.

Darren tried to flex his hand and get his trigger finger working, but his appendage wouldn't obey. He looked at the way he was being held in the shark's jaws and saw his arm was wedged between two teeth. It was within the realm of possibility that he couldn't move his fingers because circulation was no longer moving to his extremities. Or, considering the pain, he had a broken bone. Or two.

He didn't stop trying.

Whether the ocean deep would be his resting place or not, he had zero intention of going out alone. He was gonna take a shark with him, if he could.

***

"Darren!" Kinsey shouted, aiming herself towards where she last saw the monster shark. It was quickly lost from sight as it swam at a speed she didn't think was possible.

Kinsey tapped at her goggles and brought up infrared. Not the most useful when looking for a cold blooded creature like a shark, but very handy when looking for a warm blooded creature like the man she loved.

Ooooh, that came from nowhere.

She shoved the thought away. No time for bullshit.

No time for anything except diving faster.

Yet physics didn't work that way. Kinsey kicked her legs, but every time she rested, she'd lose depth, her body insisting on floating back towards the surface.

"Daddy!" Kinsey screamed. "I can't get to him! I can't see him!"

***

"Lake!" Thorne shouted.

"I heard, I heard!" Lake replied. "He's hit fifty meters and still going! I know you people have super suits on and shit, but he goes much deeper at that rate and he'll blow a gasket!"

"No gasket blowing," Ingrid interjected. "The suit will maintain his blood pressure. The suit will also adjust the compression around his body and compensate for the descent, not just the ascent."

"Then let's hope that thing slows down," Lake said. "Because if it rams into the ocean floor at that speed then super suit or not, Darren is going to be pulp!"

***

Darren pushed every ounce of his will towards moving his finger. He could feel the tip along the trigger guard. All he had to do was move it a centimeter and he'd have contact. Just one centimeter.

Blood pounded in his head and he shook it out of habit, although it did nothing to stop the building pressure.

126

The shark responded in kind and shook its head, sending Darren thrashing back and forth.

He screamed and swallowed a half-gallon of seawater, but luckily, due to the mustache, he didn't take any into his lungs.

The shark thrashed again and Darren felt like a rag doll in a Bull Mastiff's mouth. He also felt the channel gun shift slightly. He had contact.

"Fuck you," he said. Or thought he did. It was hard to tell.

Darren pulled the trigger. But nothing happened.

He thought he felt the gun kick, but couldn't be sure. He pulled the trigger again. Still nothing.

He couldn't believe he actually got his finger on the trigger, but the gun didn't fucking work!

Then it hit him. The round needed distance to really pick up speed and be effective. He had no idea where the end of the barrel was lodged inside the shark. For all he knew it was completely blocked. Once more he realized he needed to be able to move, but didn't have the capacity to accomplish that.

"Fuck!" he shouted.

***

"Where's the second one?" Max asked, his eyes searching the water all around his Zodiac.

"Not a clue, bro," Shane replied. "You'd think it would show its ugly mug. You know, just to compete with its brother shark."

"I don't think sharks are like us, dude," Max said. "Sibling rivalry isn't part of its makeup."

"They are sisters," Ballantine interrupted. "Cloned from a female."

"Right," Max said. "Because that's important now, why?"

"It isn't," Ballantine said. "I'm just making conversation while we wait to see what Captain Chambers's fate is."

"Ditcher will make it," Shane said.

"You sound confident of that," Ballantine responded.

"I am," Shane said. "Because if I didn't get the chance to kill him years ago when he bailed on Kinsey, then no shark gets the fucking chance now."

"Too true, dude," Max said. "Too true."

***

The water around Darren wasn't ink black, but it was very dark. He could feel the shark slowing and then he was floating free, let go as the shark suddenly turned its attention to something else.

Darren struggled to keep his breathing steady as his body slammed into something solid. He was able to get his left hand up and switch the spectrum on the goggles to night vision and the ocean depths were illuminated in greens and blacks; a dichotomy of light and shadow.

Turning his head to the right, Darren's eyes went wide as he realized he was flat against the hull of one of the whale subs. And the monster shark next to him had its nose buried in the cargo hold.

"You have to be kidding me," he said. "Kinsey? Lake? Thorne? Can anyone hear me?"

There was no response, not even static. His com was dead in the water.

The sub shook beneath his back as the shark wedged its way deeper and deeper into the cargo hold. Darren saw that he was missing his channel gun and figured it must still be inside the shark, swallowed whole, just like he had almost been.

White clouds escaped from around the shark as it shook harder and harder. Then it was free and whipped itself around, rocketing back towards the surface.

Darren wanted desperately to follow, but he knew he was messed up and didn't have the strength to swim a few feet let alone a couple hundred meters. The white clouds drifted closer, caught on the current, and Darren found himself engulfed. He couldn't smell it because of the rebreather that only circulated his own air supply, but as he laid there, his mouth slightly open, he could taste it.

Cocaine.

Darren hadn't ever gone full junkie like Kinsey, but he had traveled. He knew what cocaine tasted like. He also knew that it could be absorbed through contact with skin, especially the gums. He opened wide and took in as much water as he could, not just in his mouth, but also his stomach. His body rebelled and he vomited the seawater back out, watching the viscous bile float along away from him. Darren didn't dare stop, he needed the boost if he was going to get his ass out of the hell he was in.

He swallowed more. Puked more. Swallowed. Puked.

His body started to tingle and his vision brightened. His nerve endings were alive with feeling; granted that feeling was very close to excruciating pain, but it was feeling. Then the numbness took hold and Darren felt as if he was just a passenger in his own body, not actually a part of the flesh and blood itself.

He shoved off from the sub and reached out with his hands. Darren kicked his legs then looked down and saw he was missing a flipper. That must have joined the channel gun in the shark's guts. He didn't really give a shit at that moment.

One flipper on, and a belly full of cocaine laced seawater, Darren swam back towards the light.

***

"Coming back!" Lake said. "Fast!"

"Does it still have Darren?" Kinsey asked as she fought against the ocean to dive deeper.

"I have no way of knowing that," Lake said.

"What's the shark's depth?" Ingrid asked.

"One hundred meters and closing," Lake said.

"Darren isn't with it," Ingrid replied. "He's a couple hundred meters below it."

"You can tell that? How?" Kinsey asked, her eyes hunting for the oncoming shark.

"Oh, uh, depth gauge in the suits also?" Ingrid replied. "Sorry."

"Next time, less bear trap demonstrations and more actual practical operations demonstrations," Thorne snarled.

"Yes, Commander," Ingrid apologized.

Kinsey kept swimming, her channel gun strapped to her back as she used both hands to try to get down to where the ocean held

Darren. Then her goggles beeped and the image of the giant shark popped up in her left lens.

"Oh, shit," she gasped. "It's coming right for me."

She slowed herself, reached back, and grabbed her channel gun. She whipped it about and pressed it to her shoulder then sighted down the barrel at the massive mouth that opened below her.

Kinsey fired one, two, three times. She watched as the rounds sped away from the barrel, gaining momentum as they went deeper towards the shark. The creature's mouth opened wider and Kinsey screamed as it came up at her. She didn't have time to get out of its way and wrapped her arms across her face as the shark started to swallow her hole.

Then the world became nothing but white light and noise. Even muffled by the water around her, she could hear the intensity of the explosions. One, two, three, four, five, six, seven; she lost count. The blasts just kept coming and Kinsey was thrown to and fro from the concussions.

When the explosions stopped, and she was able to tell upside down from right side up, Kinsey reached for the surface and swam. Darren was still below, but there was a pain in her side that told her she needed help. And fast.

Just before her head broke the surface of the water, she looked down and saw a massive shark tooth protruding from her right side, jammed between her ribs. The suit saved her from the concussive force of the blast, but it couldn't stop a projectile, not one as sharp and pointed as an eight inch shark tooth.

She hit the surface and immediately floated onto her back.

"Hey," she croaked. "I could use some help here."

"Coming, Sis!" Shane yelled as he started up his motor and pointed the Zodiac at his cousin. "Hang on!"

She gave a weak thumbs up.

***

The sounds of the explosions, and the sudden smell of blood, both shark and human, finally tore the massive shark away from its drug binge. It reversed out of the cargo hold and whipped itself around, its nose hunting for the direction of fresh blood. Once it had locked on to the scent, the shark took off with all of its strength and speed.

***

"Holy shit!" Lake laughed. "You took that thing out, Kinsey! Way to go!"

"Thanks," Kinsey whispered. "But Darren is still down there."

"He's alive," Ingrid said. "Just hang onto that."

"I will," Kinsey said as Shane motored the Zodiac over to her.

"Shit," Lake swore. "The second one has decided to show up. It's on its way."

"Where?" Max asked.

"I see it!" Lucy cried. "Max! It's coming at you! I can see the shadow!"

"Me? What the fuck did I do?" Max shouted. "What side?"

"Starboard!" Lucy directed.

Max pulled the action back on his rifle and looked over the starboard side of the Zodiac. The shark wasn't hard to miss. It grew exponentially as it sped towards the surface. Max started firing. He watched as round after round plunged into the water, leaving a trail of white, twisting bubbles in their wake.

Then the shark hit the Zodiac and Max was sent flying into the air.

***

"Second shark has emerged, sir," the ensign said to Espanoza. "It has taken out a Zodiac with one of the snipers."

"Good," Espanoza said. "But there is still one boat left."

"Yes, sir," the ensign replied.

"I wasn't looking for confirmation," Espanzoa said, pointing out of the bridge. "I can see the fucking boat myself!"

He stood up from the captain's chair.

"Tell Diego to launch," Espanoza said. "I'm tired of waiting. The Americans will be fish food soon, anyway."

"Yes, sir," the ensign said and relayed the information.

Again, Espanoza's eye was drawn to the circling Wyrm II.

He sighed heavily then left the bridge, grabbed onto the ladder by the hatch, and pulled himself up to the small observation deck above.

"Shoot it out of the air," Espanoza said to one of the men standing by the railing.

"Excuse me, sir?" the man asked. "Did you say to fire on the helicopter?"

"I did."

The man looked at Espanoza then over at the helicopter.

"Is that an American government helicopter?" the man asked.

"No, it's a private vehicle," Espanoza replied. "Does it matter?"

"No, sir," the man said as he put the rifle to his shoulder and sighted on the helicopter's top rotor. "I just like to know how to classify my kills."

Espanoza smiled. "Good man."

***

Warning lights flashed and bells and alarms rang out in the cockpit as the Wyrm II took a sudden lurch to the side and started to spin out of control.

"What's happening?" Lucy cried. "Ballantine! What's wrong?"

"I don't know!" Ballantine yelled back.

"I thought you said you knew how to fly this thing!" Lucy shouted.

"I do!" Ballantine replied as he fought the stick for control. "It just went wild! It's like the rotor has been damaged or..."

He trailed off and looked over at Espanoza's ship.

"That asshole," Ballantine said. Then he saw the half dozen Zodiacs filled with armed men that sped from the ship towards the B3. "Motherfucker."

Ballantine used all of his skills to keep control of the helo, but the thing didn't want to obey. The best he could do was aim it in the direction he wanted to go.

He just prayed he could land it without killing himself and Lucy.

***

"What the fuck is he doing?" Lake muttered as he watched the smoking helo come at the Beowulf III fast.

Too fast. And obviously not in Ballantine's control. The helo spun about in two circles then crashed hard on one of the helipads. Flaming fuel exploded everywhere.

"Fuck!" Lake shouted as he slammed his hand down on the emergency warning system.

An ear splitting claxon filled the deck and an electronic voice began to warn the entire ship, deck to deck, of "Fire! Fire! All crew to stations! Fire!"

Then Lake saw the Zodiacs that were coming for the Beowulf III.

"Son of a bitch," Lake said and overrode the electronic voice as he put a PA handset to his mouth. "Fuck the fire, people! We're being boarded!"

He tossed the handset aside and grabbed the Desert Eagle and started to leave the bridge. Then he stopped and reached out, grabbing a fire axe off the wall.

Chapter Six: Dos

Darren had never been so thankful to have his head above water. Until he saw what the surface held in store.

One of the Zodiacs was missing, there was smoke and flame coming from the deck of the Beowulf III, and he was floating in blood and gore. Then there were the Zodiacs that were maneuvering up against the B3's hull. And armed men tossing up lines to board her.

"Hey!" Darren shouted as he saw Shane's Zodiac near by.

He grabbed the tabs and yanked the rebreather from his face. He puked up more seawater and struggled to remember how to breathe normally again. Once he had a lungful of real air, he turned towards the one Zodiac he saw.

"Hey!" he yelled. "HEY! Over here! Fucking over here you ass muncher!"

"Ditcher!" Shane yelled as he turned the Zodiac towards him and raced over.

Shane was able to pull him up into the Zodiac, and Darren found himself tumbling next to Kinsey who was splayed out on the bottom of the boat.

"Welcome to the hospital ship," Shane said. "We're a small, regional outfit, only set up for two patients at a time."

"What's going on?" Darren asked. "What the fuck is going on?"

"I don't know," Shane said as he gunned the motor, heading the opposite direction from the Beowulf II. He gave Darren a strange look, not liking the sound of the man's voice.

"Where are you going?" Darren asked. "Where are you flying this fish boat?"

"Uh...to get my brother," Shane said. "Fucking shark hit his boat."

"The sharks are high on coke, man," Darren said. "Kinsey was right. So right. Flying in a high kite with boats!"

"Fucking A I was," Kinsey whispered as she reached out and grabbed Darren's hand. "Ow." She took a breath and looked at Darren. "Did you just scream about a boat kite?"

"Ow is right," Darren replied. "Ow is hurt. How are you? Hurting much too? Too? Too?"

Kinsey studied Darren and laughed. "You're high as that boat kite you're jabbering about." She held a compression bandage to her ribs. "I think I'll live, but I need stitches. And rum. Lots of rum."

"You can't drink," Darren laughed. It was a thin, reedy noise. "No drinking for high boats a flying flyer!"

"Whoa, Ditcher," Shane said. "As much as I enjoy a good psychedelic freak out, I think you should just close your eyes and chill."

"Do you see him?" Darren asked. "Do you see the boat shark fish flyer kite?"

"No," Shane said, looking over at Kinsey. "Don't see that. Don't see my brother either. But he's out there somewhere. I know it."

"Right on, man," Darren said, pumping a fist into the air. "Fish kite boat power!"

***

Thorne grabbed the unconscious Max around the shoulders and then spun about in the water, his channel gun in hand, and fired at the shark that came at them.

The round hit the beast in the nose and exploded, ripping a huge gouge out of the monster's snout, sending it diving down past the two men. Its dorsal fin clipped Thorne and he lost his grip on Max. And his channel gun.

He reached out for the weapon, but it sank too quickly. He had his channel pistol, but he couldn't get to it and also Max at the same time. The decision was easy as he swam to his nephew and grabbed the man about the shoulders again.

Thorne reached for the surface and pulled Max with him as his head broke into the air above. He quickly yanked his rebreather off, sick of the stupid thing, and took in a lungful of fresh air.

But the air wasn't as fresh as he'd hope. He could smell burning fuel and scorched metal and he looked about for the source. The Beowulf III. Thorne saw flames and thick, black smoke on its deck and shook his head.

"Now what?" he snarled. "Never a fucking break, huh?"

Max began to come around then he struggled and thrashed, but a quick slap to the face stopped that.

"Knock it off!" Thorne ordered. "Maxwell, stop it!"

Max grabbed at his rebreather and Thorne helped it off of him.

"Maxwell?" Max asked, his voice barely a rasp. "Only Mom calls me Maxwell."

"It got your attention," Thorne said. "Just like your mom used to."

"What happened?" Max asked, his eyes looking about as the two men floated. "Whoa, what's burning?"

"The B3," Thorne said. "And don't ask why. I don't know."

"Where's the shark?" Max asked. "Did you see it?"

"I saw it," Thorne said. "And shot it. It went below, but probably not for long."

"MAX!" Shane yelled over the Zodiac's motor as he zipped towards the men. "Over here!"

"Yeah, we see you," Max said, waving. "Don't run us over."

The Zodiac came about and Shane reached over and helped Max inside then held out a hand for his uncle, but Thorne was already grabbing on and climbing in.

"Hey, the gang's all here," Max said as he sat up and checked himself out. "And I'm in pretty good shape, considering how you two look."

"I blew up a shark," Kinsey said. "And got a little blown up too. It's not bad. Just a big scratch."

"I was shoved to the bottom of the ocean and did coke with a shark," Darren said. "Then we danced the tango. There were kites. High and flying."

Max and Thorne stared at him.

"Come again?" Thorne said. "You did what now?"

"I did coke with the shark," Darren said. "Well, not really with it since the thing had its snort and took off, where Kinsey then was able to blow it the fuck up. Way to go 'Sey!" He held up a hand and Kinsey gave him a high five, just happy the man wasn't talking about kites. "Then I swallowed half the ocean, since it was mixed with cocaine, and swam my ass to the surface! Hold on."

He turned his head puked. Then puked again.

"I need water!" Darren said. "Seriously! Who's running this airship full of pickles? I need fresh water or my kidneys will attack my body! ATTACK IT!"

"You aren't supposed to drink a ton of water when high on cocaine," Max replied.

"That's extasy," Shane said. "Not coke."

"My bad," Max said. "Drink all the water you want."

"We don't have any," Shane frowned.

"Bummer."

"I was right," Kinsey said. "The sharks are on coke."

"And lovin' it!" Darren said. "The fucker was just going for it down there! Gotta get me some more of that!"

"Yeah, you do," Thorne said as he shook his head. "How about we focus and find the other one?"

"Where'd it go, Uncle Vinny?" Max said. "After you shot it, did you see where it went?"

"No," Thorne said. "But it probably dove deep since I wounded it. Sharks go to the bottom when they're hurt."

"Maybe," Shane said. "This one isn't in its right shark mind, remember?"

"We need to get out of the water," Darren said. "Get back to the B3! They have fresh water! No flying boat kites!"

"I'm really not getting what's going on," Max said.

"Don't think too hard about it," Kinsey said. "He's tripping balls."

"Coke does that?" Max asked.

"Not the coke I've tried," Kinsey said. "But maybe there was something else in there."

"Doesn't matter," Thorne said. "We do need to get to the B3."

"Not with those men scaling the side," Shane said, pointing at the ship. "That's a fucking cartel strike force if I ever saw one."

"Fuck," Thorne growled. "I'm open to suggestions."

"I said we need to get out of the water!" Darren shouted. "Coats of boats of kites of fights!"

***

Lake tucked the Desert Eagle into his waistband, lifted Lucy up and threw her over his shoulder, getting her as far away from the flaming helo as possible. He dumped her against a wall and turned back as Popeye and most of the crew started spraying fire extinguishers every which way. Soon the deck was covered in thick foam and the fire was out.

"We have company," Lake said, nodding towards the railing as he pulled the Desert Eagle back out form his pants. "Any second now."

Popeye looked at the huge pistol in Lake's hand. "Got an extra one for me?"

"No."

"Damn."

"You can have this," Lake said and handed Popeye the fire axe.

"That'll work," Popeye said. He looked about. "Where's Ballantine?"

"Here," Ballantine said as two men helped him limp over. His hair was scorched and the skin on one arm looked like a science experiment of mutant bubbles. But his eyes burned with an anger and intensity that made Popeye gulp. "And we need to get everyone below and seal up the decks. Those men coming are not navy and they won't hesitate to kill us all."

Popeye looked at his axe. "This ain't such a great gift now."

"Come on," Ballantine said. "We have to move."

"Where are we going?" Lake asked.

"Where do you think?" Ballantine smiled. "The Toyshop."

***

"Dude, relax," Shane said. "We'll get out of the water. We just have to figure out how. We can't go to the B3 because-"

The kick was hard and swift and Shane's head snapped back. He would have tumbled over the side if it wasn't for the fact he was hanging onto the stick.

"What the fuck, Ditcher!" Shane shouted.

Darren clambered to his knees and took a swing at Shane. It missed as Shane ducked away, his eye wide with surprise and fear.

"Dude!" Max yelled and lunged at Darren, grabbing him about the waist. "Knock it off!"

Darren slammed his elbow down on the back of Max's neck again and again until Max was forced to let go and shove away.

"We are getting out of the water!" Darren snarled, foam forming at the corners of his mouth. "That's a fucking order!"

"Captain?" Thorne asked in a genial tone. "Should I throw them overboard?"

Darren's chest was heaving and his pupils had gone pure black. He spun about and faced Thorne.

"What?" Darren snapped.

"Should I toss the traitors overboard?" Thorne asked. "Feed them to the shark?"

Darren seemed confused, but still raging pissed. He looked each person in the face and didn't recognize a single one.

"I don't know you," he hissed, reaching for his dive knife on his ankle. But it wasn't there.

"Yeah, first thing I did," Max said as he tossed the knife overboard.

"That was mine!" Darren screamed as he dove at Max.

Instead of getting to the Reynolds brother, he met Thorne's fist right between the eyes. He dropped to the bottom of the boat, his vision filled with floating motes of light. Darren shook his head a couple times then pushed up, ready to attack again.

So was Thorne. Another hit between the eyes.

Darren's face slammed into the bottom of the boat, but he wouldn't quit. Instead, he seemed to get angrier.

"What the fuck?" Thorne said.

"'Ren, stop it!" Kinsey yelled. "Stop it now!"

"Fuck you, whore!" Darren yelled, turning his attention on Kinsey. "I should have gutted you the day you left me! Ungrateful fucking whore bitch cunt of a-"

His words were choked off. Literally, as Thorne wrapped one arm around Darren's neck and pressed the other against the side of his head. Darren fought, but Max was able to jump on him and pin his arms down, keeping Thorne from getting his eyes scratched out.

Thorne couldn't believe the strength he felt coming from Darren. The man should have been unconscious from the chokehold, but he kept fighting and fighting. After what seemed like an eternity, Darren's struggles started to slacken as his eyes rolled up in his head.

"Is he out?" Shane asked.

"I think so," Thorne said. "But I'm not letting go anytime soon."

He eased back the choke and Darren stayed still. Max reached up and double checked Darren's pulse, just in case.

"Jesus," Max said. "His heart is racing really fucking fast."

"The coke," Shane said. "He ingested too much. He's whacked out of his brain."

"No, it's not that," Kinsey said. "I mean, it is the coke, yeah, but if it's pure, then it wouldn't make him go all psycho. He'd be amped and bugfuck nuts, but not homicidal. That's meth behavior. This shit is all wrong."

Thorne looked off at the B3 then over at the Mexican Navy ships. A thought occurred to him, and he was about to express it, when the water around them exploded and the operators were sent flying into the air.

***

"We need to get to the upper deck!" Mike said as he wheeled towards the door.

"No, don't," Lake said as he stepped in front of Mike and blocked his way, Lucy still over his shoulder. "We're going to the Toyshop. Come on."

"We're under attack," Ballantine said as he limped into view, no longer helped by the deckhands. "Espanoza is boarding us."

"Why?" Gunnar asked.

"I'm guessing because of that," Ballantine said, nodding at the pallet of cocaine. "But I don't know why."

"I think I'm close to finding out," Gunnar said. "I can't leave now. And I can't let them take the cocaine. I have to run more tests."

"Your dedication to science is admirable," Ballantine said. "But your safety is more important."

"So is hers," Lake said, nodding his head towards the unconscious Lucy he held. "She could use your help, Doc."

"Leave her with me," Gunnar said. "Set her over there. I'll check on her and make sure she's okay."

"Come on, come on!" Popeye said, hopping from one real foot to one prosthetic foot. "I can hear gunfire! They're on deck!"

"Doctor?" Ballantine said. "Let's go."

"I'm staying," Gunnar said. "I can put the lab in contagion lockdown. They won't be able to get in."

Ballantine studied the man for a second then nodded to Lake. "Set her down on that table."

"You have to be kidding?" Lake snapped, looking from Ballantine to Gunnar. "Both of you! They'll get in here and kill you!"

"I'll stay," Mike said. "I can help fight them off."

"How?" Lake asked as he walked in and set Lucy down on the table. He turned and looked at Mike's wheelchair. "No offense, but you aren't exactly in fighting shape."

"You're wrong there," Mike smiled. "I may be missing my legs, but I can still fight. Trust me." Mike nodded at the Desert Eagle sticking out of Lake's waistband. "Can I borrow that?"

Lake looked at Mike, over at Gunnar who had started to check on Lucy, and back at Ballantine, then finally at Popeye.

"Give it to him," Popeye said. "The guy wants to fight then the guy can fight."

"Fuck," Lake said and handed the gun over. "I don't have any extra magazines."

Mike popped out the magazine, checked how many rounds were inside then slapped it back.

"This will be plenty," Mike said. "If they get in here they'll be bringing me more guns anyway."

Lake snorted then shook his head. "Be careful."

"We will," Gunnar said. "Now get out so I can lock things down."

"How is she?" Ballantine asked.

Gunnar looked up from Lucy. "Bad concussion. But she looks worse than she is."

"Good," Ballantine said. "I've changed my mind. She's coming with."

"She's what?" Gunnar asked. "Why?"

"Trust me," Ballantine said. "CO Lake? Would you mind doing the honors again?"

Lake did his look at everyone thing again then shrugged and picked Lucy back up.

"One more thing," Ballantine said. "There's a panel to the right of your workstation, Gunnar. Doesn't look like much, but place your hand against it and it should open for you."

"What's in it?" Gunnar asked.

"Help. So pay attention," Ballantine smiled as they left.

***

El Serpiente made his way to the bridge and steeped up to the control panels. He grimaced at what the monitors said.

"Lockdown," he snarled, turning to the armed men that followed him in. "Fix that."

"Sir? How?" one of the men asked. "We would need their code."

Diego's snarl turned to a smile and the men flinched. "Does C4 need a code?"

"Uh, on?" the man replied.

"Then that is how you will fix it," Diego said. "Blow the hatches one by one. Get me where I need to go."

"We could blow up the ship," another man said. "With us on it."

"I don't care about the ship," Diego explained. "I care about the product. We know it is here because the tracker on the sub is here. If the tracker is here then the sub is here. If the sub is here then the product is here. Find me the product. That is your job. If the ship sinks then it sinks. Who am I to stop fate?"

"Yes, sir," the men said and hurried from the bridge.

Diego turned his attention to the different monitors and started to go through each system to see what wasn't locked down.

***

Kinsey saw it coming for her, pulled her channel pistol, and fired.

But she missed as the shark dove quickly, avoiding the round that came at it. Before it was lost from sight, Kinsey saw there was a huge chunk missing from its snout. Her dad had nailed it, but not enough to stop it.

She kicked her feet and swam to the surface, breaking the surface and gasping for air in front of Shane.

"You see it?" Shane asked. "It was just here. Dorsal fin was coming at me then it dived."

"I shot at it," Kinsey said. "But it fucking dodged the bullet!"

"The things are smart," Shane said. "Where are the others?"

"There!" Kinsey said, pointing towards where Thorne and Max bobbed up and down. "I don't see Darren!"

Kinsey closed her eyes and shook her head as a wave of dizziness hit her.

"You cool?" Shane asked. "What about your side?"

"I'm fine," Kinsey said. "Just a shitty day."

"Tell me about it," Shane said. "Lost my rifle."

Kinsey couldn't help but smile. "Asshole."

Shane winked at her then looked down in the water; his eyes searching for the monster that he knew would be coming for them.

He looked back up and was glad to see Thorne and Max swimming over to them.

"Weapons check!" Thorne ordered as soon as he was close enough.

"Pistol," Kinsey said. "Dive knife."

"Me too," Shane said. "Lost my rifle."

"Shut up," Kinsey said. "Max?"

"I lost my rifle, but I have my pistol," he said as he reached below the water and slapped at his belt. "Or not. But I have my dive knife." They watched as he tucked his legs up and reached for his ankle. The look in his eyes told them it wasn't there. "Uh…I don't have anything. What the fuck?"

"Pistol," Thorne said. "That's it."

"Probably would have been a good idea to keep the rebreathers on," Max said. "Live and learn."

"Fuck learning," Thorne said, his face twisted with aggression and anger. "Living is all that matters."

Then he was lost from sight as he dove.

***

An explosion rocked the ship then another and another.

"They're blowing the hatches," Lake said as the group, having added another four crew members, hurried from one passageway to the next on their flight to the Toyshop. "That means Gun is fucked."

"He can handle himself," Ballantine said, placing his hand against a biometric scanner set into the wall by the next hatch. It slid aside and they all hustled through. "He's a resourceful man."

The group hurried down the passageway as more explosions made the ship shudder.

"Resourceful doesn't do shit against explosives," Lake said.

"You never know," Ballantine said as he stopped by a blank wall. "We're here."

The whole group looked at the wall then at Ballantine.

"You must have hit your head pretty bad, Mr. Ballantine," Popeye said. "That's a wall right there."

"Yes, it is, Popeye," Ballantine said. "But not all walls are actually walls."

They waited by the wall, but nothing happened.

"I don't mean to argue, Mr. Ballantine," Popeye said. "But I'm thinking this is actually a wall. Just like it looks."

"No, it's not," Ballantine said. He stepped forward and smacked both hands against it.

"We can't wait here," Lake said. "We need to move. If we get to the mini-subs, we can get all of us off this ship. It'll be a tight squeeze, but between the Wiglaf II and Wiglaf III we can fit."

Ballantine frowned and turned away from the wall. "That could present a problem."

"How do you mean?" Lake asked. "We have ten here. There's room."

"But there's only one mini-sub," Ballantine admitted. "The Wiglaf II isn't here anymore. Or shouldn't be."

Another explosion echoed through the ship, much closer than the previous ones.

"What aren't you telling me?" Lake asked. "Out with it, Ballantine."

"Darby has left the ship in the Wiglaf II," Ballantine said, holding up a hand to ward off more questions. He leaned back against the wall, suddenly very tired. "I'm not going into details, so don't ask. We can get six out in the Wiglaf III. Maybe eight if two lay on the floor. But the oxygen will be depleted quickly so the escape will have to be fast and then you'll have to surface."

"There are ten of us," Lake said, nodding his chin at the still unconscious Lucy in his arms. "But you aren't coming with, are you? And she's staying too, right?"

"Right on both counts," Ballantine said. He kicked back against the wall with his heel in frustration. "Leave Lucy here. You go. You know how to pilot the mini-sub."

"I'm staying with you," Lake said. "Popeye can pilot it."

"I hate those little subs," Popeye replied.

"But you know how to pilot them," Lake said. "Since Darren isn't on the ship then that makes me acting captain. I stay." He focused a harsh gaze on Ballantine. "Unless you object to my being captain?"

Ballantine shook his head. "No objections here, Acting Captain. Except that I'd rather you left."

Lake looked at the men and nodded down the passageway. "Go. I'm staying."

They all just stood there.

"That's an order!" Lake roared.

Popeye nodded then gestured for the men to follow him. They hurried away, turned a corner, and were lost from sight.

Lake watched them go then turned back to Ballantine.

"How about we get to the real entrance of the Toyshop?" Lake said. "I'd like to set her down."

"No point," Ballantine replied. "Carlos won't let us in there."

"Why not?"

"Because I ordered him not to," Ballantine said. "Security precaution if the ship were ever taken over. If I go to the real entrance then he has orders to stay sealed shut." Ballantine rested his head back against the wall and closed his eyes. "This is the backdoor. Carlos knows to be looking for me here. Or anyone I send. If he isn't opening up then something is wrong."

Lake didn't respond.

Ballantine opened his eyes and looked at the acting captain.

"Sorry, but I don't know what else to tell you," he said and pushed away from the wall. "We need to shelter somewhere else."

Another explosion. And another.

"Don't think so," Lake said, his jaw hanging open.

Ballantine slowly turned and grinned at the sight. The wall was nearly transparent and there stood Carlos and Ingrid, both holding very large automatic rifles.

Ballantine waved and part of the wall slid aside.

"I didn't bother you two, did I?" Ballantine said as he pushed past Carlos and Ingrid into the Toyshop.

"Carlos forgot which wall it was," Ingrid said.

"I did not," Carlos argued. "I narrowed it down between two walls."

"He forgot," Ingrid said, hurrying Lake inside. She pressed on the wall and it sealed then turned dark, looking like a normal ship's wall.

146

"Set her on that long cart," Ingrid said. "I have a prototype med bay in sector eight I can wheel her to."

"For the record, I did not forget," Carlos announced as Ingrid wheeled Lucy away.

"Don't care," Ballantine replied. "We need guns."

"We have those," Carlos said, holding out the rifle to Lake.

"No, I'd prefer a pistol," Lake said. "The bigger the better."

"I'll get your usual," Ingrid said.

"Point me to the control station," Ballantine ordered Carlos as he looked at the many rows of equipment that surrounded them. "And two of whatever weapon Lake gets."

"This way," Carlos said and turned right. Then stopped and turned left. "This way."

***

Her systems told her she was past the Mexican naval blockade, but that didn't ease Darby's tension. She looked at the coordinates of her destination and was not happy with the amount of open water she'd have to move through to get there.

That left a lot of space for a shark to come at her.

She knew the risks of what she was doing, but it didn't make it any easier. Her paranoia was ratcheted up all the way and her eyes kept moving from the windows in front of her to the sonar to the radar to the navigation system and back to the windows.

She took a deep breath and slowly let it out her nose. There was nothing else she could do, but keep going and hope the sharks were occupied.

***

Espanoza's men ran through the passageways, their Ak-47s barking lead as they killed anyone that was unlucky enough to be in their way. The crewmembers of the Beowulf III, men that had signed on knowing there would be danger and that the B3 was a very different ship, fled from the death that stalked them.

Thinking they were safe behind locked and sealed hatches, the men found out the hard way they weren't as the metal exploded in at them and bullets followed. Blood and the acrid odor of C4 filled the passageways as Espanoza's men blasted their way from deck to deck.

***

Thorne burst from the surface and spun about, trying to look in all directions at once.

"Where is it?"

"Did you see it?"

"Daddy? What's wrong? Did you see Darren?"

Thorne looked over at his daughter and two nephews as they treaded water. "I don't know."

"Don't know what?" Kinsey asked. "Don't know if you saw the shark? If you saw Darren? What don't you know?"

"Shadow!" Max yelled as he looked down into the water. He ducked his head below for a better look then came up spluttering. "It's coming at us!"

"On it!" Shane said as he dove under, his channel pistol in hand.

He saw the shark coming up fast and emptied the magazine. It was a rookie move, but he knew he didn't have time to take careful shots.

The rounds sped at the shark and the monster swam out of the way, but three hit their mark and exploded against the shark's side. The creature jerked and flipped about, changing directions instantly.

By the time Shane saw what was about to happen, it was too late.

The shark's tail slammed into his body and he found himself flying up out of the water. He would have laughed at the look on his brother's face as he soared over his family, but he was too busy screaming. And bleeding.

***

Popeye hustled through the passageways as fast as possible, leading the other men from hatch to hatch. As boatswain his biometrics were loaded into the ship's system so the hatches opened for him. He didn't want to think what would have happened to the men if he hadn't been there. The ability for "authorized" personnel to only be able to access hatches during lockdown was an argument Popeye had heard Darren and Ballantine have on more than one occasion.

They hit a set of stairs and slid down to the next deck then proceeded down the passageway to the next hatch, opened it, hit the next set of stairs, the passageway, the hatch, more stairs.

Finally, Popeye held his hand to the hatch to the mini-sub bays. The hatch opened and he hurried everyone inside, making sure the hatch sealed behind him. One of the bays was still purging water from Darby's launch, so Popeye pointed at the hatch to the other bay.

"In there," he said as he pressed a hand against the scanner. It didn't open.

"Pop?" one of the men asked.

"Hold on," Popeye said as he tried again.

It still didn't work. He slammed his considerable fist against the scanner again and again until the high impact plastic cracked. The hatch slid open and Popeye smiled.

"Technology got nothing on these ham hocks," he grinned as he pointed at the mini-sub docked in the bay. "Get your asses inside! Now!"

***

Diego grinned as he figured out how to override part of the ship's systems. He couldn't gain control of the helm, or unlock the hatches, but he could make sure all hatches stayed locked. He'd watched as hatch after hatch below deck had opened then closed. He knew it was the crew escaping, and after some study, he realized where they were escaping to.

He pulled a radio from his belt and put it to his mouth.

"Where are you?" he asked.

"Getting close to the galley," a man replied. "Should we bother with that?"

"Are you hungry?" Diego asked.

The man paused then replied cautiously. "No?"

"No, you are not hungry," Diego responded. "So why would we bother with the galley?"

"We wouldn't, sir," the man replied.

"Then leave the galley alone," Diego replied. "You need to get to the sub and the product. You are not there yet. Get there."

"Yes, sir," the man replied.

An alarm sounded and Diego looked at the monitor. Someone had opened a hatchway to the mini-sub bay despite Diego's override.

"Get to the mini-sub bays first," Diego ordered. "There's a breach."

"The mini-sub bays?" the man asked. "Is that not where we are going?"

"No, you are going to the specimen bays," Diego replied as he studied the schematic of the ship on the monitor in front of him. "The mini-sub bays are fully aft and just above the specimen bays. Go there now. I don't want to have to come down there and do your job for you."

"Yes, sir," the man replied. "I mean, no, sir. You do not have to come down here. It is handled."

Diego placed the radio back on his belt then started to try to hack into the navigation systems, and hopefully, the helm.

***

The mess was dark and empty. Except for Chief Steward Beau McWhitt.

After what had happened in Somalia, Beau had pretty much kept to himself, occupying his time running the galley, the mess, and making sure the Beowulf III was well supplied with whatever the men needed.

At five feet six, he had the features of a teenage boy. But, being twenty-four, Beau wasn't a boy and had been through hell like a man. He had constant nightmares of the galley filling with water, ready to drown him and take him down deep below the surface of the sea. When the Beowulf II had encountered the monster sharks off the coast of Somalia, and the ship had started to sink from the shark attacks, Beau had been left behind.

No one came looking for him as he tried to get his mess crew out the hatches and up to safety on the deck above. They'd fled, but he'd stayed behind to make sure no one had been forgotten.

Turned out he had.

The ship had fallen apart around him and he'd made a mad dash through the flooding passageways until he found himself in front of the Toyshop. Hands grabbed him and he had been yanked inside just as the Toyshop became something else.

All of those thoughts went through his head as he hid in the shadows of the B3 mess and watched as brown faces appeared at the hatch, looked about, then went away. He had heard a man speaking to someone in Spanish, so he figured the Mexican Navy had boarded the B3, he just didn't know why.

And didn't really care. Because here he was, forgotten again. He'd sent his crew out as soon as the claxons blared. Then the explosions started. And gunshots. He had no idea if anyone had survived or not.

But Beau planned on surviving.

He looked at the meat cleavers he gripped in each hand then looked at the hatch. He counted to ten then walked towards the hatch, took a deep breath, stuck one of the cleavers in his belt, and pressed his hand against the biometric scanner. Nothing happened. He flipped a cleaver around and smashed the scanner. The hatch opened, he grabbed the other cleaver from his belt, and stepped out into the passageway.

***

All of the men were crammed into the Wiglaf III and Popeye started to close the top hatch when Espanoza's men rushed into the mini-sub bay. They saw Popeye and opened fire. Bullets pinged off the Wiglaf III as Popeye ducked inside, slammed the hatch closed, and locked it tight.

Bullets kept hitting the mini-sub as Popeye went through the launch protocols.

"Pop?" a man asked.

"I know, I know," Popeye said as he struggled to get the mini-sub operating. "Give me a damn minute!"

More bullets hit the mini-sub and the distinct sound of gas escaping some valve reached everyone's ears.

"There!" Popeye yelled as he pressed a button and a claxon rang out in the bay.

Espanoza's men fired some more then quickly retreated from the bay and behind the hatch that sealed tight as soon as they were through it. One of the men, the one that had spoken to Diego before, watched through the porthole as the bay filled with water. Bubbles streamed from the end of the Wiglaf III once the water had completely filled the bay then the far wall opened and the mini-sub shot out, gone from sight in seconds.

The man didn't want to, but all eyes were on him and he knew what had to be done. He took the radio from his belt and put it to his mouth.

***

Diego slammed his hand on the control panel again and again, ripping part of his palm open. He looked at the wound then put it to his mouth and sucked on the blood, savoring the salty flavor.

"Get to the specimen bays," Diego said into the radio. "I will join you there shortly.

***

"What's the plan?" Lake asked, looking from Ballantine to Carlos to Ingrid. "This thing can become an escape pod, right? Then let's escape."

Carlos looked over at Ballantine and glared. Gone was the look of embarrassment and subservience from before. Lake was puzzled by the look of rage that now clouded the man's features.

"What did I miss?" Lake said. "No, let me guess. This doesn't turn into an escape pod, does it?"

"Those modifications weren't completed," Carlos said. "Against my protests."

"There was other work that needed to be finished first," Ballantine said, matching Carlos's glare. "Such as the specimen bays. I told you we would complete your modifications once we returned to the company's Manila facilities. They have the skills to do it right."

"I did it right on the Beowulf II," Carlos snapped.

"Excuse me?" Ingrid said.

"With some help," Carlos said, waving Ingrid away.

"Fuck you too," Ingrid said and stormed off into the shelves.

"Then why didn't you complete the mods yourself again?" Lake asked.

"Because he specifically told me not to," Carlos snarled, pointing at Ballantine.

Ballantine stepped closer, letting the accusatory finger stab him in the chest.

"Whoa, whoa, knock it off," Lake said. "None of this bullshit matters now. We need to figure out how we'll get out of here. Eventually, they'll blow their way inside."

"Not hardly," Carlos snorted. "You can't get into the armory."

"Carlos doesn't like to share his toys," Ballantine said.

"Don't call them toys!" Carlos yelled.

"Knock it off!" Lake shouted, shoving the men away from each other.

"Hey, guys?" Ingrid asked, coming back to where they stood, her face white with fear. "Where's Moshi? I can't find her."

"Just yell for her," Carlos said, putting his hands to his mouth. "Moshi! MOSHI!"

"Not like she can respond," Lake said.

"She's shy, not mute," Ingrid said.

"Really? I didn't know that," Lake replied. "I thought she couldn't speak at all."

"Moshi!" Carlos yelled again.

"Moshi!" Ingrid echoed.

"Stop," Ballantine said, but was drowned out by the others' yelling. "Stop!"

"What? Why?" Ingrid asked.

"I know where she is," Ballantine said. "I know *exactly* where she is."

***

The sounds from above made Moshi cringe and shake with fear. She was a weapon smith and she knew immediately that C4 was being detonated and AK-47s were being fired. There was small arms fire as well -9mms, .45s, .38s, and even a couple of .22s- but those sounds were sporadic and Moshi knew they could be from the attackers or the B3's crew. But the explosions and machine guns were not.

Her hands flew across the controls of the whale sub and she began flipping switches and turning knobs. The sub powered up, but she didn't engage the tail motor since the specimen bay was empty of water and the sub was dry docked. If she engaged the motor without the tail being submerged, she'd warp the sub and most likely rip it completely apart.

She heard the hatch above on the catwalk open and she froze, terrified to move or even breathe. Boot steps echoed through the bay and she pressed her body as far into the sub's cockpit as possible, hoping she was out of sight from whoever was coming. Her view out of the sub was limited, since the hatch was so small, and she hoped the view into the sub was just as obscured.

Men's voices called out in Spanish and she picked out a few choice curse words here and there. She heard boots descending a ladder then land on top of the sub. There were more curse words and then a loud thump.

Someone was inside the cargo hold. She hadn't closed the hold doors after the cocaine was removed and the men must have decided to double check to make sure none of the cargo was left behind. Her teeth began to chatter as her heart crawled into her throat. She stank of fear and hated herself for it, but she didn't break. She stayed quiet, her natural default mode anyway, and waited.

The sub shook as she heard the man leave the cargo hold and begin to make his way atop the sub to the cockpit hatch. She could hear him speaking to someone over a radio and the voice that replied was very angry. Moshi almost lost it, but shoved the fear down, as she looked about the cockpit, desperate for an answer to her predicament.

There, easily within reach, was her tablet. She had been taking notes on it and uploading her findings to the Beowulf II's mainframe. She'd even used it to get the backtracked coordinates to Darby and her mini-sub.

But now she needed it for something else. She snatched it up and flipped through page after page until she found the system she needed. She was surprised to find an override already in place, but she easily bypassed that and took control of all the hatches.

A loud claxon rang out as the hatch by the catwalk above slammed shut.

Men began shouting and she heard the boots on the sub stop then turn and run. Boots on the ladder, boots on the catwalk, hands pounding at the sealed hatch.

Moshi shoved away from where she'd wedged herself and threw switches and yanked at levers. The cargo hold hatch doors shut on the sub and so did the hatch above her. She scrambled to it and twisted the wheel, making sure it was completely sealed before she turned her attention back to her tablet.

She let out a breath she didn't know she was holding and began the protocol to fill the specimen bay with water. Even through the hull, she could hear men shouting and yelling. Then gunfire as they started to shoot at the sub.

She shrieked as bullets impacted the faux skin of the whale and metal hull it hid underneath. She settled her hands on the controls and waited for the sound she needed to hear. While she struggled to ignore the sounds she didn't want to hear. More gunfire and then muted screams as water filled the bay and rushed up over the sub.

There was nowhere for the men to go. Moshi didn't want to kill them, but in order for the specimen bay doors to open, the bay had to be completely filled. The pressure had to equalize or the bay doors wouldn't budge.

Tears streamed down her face as the screams were finally silent and her tablet chimed. She pressed the button that flashed red and the doors in front of the sub split down the middle, opening up for her escape.

***

The ocean water distorted his view through the hatch porthole as Diego stood there, having joined the men below, and watched the sub escape into open waters. The corpses of his men that had been trapped inside floated about the specimen bay. Some were sucked out of the bay by the sub's passage, but others just bobbed up against the ceiling and the catwalk.

Diego didn't flinch as a man's face appeared at the porthole, his eyes bulged and mouth wide open. The man's corpse kept floating and was soon lost from sight.

None of the men that stood behind Diego said a word. They just waited for their boss to decide the next plan of action. Most of them hoped the plan wouldn't be to turn and kill them. Diego was cold and calculating, and wasn't known for brutally killing his own men in frustration, but then he wasn't called El Serpiente for nothing.

Diego turned about and the men flinched. He smiled slightly at that.

"There is another place the product could be," Diego said.

"Men have checked the main cargo hold, sir," a man said, the rifle in his hands shaking slightly. "There was no sign of the product there."

"I doubt they would put that type of cargo where any sailor could get at it," Diego sneered. "Do you? Is that what you really think a person like Ballantine would do? Or any of these Grendel operators?"

"No, sir," the man replied. "I was only making sure you knew we checked there. I wanted you to know we were thorough."

"Does that look thorough?" Diego asked, looking back over his shoulder at the porthole. "It looks like anything but thorough."

"Yes, sir. My apologies, sir."

"I don't need your apologies," Diego said as she shoved past the men and headed for the stairs. "I need your guns. Follow me. I'll show you thorough."

***

"She's gone!" Ingrid cried. "She made it out! See!"

Ingrid showed the men her tablet and the view of a happy Moshi waving at them from the sub's cockpit. Then the image started to pixelate and went black.

"Where'd she go? What happened?" Ingrid asked.

"She was using the camera on her tablet," Carlos said. "She's out of the ship's Wi-Fi range."

"Oh, right," Ingrid said.

"She's out. Good," Lake said. "But what is she going to do with that sub?"

"Whatever she wants," Ballantine responded. "She is a highly capable, intelligent woman. I am sure she will find a good use for it."

"She'll find a good use for it? That's your answer?" Lake snapped. "That doesn't help us or anyone on this ship!"

"Moshi won't abandon us," Ballantine said. "I know the woman well. She is not a coward."

"She hides whenever anyone comes into the Toyshop!" Lake yelled.

"Don't call it the Toy-" Carlos started to say then was stopped by Lake's fist.

"Acting Captain Lake," Ballantine warned, pressing his hand against Lake's chest. "Calm. The. Fuck. Down."

The tone of Ballantine's voice resonated with Lake and he took a step back, shook his head, then frowned at Carlos.

"I'm sorry," he said. "I lost my temper. I'm supposed to be the one on this ship that always keeps his cool. It won't happen again." He took a deep breath. "But I still don't think that woman can help. She doesn't ever speak, for God's sake."

"Maybe she just doesn't have anything to say," Ballantine smiled at the acting captain.

***

"He's coming around," Max said, holding onto his brother as they floated in the ocean water. "Shane? Can you hear me, dude?"

"I can," Shane said. "And smell you. You need a mint."

"Fuck off," Max said and shoved his brother away, causing the man to dip under water.

Shane came up sputtering and held out a hand. "Sorry, sorry."

"Did you see Darren down there?" Kinsey asked, her voice panicked.

"Just now? No," Shane replied. "And not before I flew the sharky skies, either. There's no sign of him?"

"No," Thorne said tersely as he continued to look at the water underneath them. He bobbed his head down then came up for air. "I don't see any of them."

"Any of them?" Shane asked. "Any of who? The shark and Darren?"

"Yes," Thorne said. "And another."

"Another?" Kinsey asked. "Who else is down there?"

"I don't know," Thorne said. "Maybe I was seeing things. One shark is dead and the other attacked Shane so that makes two."

They just watched the commander as he tried to work something out.

"If the timing was right then there's only one more," Thorne said. "But…"

"But what?" Kinsey asked. "Daddy did you see another shark?"

"I don't know," Thorne replied.

"Whoa, whoa, whoa!" Max said. "There might be a third? But we saw the videos! It was obvious only two were attacking all those people!"

"Yeah, how could there be a third?" Max asked.

"How the fuck should I know!" Thorne snapped. "But Ballantine did say there could be a third. Or even a fourth."

"Well, that's comforting," Max muttered.

"What's that?" Kinsey asked as several meters away bubbles started to come up to the surface. "Is that one of the sharks?"

In seconds it became clear it was. And so much more.

The shark exploded from the water, launching itself high into the air. And holding on for dear life, with one hand on the shark's dorsal fin, while the other pressed a channel pistol to the monster's side, sat Darren. He was screaming his head off, spewing every vile epithet he knew at the beast as it flew through the air.

He was also pulling the trigger over and over on the channel pistol. Despite the gun's limitations out of the water, it was obvious Darren was doing some damage as blood sprayed in all directions and the rest of Team Grendel watched in awe as holes burst open on the side of the beast.

The shark slammed into the water on its side and Darren was thrown free. He landed just feet from Kinsey and she swam to him, taking him up in her arms. He held the channel pistol in his hand and was still pulling the trigger over and over even though the magazine was long since emptied.

Emptied into the shark that floated on the surface of the water for a minute then started to sink.

"I'm going to make sure," Thorne said as he dived down and swam towards the shark corpse.

The beast kept sinking fast and Thorne stopped, settled himself as best he could, took aim, and fired until his own pistol clicked empty. He watched as far below more holes opened up in the shark's side then several small explosions ripped the monster in half.

He swam up quickly and grinned at his Team.

"Done," he smiled. "That one isn't coming back."

"Then what's that there?" Shane asked as large bubbles broke the surface of the water.

Then the whale sub surfaced. The Team stared.

The cockpit hatch opened on the sub as did the cargo hold doors.

Moshi peeked her head out of the cockpit and grinned at the Team. She gestured for them to get into the cargo hold and none of the operators needed to be told twice. They swam as fast as they could, Kinsey helping Darren, then climbed aboard.

Max and Shane scrambled up into the cargo hold then reached down as Thorne and Kinsey tried to help boost Darren up to them.

"Jesus he's heavy," Max said as he snagged one of Darren's arms.

"No shit," Shane said.

"Did you guys see that?" Darren mumbled. "I rode a shark. I fucking rode it like a flying kite. Killed the fucker too. I'm a shark cowboy."

"Yep, you rode and killed a shark, pardner," Shane said, finally able to get his hand up under Darren for better leverage. "You'll be telling that story the rest of your life."

Kinsey and Thorne steadied Darren as Max and Shane lifted him up into the cargo hold. Then the brothers appeared again and held down their arms.

"Come on," Max said.

"You're next," Shane added.

"You first," Thorne insisted. "Then me."

"But-"

"Don't argue, Kins," Thorne said. "Just get up in the whale sub."

"Mark that on the list of shit you thought you'd never say," Shane said as he got a hold of one of Kinsey's hands while Max grabbed the other.

"That is going to be a long list before our time with Ballantine is done," Max laughed. "I can guarantee that."

Kinsey was pulled all the way up and she spun about and reached for her father.

Thorne started to reach up then stopped, his attention drawn to the water.

"Daddy?" Kinsey asked.

"It's okay," Thorne said. "Thought I felt something, but you can see there's nothing there."

He reached up and his finger tips touched Kinsey's. And then he was gone.

But instead of being pulled under the water, Thorne was dragged across it, his body sticking up like he was a dorsal fin himself. Surrounding his body was the massive mouth of a shark, yet this one wasn't quite like the others. It was scarred and beaten up, parts of it chunked out in long, red gouges. It had seen better times.

"DADDY!" Kinsey screamed as she watched her father get taken further away. And then he was gone as the shark dove. "Daddy!"

"Get in," a quiet voice said behind her.

Kinsey, Shane and Max all turned to see Moshi waving at them.

"Get in the hold," she said quietly. "We'll go get your father."

She slammed the cockpit hatch shut and the three operators scrambled to get into the cargo hold and seal the doors so they could go get their father, uncle, commander.

Chapter Seven: Tres

Loud pounding drew Gunnar's attention to the hatch and he flipped off the man that looked in through the hatch's porthole.

"That's a great idea, Gun," Mike said as he slipped down out of his wheelchair, the Desert Eagle tucked in his waistband up against his back. "Taunting the enemy never backfires."

"They can't get in here and I could give two shits," Gunnar said. "I'm so close to working this all out."

"What does it fucking matter?" Mike asked. "Answers aren't worth your life!"

"They are to me!" Gunnar snapped. "Answers are all I have! I'm not a SEAL, I'm not a captain of a ship, I'm nothing except for my research!"

"But this shit isn't your research!" Mike countered. "You study marine life! Fucking ghost whales and giant sharks! Not fucking cocaine!"

"I study the cocaine if it affects marine life," Gunnar said. "And it's not cocaine."

"It's not...what?" Mike asked. "You said your tests came up as cocaine every single time. What the fuck is it?"

"I think it's-" Gunnar began to reply, but the hatch suddenly opened and several men walked in, rifles pointed at him. "Oh...crap..."

Gunnar dove out of the way as bullets flew towards him, but the slugs obliterated the counter where he had just been working at, destroying everything

"FUCKERS!" Gunnar shouted. "YOU FUCKS!"

More men streamed into the lab and found him where he laid, their rifles pointed at his head and chest. He looked around, but Mike was nowhere to be seen.

"Hello, Doctor Peterson," Diego said. "I am Diego Fernandez." The man pulled a long knife from a sheath on his belt. "I am also known as El Serpiente." He pointed the knife at the pallet of cocaine. "That belongs to my boss, do you mind if we take it off your hands?" He kneeled down next to Gunnar. "If you do mind then I can also take your hands. Your choice."

"Don't really have much choice, do I?" Gunnar replied. "You'll kill me and take it or take it and kill me. Two sides of the same coin."

"More than likely," Diego shrugged. "But I like to give those I'm about to kill at least the illusion of choice. It eases their minds."

"Hey," Beau said from the hatch, the two meat cleavers in his hands dripping with blood. "Step away from the doc."

Diego looked at Beau and the gore and blood smeared apron he wore over his black tank top. The man was short, but Diego came from short people and knew that didn't make a goddamn bit of difference. His uncle had been barely five five and Diego watched him rip a dog's head off with his bare hands.

It had been Diego's dog. His uncle didn't live long after that. Actually, he did live long, just not very comfortably.

Diego watched Beau for a minute then stood up, knife in hand.

"You any good with those?" Diego asked.

"The blood isn't answer enough for ya?" Beau replied.

"It is," Diego said and nodded to his men.

They all brought their rifles up and took aim.

Then one started screaming. And another. And another.

Diego looked at his men then looked down at the ground and the crawling form of Mike Pearlman, with a blood coated scalpel in his hand. He slashed out and cut right through another man's boot and into his Achilles' tendon.

"You," Diego snarled. "I know you."

He threw his knife, but Mike rolled out of the way. It bounced off the metal floor and skidded across the lab. Mike slashed another man's leg then pulled his pistol and fired at Diego, but Diego was called El Serpiente for many reasons, not just his cold-blooded nature. He also happened to be very fast.

As Mike fired, and Diego ran across the lab, staying ahead of Mike's aim, Gunnar pushed up from the floor and ran to the place on the wall Ballantine had indicated earlier. He pressed his hand on the wall and a compartment popped open. He looked inside and smiled.

"Down!" Beau shouted and Gunnar hit the deck.

Gunfire rang out then a thud and a scream. Gunnar looked over and saw a man fall to the floor, a meat cleaver stuck between his shoulder blades. The rifle he held clattered to the floor as he tried to reach back and pull the knife free.

"No, no, no," Beau said as he walked in and swung away with the other cleaver. The man's head tumbled to the deck. "Blades stay where I put them." He looked at Gunnar. "You okay?"

"I am," Gunnar said. "Behind you!"

Beau dropped to a knee and spun around. Lashing out with the cleaver. It buried deep into a man's belly. Blood and intestines spilled out around Beau's wrist and he tried to pull back, but the cleaver was stuck. Beau had swung so hard that he cut all the way to the man's spine.

The dying man reached for Beau, his fingers trying to find the Chief Steward's throat. Beau wrenched at the cleaver and the man screamed, his hands instinctively going to his belly. The man was tossed to the right as Beau wrenched again then to the left as Beau kept struggling to get the cleaver free. Finally, he stood up and shoved the man back against the counter, lifted his leg, and kicked the handle of the cleaver as hard as he could.

The snap of the man's spine echoed in the lab, and his torso started to bob and weave like a child's spring animal toy. Beau reached into the man's guts and pulled the meat cleaver loose, wiped the gore on the man's shirt, then buried it between his eyes.

He tried pulling back, but it was stuck again.

"Motherfucker!" Beau yelled.

"Here," Gunnar said as he smacked the handle down with the flat of his hand. The cleaver fell and Gunnar caught it easily.

"Thanks," Beau said then turned and hurled the cleaver as a man came running at them.

The cleaver slammed into the man's chest, but handle first, and only knocked the man down. As Beau ran towards the man, Gunnar spun about and grabbed what was in the small compartment in the wall.

He pulled out the two 7" carbon steel, fixed blade combat knives and smiled. Then saw a piece of paper and picked it up, stuffing it in his pocket. Spinning the knife in his right hand so it was blade down while he kept the one in his left hand blade up, Gunnar turned his attention quickly back to the fight. He closed on a man that was about to open fire on Mike and stabbed him in the side of the neck. Blood spurted everywhere as the artery the man's body of blood across the room like a fountain. Gunnar slammed his right hand into the man's chest, burying the second blade deeply into the bleeding man's heart.

The body fell and Gunnar kicked the dead man's rifle over to Mike just as the Desert Eagle clicked empty. Mike nodded his thanks, picked up the rifle, and kept firing as Diego jumped over a table and turned to run towards the hatch.

Beau hacked a man's arm off then turned the cleaver about and cracked open the man's skull. He shoved him aside and stepped towards the hatch, changing Diego's mind. El Serpiente switched directions again, this time going straight for the pallet of cocaine.

Bullets ripped up the ceiling above Diego as Mike tried to get a bead on the man, but his position was too low and he couldn't get a good angle. Diego dove behind the pallet and Mike swore.

"You can't stay back there forever, dipshit!" Mike yelled.

There were more gunshots and Beau jumped away from the hatch as six more men came through. He turned in the air and slashed with the cleaver, but found only open air as the man he was going for rocked back on his heels, keeping his chest from being slashed open. More gunfire and Beau dove then rolled over and over, keeping himself from being shot up, before stopping behind the same table Mike was hiding behind.

"Hey," Beau said.

"Hey, what's up?" Mike replied.

Gunnar tossed one blade and it hit a man between the eyes then he sprinted to the others, his left hand slashing back and forth. A rifle barked and Gunnar felt a searing pain in his side, but he ignored it and kept attacking. He was able to push the men back, his attack so frenzied that they were stunned and confused by the constant movement of the knife.

That gave Mike and Beau time to regroup. Beau stood up and threw his cleaver. This time it didn't bounce off the target, but landed firmly in a man's shoulder as the guy was about to shoot Gunnar. Mike rolled to the side and came out from behind the table, the rifle in his hands firing non-stop.

Two men, then a third fell as their heads were ripped apart by hot slugs. Gunnar ducked down, turned and gave Mike a reproachful look, then turned back and hamstringed the man in front of him. The man tumbled on top of Gunnar, and he started to shove him off, then pulled the man back on top as another man opened fire. The man on top of Gunnar shuddered as the bullets ripped into him.

The gunfire stopped and Gunnar looked out from under the fresh corpse that covered him. Beau had regained one of his cleavers and had embedded it in the firing man's crotch. He let go and the cleaver just bobbed there, a poor substitute for what it had just severed. Beau grimaced and wiped the blood off his hand.

"Come on out, asshole!" Mike shouted as Gunnar got up and helped him into the wheel chair.

All about them men were dead, dying, or begging not to die. Beau demonstrated his lack of mercy and silenced the beggars while leaving the silent to suffer.

"I said come on out!" Mike yelled at the pallet of cocaine. "Or I just start shooting!"

Gunnar leaned down and whispered in Mike's ear. "You don't want to do that. We breathe that shit in and it's not going to be a fun party."

A poof of white powder lifted up from behind the pallet and Gunnar gasped.

"Oh, shit, not good," he said just before Diego leapt from his refuge, a maniacal war cry coming from his throat.

***

"We can't see anything in here!" Kinsey shouted, frustrated by the lack of portholes in the cargo hold. "I don't know what's happening to my father!"

"I see him," Moshi's voice said from a tiny speaker set into the wall of the hold. "The shark is fast, but so is this sub now. I fixed it. Made it better. I'll catch him."

"Then what?" Max asked. "We don't have rebreathers or scuba tanks. How will we get him in here without drowning?"

"You hold your breath," Moshi said. "Your suits will keep you from being crushed. You get him and put him in the hold. Then I pump out the water and we go."

"Whatever works," Shane said. "We can't let Uncle Vinny die."

"I can hold my breath forever!" Darren yelled. "FOREVER! LIKE A KITE!"

The brothers looked at Darren then at Kinsey.

"What do we do?" Shane asked.

"What do you mean?" Kinsey said.

"With Ditcher," Max said. "He's obviously on some bad shit. What did you do when that happened to you? When you took some bad shit?"

"I usually fucked some people up," Kinsey said. "Most of the time I blacked out and when I came to I had some cleaning to do if it was my place or I just got the fuck out of there if it wasn't."

"Cleaning? What the hell did you clean?" Shane asked.

"Blood," Kinsey said. "Bodies. Whatever I had to."

"Jesus, Sis," Max whispered. "There's a lot of shit you haven't told us, isn't there?"

"You don't know the half of it," Kinsey frowned.

Her arm was grabbed and she found herself yanked close to Darren's face.

"Are we going to kill another shark?" Darren asked. "That was some sweet, sweet shit. I could kill sharks all day."

His pupils dilated, closed, dilated. It was like nothing Kinsey had ever seen before.

"Let go of me or I toss you out the hatch," Kinsey snarled.

"You'll kill us all!" Darren shouted then winked.

"How about this?" Shane asked then hammered blow to Darren's temple.

Darren turned his head slowly to look at Shane and he grinned wide.

"You think you can take me?" Darren asked as he tried to get to his feet. "Is that what you think, you little hippie fucker? You don't have the kite balls to do it."

"Is he calling me a hippie or a guy that fucks hippies?" Shane asked, scrambling away from Darren until his back was up against the cargo hold wall. "Because one is kinda an insult and one I don't mind at all."

"You're dead," Darren said, pointing at Shane.

He lunged, but was knocked to the side as Max slammed a foot into his ribs. Kinsey grabbed Darren by the collar and pulled him close, sticking her face in his.

"Calm the fuck down or I calm you down, 'Ren," Kinsey said, her voice hard and even. "Are you listening to me? I will hurt you if I have to."

"You won't hurt me, 'Sey," Darren said. "You love me too much. The question is whether I love you?"

"Let me help you with the answer to that question," Kinsey said just before she slammed her forehead into Darren's face.

The captain's eyes rolled up and Kinsey let him drop away, unconscious and finally out of everyone's hair.

"Whatever that shit is, it's worse than coke and meth combined," Kinsey said. "There's a lot more chemistry going on in there than coca." Kinsey tapped Darren's forehead. "I just hope the shit doesn't do permanent damage."

"How will he know to hold his breath if he's out cold, Sis?" Shane asked. "Didn't think about that, did ya?"

"Oh, I did," Kinsey said, placing her hand on Darren's crotch. "A hard squeeze will bring any guy awake like that." She snapped her fingers.

"Except he's wearing a suit," Max said. "He may not feel it."

"We'll deal with that when we need to," Kinsey said. "But if the time comes, I'm picking my dad over Darren, got it?"

"Got it," Max said.

"Got it," Shane replied, giving a thumbs up as he looked at Darren. "Nice knowing ya, kite boy."

***

Thorne's lungs were ready to burst and he knew he was only seconds away from drowning when the shark suddenly let him go. He slammed into the whale sub that appeared before him on the ocean bottom and almost lost his lungful of air, but he was able to fight the urge to breathe and looked about.

He quickly saw he was right next to the cockpit hatch of the sub and he pulled himself down inside. His arms were heavy from the lack of oxygen, but he forced them to work as he searched the inside of the cramped cockpit for something, anything that may have had air trapped in it.

Then he saw the bright red cross of an emergency kit and he yanked it open, slamming his elbow into one of the control panels. Thorne almost cried when he saw the small canister of oxygen with a plastic mask already attached. He twisted the nozzle and bubbles spewed from the mask. Thorne pressed the mask against his mouth and nose and breathed deep.

It was like the first time he'd had a drink, the first time he'd had sex, the first time he'd killed a man, the first time for everything all rolled into one.

The oxygen went straight to his brain and the world clarified around him. He rocked back and forth and put out a hand to steady himself as he took another deep breath then twisted the oxygen tank closed. He knew he had to conserve the air.

He rocked some more despite the fact he was in a space that could barely hold his bulk and realized that he wasn't the one moving, it was the sub. He debated whether to climb up and look or not. He knew the shark couldn't get him in the cockpit, since he barely fit himself. But then the shark wasn't exactly a problem solver. If it wanted a square peg to go in the round hole then it would damn well slam that peg through.

Thorne shook his head and cleared the lousy toddler metaphors from his oxygen addled brain and went on instinct.

Decision made, Thorne took a short pull off the tank then yanked himself up so his head and shoulders were out of the hatch, but the rest of him was still inside. He almost lost the precious breath he was holding.

The shark was ripping into the cargo hold and cocaine plumes filled the water.

He would have said, "Holy shit, are you kidding me?", but without the rebreather that would have been a bad idea. Instead, he slowly lowered himself into the cockpit and turned to the controls, hoping maybe he could get the com system working. Otherwise he was going to be out of oxygen and dead very soon.

***

Beau, with both cleavers back in hand, swiped at the madman coming towards him, but Diego dodged then blocked and grabbed Beau's arm, slamming it down on his knee. Beau cried out as he lost his grip on one cleaver and the knife went skittering across the floor. Diego didn't stop there, his elbow came up and obliterated Beau's nose.

Beau stumbled away and swiped with the other cleaver, but Diego bent backwards, letting the blade slice the empty air he just occupied. When he came back up, he sent two jabs into Beau's shattered nose and down went the Chief Steward. Beau's head slammed into the edge of the lab counter and his eyes rolled up as conscious thought took a vacation.

Gunnar came in fast with his knives, but Diego was faster, expertly blocking every stab, swipe, slash, and hook. Gunnar's forearms were nothing but bruised flesh after the defensive moves Diego pulled off. Then his gut joined in the pain as Diego dropped and smashed both fists into Gunnar's stomach. He stood quickly and jammed an open palm into Gunnar's sternum, sending the doctor flying backwards over a table.

Diego, barely breathing hard, twisted his head and looked across the room to where Mike had wheeled himself. The double amputee grinned as he pulled the trigger on the AK-47 he held. Diego ran as fast as he could, keeping just ahead of the bullets that ripped apart the lab even more than it already was. He dove back behind the pallet of coke again as Mike's rifle clicked dead.

Wheeling forward as fast as possible, Mike reached down to grab another rifle that lay in the dead hands of one of Diego's men, but the bullet to his shoulder changed that plan.

Mike dove from the chair just before it was torn apart by gunfire. He rolled behind a table and searched for a weapon, but all he saw was a beaten Gunnar sitting there, eyes wide, nose pouring blood, shirt stained with more blood, and hands gripping knives that weren't very effective against sub-machine gun fire.

"You okay?" Mike asked.

"Yeah! You?" Then Gunnar saw the shoulder wound. "Shit!"

"Fucking punta bitches!" Diego screamed as he kept firing. "I will do this all day until I have your heads on my dick!"

"Interesting choice of words!" Mike shouted.

"Fuck yourselves!" Diego replied. "Faggot ass fuckers!"

"So much hate," Gunnar grinned then winced at the severe pain the smile caused.

"What now?" Mike asked.

The gunfire stopped and they both heard some very loud snorting.

"Jesus, he's really going for it," Mike said.

"Time to die, little maricónes!" Diego screeched.

"Why he gotta be gay hating?" Mike said as he held out a hand.

Gunnar gave him one of the knives, nodded then stood. Gunnar jumped and slid across the table.

Diego was waiting for him. He fired off round after round, hitting Gunnar in the left arm, but it didn't slow the doctor as he hit the ground and pushed up, coming at El Serpiente in full fury.

Behind Gunnar, Mike pulled up onto the table and steadied himself. He watched as Gunnar dove at the Mexican madman, tackling the killer around the legs. But it only shoved the man back against the pallet and not onto the floor. Diego's rifle clicked empty and he flipped it about using the butt to batter Gunnar between the shoulder blades again and again. Mike heard Gunnar cry out then took aim and threw his knife. But Diego saw it coming and batted it away like it was an insect, not 7 inches of deadly steel. The man stared at Mike as he hammered down on Gunnar over and over until the doctor collapsed in a heap at his feet.

"You think you can take me, cripple?" Diego asked. Half his face was coated in white powder and his eyes gleamed with manic evil. "You want to try? How about I come over there since you can't come to me?"

Diego kicked Gunnar aside and casually strolled to the table Mike sat upon.

"Look at us!" Diego laughed. "With you up there we are the same height! Now it is a fair fight!"

The two men faced off, eyes studying each other, waiting for who would make the first move.

Then fists flew.

Diego hooked with his right and Mike brought up a forearm to block the blow, countering with his own right hook which Diego blocked also. They twisted their arms about, each trying to get an advantage, but their skills were too matched. Even with Diego's drug fueled drive, he couldn't get in at Mike since the man had been using only his arms for a long while. Likewise, because Mike didn't have the stability of his lower legs, he couldn't get the leverage he needed to take advantage of Diego's mistakes.

Mike grabbed Diego's wrist and twisted, causing the man to tilt to the left, but Diego jabbed two fingers in Mike's armpit and he lost his grip. Diego then boxed Mike's ears, but the ex-SEAL shook it off in time to counter the jabs that came at his face. He blocked and swiped one arm to the side then blocked the other as he brought his head forward, trying to head butt Diego, but the man used the momentum of Mike's blocks to duck down and Mike only hit the top of Diego's head, not the target between the eyes he'd been going for. Diego lunged up, slamming the top of his head into Mike's chin. His jaws snapped shut and Mike tasted blood as he was pretty sure he just lost the tip of his tongue.

Rocked back by the blow, Mike was barely able to fend off Diego's next attack as a powerful roundhouse kick came up over the table, aimed for Mike's head. He got both arms up in time, but he was sent rolling down the table. He skidded to a halt just before falling off and tucked his shoulder, rolling back the way he came.

Mike knew Diego would use that as an opportunity and he was ready when the fists came down at him.

On his back, Mike brought his forearms up again to block the blows Diego hammered down at him. If he'd had legs he would have been able to twist and kick the man. He just fended off the attacks, not quite as helpless as a turtle on its shell, but not as agile as he wished he was.

A fist got through and Mike gasped as his solar plexus exploded in pain and the air left his lungs. He tried to breathe, but the blow stunned his diaphragm and the wide muscle only spasmed, refusing to do its job and draw in breath.

"Little fishy can't breathe?" Diego laughed. "Maybe I can help with that."

Mike started to move, but Diego hit him in the same spot again and again, keeping him in place.

El Serpiente looked about then smiled. He reached down and picked up one of Beau's meat cleavers. Looking Mike up and down he finally settled on grabbing him by the wrist, immobilizing the stunned man's left arm.

"You are a little out of balance," Diego smiled. "I like symmetry, don't you? Let's take care of that for you."

Mike thrashed, fighting through the lack of ability to breathe, but Diego slammed the handle of the meat cleaver right between Mike's eyes and the world went fuzzy and swam before him.

"Hold still," Diego said. "This will be over in a second. Then we can take care of that other pesky arm of yours."

He raised the meat cleaver over his head and laughed.

***

"I can see it," Moshi said, her voice barely above a whisper.

"What did she say?" Max asked.

"She said she could see it!" Darren yelled, suddenly wide awake. "I can hear everything! I can hear the WHOLE UNIVERSE!"

"Jesus!" Max jumped. "The guy won't stay down!"

"Okay, I'm tired of the batshit nuts routine," Shane said. "Just want that officially out there."

"It isn't his fault," Kinsey said. "Darren is a lightweight. He only drinks and he's no good at that either. I don't know what this shit is doing to his brain, but sane Darren isn't in there right now."

Darren grabbed her wrist and pulled her close. "Sane Darren is a pussy."

"I've been saying that for years," Kinsey smiled as she pulled her wrist away.

"I think you're digging this a little too much," Max said. "Not cool to take advantage of the stricken."

"The shark is eating the whale," Moshi's voice said.

That got their attention and they all looked up at the tiny speaker.

"What?" Shane finally asked.

"The shark is eating the whale," Moshi repeated. "The whale sub like this one."

"Oh," Max nodded. "Uh, can it do that? I've heard of tiger sharks eating tires and license plates and crap, but can a shark eat a freakin' sub?"

"It wants the candy center," Darren said. "The sweet, sweet candy center. Swimmin' down to Crystal Candy Coke Mountain!"

He moved his hands in a weak air banjo imitation.

"We should just keep him high and sell him to the circus," Max said.

"That's a good idea until he snaps and thinks some overweight housewife is another shark and goes all rodeo on her," Shane countered.

"Good point," Max replied.

"I will get you close," Moshi said. "Then open the cargo hold and you can kill the shark."

They sat there for a second.

"We're gonna need a way better plan than that," Shane said.

"Give me your pistol," Kinsey said.

"Do what?" the brothers asked.

"Give me your pistol," Kinsey said. "I go out and kill the fucking shark. I'm the best with a pistol. You two are rifle jockeys, not pistoleros."

"Pistoleros?" Max laughed. "You've been in Mexico for a day and you've gone native."

"It's been a big day," Kinsey said, holding out her hands. "Give."

Shane checked his channel pistol's magazine then handed it over to Kinsey. Max looked about and smiled.

"Looky here," he said, picking up another channel pistol. "Ditcher must have still had one on him."

"Good," Kinsey said, taking the pistol from Max

Kinsey tucked the two pistols into her belt, made sure they weren't going to fall out, and then looked up at the hatch.

"Ready, Moshi," Kinsey said.

"This will not be fun," Moshi replied as the cargo hold's hatch started to open.

The three members of Team Grendel felt the change in pressure instantly.

"Hold your breath, Ditcher!" Max yelled at Darren.

"I can hold my breath longer than you!" Darren shouted then took a huge breath, his cheeks poking out like a chipmunk's full of seeds.

"Keep doing that, buddy," Shane shouted over the roar of the ocean.

They all took one last breath and braced themselves as the cargo hold filled completely up. Once the hold was full, the pressure equalized and the hatch opened wide. Kinsey swam out fast. She didn't waste a second thinking about what she had to do, she just did it.

Once out she spun around, looking for the sub and the shark. She found both. The sub was downed and in bad shape while the shark was busy eating it, but Kinsey instantly saw what it was "eating" as white clouds puffed out from its gills. Not good.

And to her great surprise, she also found her father looking up at her from the cockpit hatch of the downed sub. He gave her a thumbs up and waved the oxygen tank at her then took a deep breath from it and waved it again.

Kinsey swam towards him, but as she got to the sub she risked a glance over at the shark. It had stopped its coke gorge and was slowly backing away from the crushed cargo hold. A black eye found her and the shark whipped about, its tail sending it shooting right to her.

Thorne grabbed her and yanked her right on top of him, stuffing the cockpit with Thornes. She had just pulled her legs in when the shark's jaws snapped closed an inch from the cockpit hatch. Kinsey didn't waste her opportunity and aimed a pistol up through the hatch. She fired into the shark's belly as it swam by. The tail had just cleared the hatch when the distant whumping sounds of small explosions found their ears.

Kinsey pushed up through the cockpit and then reached back for her father. He handed her the oxygen tank instead and pointed at it. She nodded, took a grateful hit of oxygen and handed it back. Then she pulled the other channel pistol from her belt and spun around, hunting the murky waters for the monster.

Its blood mixed with the drugs leaking from the cargo hold and the gloom turned a shade of pink, adding a very surreal element to the entire scene. Kinsey didn't see the monster and she gestured for Thorne to come out. He quickly swam from the cockpit and held out his hand; Kinsey gave him one of the pistols. The two Thornes swam their way to the cargo hold of the waiting sub, their eyes watching for the shark everywhere, but there was still no sign of it.

When they crawled into the cargo hold, Thorne handed the oxygen tank to Shane. He took a deep breath then handed it to Max as Moshi forced the hatch closed and started to pump the water out. Max took his breath then jammed the mask against Darren's face. The man shook his head, pointed to his puffed out cheeks and than gave a thumbs up.

Thorne looked at Kinsey and she just shrugged. Once there was enough room for their heads, Max yanked Darren up to the air so he could breathe. But he didn't, just kept holding the same breath, a tight lipped smirk on his face.

Kinsey punched him in the nose. He breathed.

"Hey!" he shouted. "I was winning! I WAS WINNING!"

He started to take a swing at Kinsey, but she just head butted him between the eyes again and he rocked back, stunned.

"No!" she yelled, wagging her finger in his face as if he was bad dog that had gotten into the trash. "No, 'Ren! No more fighting!"

Darren glared at her and began to struggle some then the skin around his eyes started to twitch, followed by the corners of his mouth. In a split second he was in a full seizure and it took Kinsey, Max and Shane to hold him down as the last of the water pumped out of the hold.

"What the hell is happening?" Thorne asked.

"Too much coke," Kinsey said.

"You said it wasn't coke," Max said then saw the look Kinsey gave him. "Right. Not the time to quibble."

"He's seizing and if we don't get him some help he could fry his brain," Kinsey said. Then Darren stopped shaking and his whole body went limp. Kinsey immediately checked his pulse. "Or he could die!"

She started to do chest compressions, but the specialized wetsuit fought her.

"Get this shit off him!" Kinsey yelled as she tilted his head back, pinched his nose, and blew.

Max and Shane struggled to get the wetsuit off, but they were only able to get it down his chest and arms before Kinsey shoved him out of the way. She pounded on his chest four times then straddled him and began chest compressions once more.

"What can we do?" Shane asked.

"Fucking pray!" Kinsey said as she leaned in and gave Darren mouth to mouth once more.

"Uh...hello?" Moshi's little voice asked. "The shark is back. I am taking us to the surface, but it will probably catch us."

"Fuck," Thorne said. "I am so fucking done with monster sharks."

***

As the meat cleaver fell towards Mike's arm, Diego screamed, his head upturned, his neck muscles bulging. The cleaver came down just above Mike's shoulder, nicking him some, but leaving his arm intact. Mike shoved Diego away and the man stumbled back.

"Fuck you, asshole," Beau said, yanking his meat cleaver out of Diego's leg as the man fell to the ground. "And fuck your leg."

Diego's left leg was hanging by a thread at the knee. Beau severed that thread. Diego screamed again and took a swipe at Beau with the meat cleaver he still held. Beau ducked under the swipe then came up, both hands on his cleaver, and slammed the massive knife into Diego's other knee. There was a pop and the leg came free from the knee down.

Diego's screams intensified and he swung back with his own cleaver, catching Beau in the side. The Chief Steward fell away and dropped his cleaver; his hands went to his side and he tried to hold back the gush of blood, but it just streamed from between his fingers.

"You fucking asshole," Beau said as he collapsed all the way to the floor. "You fucking, fucking asshole..."

His head rested against the cold metal floor and his eyes glazed over as the life left him.

Diego kept screaming and swiping with the knife even though there was no one to fight. He looked up and saw Mike staring at him from the table.

"I WILL FUCKING EAT YOUR SOUL!" Diego screamed. "I WILL SWALLOW IT WHOLE, YOU FUCKING PUNTA!"

"Yeah, you do that," Mike grinned. "Why don't you stand up and come get me."

He looked down at the still form of Beau and sighed then looked over at Gunnar, as the man lay against the pallet, still unconscious.

"Fuck," Mike said as he lifted himself up by his arms and started to swing forwards and backwards. "Guess it's up to me."

He aimed his body away from Diego and launched off the table, landing hard on the floor just past Beau's corpse. Diego lashed out with the meat cleaver, but Mike tucked and rolled out of range. Diego spat and foamed at the mouth, hurling Spanish expletives like a monkey flung feces, but Mike ignored the man as he worked his way over to his wheelchair. He climbed up and then spun it around to face Diego.

"I don't know what's in that shit," Mike said. "But it's bad news, hombre. I think you need to get clean."

Mike wheeled over to an AK-47 and picked it up. He checked the magazine, slapped it back in, pulled back the action, then took aim at Diego.

"Uh, hello there, Mr. Pearlman," Ballantine's voice said from the PA system. "Please don't do that."

"Did you see what this fucker did?" Mike shouted, recognizing Ballantine's voice as he looked about for the video camera.

"I saw it all," Ballantine replied. "And he will die for what he did. But for now we need him alive. Can you do that?"

"Keep him alive? No, I'm not a doctor," Mike responded. "And the way he's bleeding he won't last long. So how about giving me the satisfaction of killing him?"

"While I'd normally agree, this time I have to ask you to refrain," Ballantine said. "Is Gunnar wearing his com?"

"I don't know," Mike said. "I'm across the room and can't tell."

"Well, we're about to find out," Ballantine chuckled.

There was a pause and then Mike could hear a faint whining. Gunnar's eyes shot open and he jumped up from the pallet, clawing at his ear.

"WHAT THE FUCK?" he shouted. The whining stopped. "Jesus, what was that?"

"I apologize, Dr. Peterson," Ballantine said from the PA. "I needed you awake. How is your arm and your side?"

Gunnar looked about the room, his eyes finding Mike then Diego and finally Beau.

"Gunnar?" Ballantine asked again. "How are you?"

"What the fuck happened to Beau?" Gunnar asked Mike.

"Gunnar!" Ballantine shouted. "We'll grieve later! Right now I need to know your medical status!"

Gunnar froze for a moment, shook his head, then looked at his arm "It's a through and through," he replied. "No broken bones, but it's useless right now."

"The bleeding? Can you stop the bleeding?"

"Yeah, I can do that," Gunnar replied. "I'll get right on that."

"Are you bleeding bad?" Ballantine asked.

"No, not bad," Gunnar said. "I can tie it off and that'll hold until I can stitch it up."

"And Mr. Pearlman? How are you?" Ballantine asked.

Mike looked at his wound and grinned. "It's a graze. Already stopped bleeding."

"Good," Ballantine said. "Help Gunnar tie off his wound fast then save Mr. Fernandez's life."

Gunnar had started to walk towards Mike, but he stopped and looked around for the PA speaker. "Are you fucking nuts? I'm not saving that fuck!"

"I actually need you to, Gunnar," Ballantine said. "Please. You seem to forget that we are surrounded by half the Mexican Navy. If we want to survive this then I need leverage. And Mr. Fernandez is all the leverage we have. That and the cocaine."

"It's not cocaine," Gunnar said. "It's something designed to mimic cocaine. Even down to a chemical test. But there isn't a molecule of cocaine in that shit."

"Hmmmm," Ballantine said. "I sometimes underestimate your scientific abilities. I apologize for that. Now, please save Mr. Fernandez's life. El Serpiente is key to us not getting blown out of the water."

"Fine," Gunnar said. "But I get to kill him when the time comes."

"There will be a long list for that privilege, I'm afraid," Ballantine said.

"Put my name at the top," Gunnar replied as he clutched his wounded arm and walked to the supply cabinets.

***

Kinsey nearly cried when Darren gasped for breath. Max immediately put the oxygen mask over Darren's mouth and nose. He cranked the valve and Darren sucked deeply.

"You'll be fine," Kinsey said, leaning close and whispering in his ear. "You're going to be fine."

He mumbled something, but it was hard to understand either due to the mask or Darren's drug induced incoherence. Kinsey kissed him on the cheek then sat up and took a deep breath of her own.

"You have wounded the shark considerably, Kinsey," Moshi's voice said. "It is not gaining on us."

"Good," Kinsey replied as she wiped the sweat from her forehead. "Hopefully the fucker will just die."

There was a jolt and everyone tensed, waiting for the sounds of the sub being attacked. Instead, they felt a change in the pressure and the hatch opened to the ocean air above.

"Moshi?" Kinsey asked.

"Here it comes," Moshi said. "Please finish it."

Kinsey didn't have to be told twice. She held out her hands and Thorne slapped a channel pistol in one while Shane slapped a second in the other. She nodded to the men, stood up and pulled herself outside.

The sun was starting to set and it hit Kinsey that she had woken up in her own bed just that morning. Or at least she had woken up in Gunnar's guest bed. Back in a condo that was destroyed. She realized it was probably a good time to go apartment hunting.

But she had something else she needed to hunt for first.

"Hey!" she yelled down into the hatch. "Toss me up Darren's wetsuit!"

Shane yanked it off Darren's legs then tossed it onto the top of the sub. Kinsey put both pistols into her belt, bent down, grabbed the wetsuit and threw it as far out into the water as she could. Without hesitating, she grabbed the pistols once more and was ready when the shark came exploding out of the water, its mouth chomping down on the wetsuit.

The shark was leaking blood and seawater from the gaping wounds in its belly, yet the thing was still terrifying. But not terrifying enough for Kinsey to hesitate from emptying both pistols. Despite the gun's design limitations, Kinsey hit the mark with every round. Its right pectoral fin was shredded as the rounds slammed into it. Then one by one, the rounds exploded and the shark was ripped in half.

Blood and gore burst towards Kinsey and she didn't have to time to duck and cover. She was dripping with shark when Shane climbed out of the cargo hold.

"Nice look, Sis," Shane said, wiping the yuck from Kinsey's face. "It suits you."

"Go fuck a whale, cuz," Kinsey said. She looked at the pistols. "Remind me to let Carlos know that in the right hands the pistols work out of water. He needs to duplicate that with the rifles."

"No shit," Thorne said from below. "He also needs to make the rifles work in close quarters."

Then large caliber gunfire opened up on them from the Beowulf III's deck, pocking the water around the sub.

"Aw, fuck!" Shane said as he pulled Kinsey into the cargo hold. "I forgot about those guys!"

The sub dove back under the water once again as bullets flew at it.

***

Diego was unconscious on the table thanks to a few well placed hits from a rifle butt. One hit, two hits, three and out went El Serpiente.

At least until Gunnar applied the torch to his open and bleeding leg stumps. He woke right the fuck up then.

"Mike," Gunnar said.

Slam went the rifle butt. They had pulled a second table next to the one Diego lay upon so Mike could keep watch over the prisoner. He was glad to apply the anesthetic.

Gunnar bandaged and taped the stumps, trying not to gag from the cooked meat smell that filled the lab.

Then he looked down at Beau.

"We need to do something with him," Gunnar said.

"We will," Ballantine said. "Don't you worry."

"How many men are still onboard the B3?" Gunnar asked. He looked at Mike, who had his rifle to his shoulder, and nodded towards the hatchway. "Can you see if they are close?"

"They are," Ballantine replied.

Gunnar finished strapping Diego to the table then went and fetched a rifle for himself.

"Can we take them?" Gunnar asked.

"You can certainly hold them off," Ballantine replied. "Don't worry about taking them. Help is on the way."

"You realize how stupid that sounds, don't you?" Gunnar laughed as he pulled back the action and chambered a round. "We were supposed to be the help on the way today."

"Life changes on a peso," Ballantine said. "Hold tight."

***

Moshi piloted the sub into the specimen bay as if she had been doing it her whole life. As soon as the bay cleared of seawater, hatches were thrown open and Kinsey, Thorne, and the Reynolds bolted from the sub.

"We'll need weapons," Kinsey said.

"Hello, Team Grendel," Ballantine's voice said from the PA in the bay. "You are a sight for sore eyes. Where is Captain Chambers? Please tell me we didn't lose him."

There was some loud mumbling and shouts from the cargo hold.

"Ah, I see he is under the weather," Ballantine said. "Will he be okay?"

"He'll live," Kinsey said. "But we have no idea what the long term is for him. He drank a ton of seawater with cocaine."

"It is not cocaine, as you already know, I'm sure," Ballantine responded. "And you'll want to get him to start drinking fresh water ASAP."

Moshi exited the cockpit and nodded at the Team.

"Can you watch him and get him some water?" Kinsey asked.

Moshi nodded again, back to her quiet self.

"Thanks."

"Punch the fuck out of him if you need to," Shane said.

"Let's move," Thorne said, limping his way to the ladder that led up to the catwalk and the hatch out of the bay. "Do you have eyes on the passageways, Ballantine?"

"We do, Commander," Ballantine responded.

"Who's we?"

"Acting Captain Lake, Carlos, Ingrid and myself," Ballantine replied. "I'll guide you to the Toyshop, but you will need to hurry. We don't have much time before this ship is sunk."

"Sunk?" Thorne asked. "Has the hull been breached?"

"No, not that kind of sunk," Ballantine answered. "I mean sunk by artillery. If I know Espanoza, he will use the cover of night to attack. That way any story he makes up will be hard to refute."

"How much time?" Thorne asked.

"An hour," Ballantine said. "Maybe more, maybe less."

"Fuck," Thorne said. "That's not enough time to do a full sweep of this ship."

"I know," Ballantine replied. "'But I have a plan. I'll get you to the Toyshop then we'll go from there."

"We know where the Toyshop is," Shane said as he looked through the porthole in the bay hatch. He took not getting his head blown off as a sign the coast was clear.

"You don't know what I know," Ballantine said. "Just follow my voice and all shall be revealed."

"That guy enjoys drama way too much," Max whispered.

"No shit," Shane said as he tried to shove the hatch open. But it didn't budge. "Crap. No go."

"Must have been damaged when Moshi escaped," Ballantine said. "You'll have to go up. Once out then just follow my voice."

"Creepiest breadcrumbs ever," Max said.

***

Long cables shot from the bottom of the mini-sub and the machine slowed then came to a full stop as Darby reeled in the cables until the lines were tight and the mini-sub stable. She checked her gear, put on a rebreather over her gear, and opened the small hatch set into the floor of the mini-sub. Water splashed up over the threshold, but she ignored it as she dropped a small ladder through.

She climbed down, affixed her mouthpiece, then dropped all the way into the seawater. The light from above was dim as the sun set over Baja Mexico. But Darby didn't need much light. She oriented herself and swam away from the mini-sub, headed to where the day had all started.

Chapter Eight: What Happens At Sea, Stays At Sea

The sun was blindingly bright as it set across the Pacific Ocean, and Espanoza smiled as he waited for Diego's report. And waited. And waited. The smile slowly left his face as he turned to the ensign manning the communication's station.

"How late is he?" Espanoza asked.

"Ten minutes, sir," the ensign replied.

"That is not like Diego," Espanoza said. "Something must have happened."

"Should I hail the Beowulf III, sir?" the ensign asked.

"No," Espanoza said. "We wait another two minutes, and then I'll decide the fate of the Beowulf."

Espanoza stood up from his chair and walked towards the wide windows of the bridge. He looked out at the Beowulf III as it floated in the center of the semicircle of Mexican naval ships. If his brother did not contact him within the next two minutes he had every intention of firing all guns on the research vessel.

Research vessel.

The thought made him laugh. He knew the Beowulf housed almost as much munitions as the ship he was presently on. And he also knew Ballantine could care less about the research the vessel was registered to complete.

A giant, prehistoric whale? He had nearly shot tequila out his nose when he'd heard that was what Ballantine was using as an official story. YouTube video or not, it made no difference.

Ballantine was a company man and he used the ruse of research to hide the work the company expected him to complete.

And Team Grendel? Burnouts, washouts, losers, all of them. Yet they were dangerous, he knew that. Commander Thorne had a solid reputation before he left the SEALs in disgrace. Darren Chambers was known as a deadly operator, despite his Moby Dick obsession. The brothers Reynolds were legendary snipers, even after they retired and decided to train hippies on how to protect their pot fields. Those two he would like to get alone in a dark room with two pans of water and a car battery hooked to their balls; payback for the trouble they had caused him and his associates when they had looked to a Northern California expansion.

Then there was Kinsey Thorne. The woman that almost became the first female Navy SEAL in history. Instead, she became just another junkie. Well, almost. He had his suspicions about the woman. Rumors filtered down across the border of the "loco chica" that liked to cut up her dealers instead of paying them. His organization had lost some good providers during the time she was holed up in a San Diego apartment complex known for prostitution and child porn.

Then the providers stopped disappearing. About the same time Kinsey Thorne was ripped from that life by her family and given a second chance with Team Grendel. Espanoza wasn't one to just let a coincidence like that go and he planned on having a word with Senorita Thorne. If she lived. If not then he didn't need to worry about it.

There was one he did worry about: the woman called Darby. He had hunted through every database he had access to, and paid quite a few bribes for information where he didn't have access, but she came up a blank. The official story was she was ex-Israeli Special Forces and Intelligence. Yet, there were no details on missions, or connections to any current members of Israeli command, no way to confirm any of it. And she only had the one name.

Darby.

No first or last name, just Darby.

She was a true ghost in the business and Espanoza did not like ghosts. They had a way of appearing during the most inconvenient times.

"Sir, there's an incoming message from Naval Command," the ensign said, bringing Espanoza out of his thoughts. "They are recalling the ships immediately."

"Recalling? Why? For what reason?" Espanoza asked, whirling on the young man. "Explain now!"

The ensign flinched and looked around at the other sailors on the bridge for help, but all eyes were quickly averted.

"There is a hostage situation with a cruise ship in international waters," the ensign said. "I don't have any other details, but every ship is needed."

"Well, they cannot have every ship," Espanoza said. "Respond that we have sustained damage and will be doing repairs through the night."

"Sir?" the ensign asked. "What damage?"

"I don't care what damage!" Espanoza roared. "Make some damage up! Tell them what you need to tell them so they leave me and this ship alone!"

"Yes, sir, of course, sir," the ensign replied and began relaying the information to Mexican Naval Command.

Espanoza turned to the rest of the crew on the bridge. Technically, he wasn't their captain, but he could give a shit and a half about technicalities at that moment. Ballantine had obviously called in a favor and made a move. Which probably meant Diego was dead. Or worse.

"Does anyone here have a problem with my command of this ship?" Espanoza asked. "If you do then you may leave immediately. I do not want troublemakers on board my ship."

There were plenty of scared faces, but no objections were spoken.

"Good," Espanoza said. "I want all men to battle stations now. I am not going to sound the alarm. That would alert our enemy. Just make it happen."

The men all stood there at attention, unsure of what to do next since pretty much every protocol had been broken since Espanoza had stepped foot on the ship.

"Do I need to shoot someone in order to be heard?" Espanoza asked.

The men moved then, all hurrying to their stations so they could issue orders and prepare for battle.

Espanoza sat back down in the captain's chair and frowned. He didn't like how things were going. He had no doubt he would be triumphant, and retrieve his product, but he was tired and wanted it to all be over.

***

"The call has been made and ships are on the move," Ballantine said to the others. "Now open the wall so we can get the B3 back."

Carlos opened the secret entrance to the Toyshop and rolled his eyes at the disbelieving stares from Team Grendel, who stood gaping at the suddenly missing wall.

"I'm not going to explain it," Carlos said. "Just get in here so you can get your gear and do your jobs killing people."

"It is good to see you all," Ballantine said as Team Grendel walked into the Toyshop and the wall behind them became just a wall once again. "I have to say I was getting separation anxiety with you off the ship. Let's never part again."

"Shut up, Ballantine," Thorne said. "I'm in no mood, or shape, for your weird bullshit. Talk sense or get some knocked into you."

"Direct and down to business," Ballantine laughed. "That's why I hired you."

"You hired me because I knew how to put together a Team and do the job I'm given," Thorne said. "Did you notice how I didn't list 'listen to crazy talk' in there?"

"Hey," Lake said. "Darren going to be okay?"

"He'll be fine," Kinsey said. "I hope."

"Good," he nodded and stepped out of the way.

"Modified M-4s," Ingrid said as she pushed a cart past Lake and over to the operators. "Six extra magazines apiece. Full body armor as well as NVGs."

"NVGs?" Shane asked. "What are we going to need night vision goggles for?"

"Because I'm having the lights turned off," Ballantine said. "In fact, I'm going to shut down all of the power to the ship except for emergency backup."

"You can do that from here?" Max asked.

"No, unfortunately, or I would have employed that trick earlier," Ballantine replied. "But I know a guy." He nodded to Ingrid and she handed each of them new coms.

"Scrambled frequency," Ingrid said. "I just put the code together a few minutes ago so it'll be hard for Espanoza to tap into. We'll have the ship back before he gets through."

"Thank you, Ingrid," Ballantine smiled. He cleared his throat and activated his com. "Cougher? Can you read me?"

"Yeah, I hear ya," Cougher said. "Are we on?"

"We are," Ballantine replied. "In exactly five minutes, I need you to cut the power to the ship. Do not disable the ship, we will need to be mobile at some point soon. But just make it so the power is out and if anyone comes to investigate, as we know they will, they won't be able to get the ship operational for some time."

"But you want me to be able to get it operational right away once the bad guys are dead, right?" Cougher asked.

"Exactly," Ballantine said. "Will you be able to do that?"

"Yeah, I can do that," Cougher said.

"Good," Ballantine replied. "Now take the com out of your ear and destroy it. Don't use that com again. You'll know when we need the power again."

"You got it," Cougher said.

Ballantine smiled at Team Grendel. "You'll probably want to get suited up. The clock is ticking and we need to get you out of the Toyshop before we lose power." He turned from the Team and tapped his com again. "Gunnar? Can you hear me?"

***

"I can," Gunnar replied as he fetched a tube of smelling salts from the med kit on the counter. "You sure about this?"

"I wouldn't be doing it if I wasn't," Ballantine said over the com. "Now, is our guest in place?"

"Yes," Gunnar said as he looked over at the unconscious and bandaged form of Diego. The man was strapped to a table in the far corner with Mike sitting directly underneath. "It's going to get very dark in here when that power goes out."

"That's the point, Gunnar," Ballantine said. "Just get to a secure part of your lab and wait it all out."

"I've been more than just a bystander today, Ballantine," Gunnar said. "I've held my own."

"I know you have," Ballantine replied. "You are also wounded. Get someplace safe, Gunnar. I'm not saying that because I don't think you are capable of fighting the good fight, I say that because you are too valuable to waste in a firefight."

"Fine," Gunnar said. "How much time do we have?"

He walked over to the table Diego was on and handed Mike the smelling salts.

"Two minutes," Ballantine said. "Good luck."

"Yeah, you too," Gunnar said.

***

"Half of you will need to head to the engine room and the other half to Gunnar's lab," Ballantine said. "I would engage silently, if you can, until you reach your destinations. The idea is to draw Espanoza's men to the two locations. Thus splitting them in half and making sure we know where they are."

Thorne watched Ballantine for a minute then smiled. "That's plan's not half bad, Ballantine."

"That is a high compliment coming from you, Commander. Ready?"

"Team Grendel? Ready?" Thorne asked.

"Ready," they responded.

"Then lets get out of this Toyshop," he said.

Carlos audibly groaned.

The wall went away and they stepped out into the passageway. Then the lights went out.

"Cougher was early," Ingrid said.

"It appears so," Ballantine sighed. "That means we are exposed with this wall open. Good thing we know where the guns are."

Team Grendel powered up their NVGs and the world was illuminated in greens and greys.

"You sure you'll be okay exposed like this?" Thorne asked, looking at Ballantine.

"We're good," Lake said. "We do have flashlights, you know."

"No lights," Ballantine said. "That'll draw them to us. We don't want that."

"Just saying," Lake said. If there had been light they would have seen him shrug.

***

The last rays of the sunset faded to purple then to dark blue and finally black. The lights on the Beowulf III's deck twinkled in the night then went dark.

"What's happening?" Espanoza asked. "Why did they go dark?"

"Sir, their engines have shut down," the ensign said. "They may have had some malfunction due to damage."

"What damage?" Espanoza asked. "The ship has been just sitting there all day long!"

"Perhaps during a gunfight the engines were damaged," the ensign suggested. "Not that there were officially any gunfights on the ship. They are our ally and there would be no cause for gunfire at anytime."

Espanoza's eyebrows raised and he laughed.

"I like you," he said. "There may be a place for you in my other endeavors."

"Yes, sir," the ensign said. He had zero intention of joining Espanoza in any other endeavors. He just wanted to live through the one he was stuck in.

"Get me someone on the radio," Espanoza ordered. "I don't care who it is. Juts get me someone that will answer their damn radio. I want to know what exactly is going on over there."

"Yes, sir."

***

Rising slowly from the water, Darby estimated the distance to the marina hangar bay as close to one hundred yards. With her NVGs activated, she counted no less than ten men standing on the dock outside of the hangar, walking back and forth, their attention on everything from the sky to their shoes.

Amateurs. At least by Darby's standards.

But heavily armed amateurs.

Keeping her legs kicking below in a slow rhythm, Darby lifted her hands out of the water an inch at a time so there was zero noise except for the lapping of the waves against the dock's pilings. She held an H&K MK23 with a KAC sound suppressor attached. Underneath the barrel was a LAM (laser aiming module) that allowed her to put three dots that were only visible to her NVGs on any man she wanted.

She watched the random movements of the ineffective sentries and took aim. She squeezed off ten rounds. Each man fell, some into the water, some onto the deck. Darby slipped back under the water as rifles clattered against the deck boards. By the time other men came out to investigate, she was lost from sight; the night returned to gentle waves and the sounds of sea birds.

***

Kinsey and Max made their way towards the engine room, their steps careful and quiet as they walked through the passageways of the B3. They could hear men shouting back and forth and the bark of radios echoing to them. It was only a matter of seconds before they had to engage.

The first man came around the corner, a dull LED flashlight in hand, and just stared at the goggled operators. Kinsey and Max aimed their M-4s, outfitted with modified flash and sound suppressors, at the surprised man. He never had a chance to even lift his TEC-9 before Kinsey put two rounds in his chest and one in his head.

The two operators stepped past the man's body, easily avoiding the pooling blood as it showed up as dark black in their NVGs.

***

The second the lights went out Mike snapped the smelling salts and tossed it up onto Diego's face. He ducked back under the table and waited for the man to come around. When he did, it was with a loud gasp of surprise. Then screams of pain.

"My fucking legs!" Diego yelled. "Motherfuckers took my legs!"

He thrashed against his restraints, his arms straining to get free, but he was held tight and all he could do was yell.

Mike had to fight the urge to reach up and smack one of Diego's stumps; he wanted to hear the man really scream. But El Serpiente was making enough noise for their needs so he just waited under the table with two AK-47s, ready to open up on anyone that got too close.

***

Thorne, with Shane right behind him, rounded a corner and came face to face with four of Espanoza's men. He jammed the suppressor on the end of his M-4 up under the first man's chin and squeezed the trigger. Before that man fell, Thorne grabbed him, spun the body around so it was facing the other men and used it for cover as those men opened fire.

Shane took a knee and spun around the corner, the muzzle flashes from the men's guns like fireworks in his night vision. But they also told him exactly where to shoot. A shot to the chest and one to the head each and the men dropped to the floor.

"Clear. You good, Uncle Vinny?" Shane asked as he stood up and went to his uncle.

"Solid, kid," Thorne replied, letting his shield corpse drop. "This guy was wearing body armor. Good thing I gave him a shot to the chin."

"Just a nudge," Shane replied.

"A simple tap," Thorne grinned. "Come on, I can hear the party has started."

The far off sounds of Diego's screaming drifted to them.

"Well, we'd hate to be late for that party," Shane laughed.

***

Men ran towards the sound of their boss screaming his head off, their flashlights bobbing up and down as they sprinted through the B3's passageways. Five, ten, twenty of them. A good amount more than Ballantine estimated. While the surveillance system in the Toyshop was top notch, many of the cameras had been damaged by bored men looking to just break shit. It was the bane of any commander's existence: bored men.

Several reached the hatchway at the same time and they rushed inside, unable to ignore the wails of Diego. They all knew they could be rewarded well if they were to rescue him. They also knew they would be punished brutally if they didn't. Not just them, but possibly their families.

Six of them got all the way to Diego before Mike opened fire, ripping their legs apart. As they fell he put several bullets in each head then set the empty AK-47s aside and grabbed the rifles from the dead in front of him.

Lights flashed into the lab from the hatchway and Mike focused on those, taking careful shots instead of the wild sweeping automatic fire from before. He'd drawn in the men so he could get more ammunition, but now that he had it he needed to conserve rounds. He had no idea how many were actually out there and how long it would take part of Team Grendel to get to him.

Like a true SEAL, he knew he wasn't alone, but he had no illusions as to his safety. It was up to him to keep the men outside the lab, or at the very least pinned down, so he and Gunnar could stay alive.

Shots rang out and Diego screamed.

"You fucks! YOU FUCKS! YOU SHOT ME! FUCKING ASSHOLES!"

Mike smiled as the wild gunfire stopped. He focused on a flashlight and took another shot. The light went dark, the man fell dead.

"GET ME OUT OF HERE!" Diego screamed.

Mike welcomed the idea.

Come on in, fuckers, he thought. *Come and get it.*

***

Darby surfaced in the corner of the marina hangar, her head melding into the shadows of the dock. The inside of the hangar was lit up enough that she didn't need her NVGs and she slowly lifted them so they rested on top of her head. She wedged herself against the pilings that made up the corner of the dock and watched as men walked this way and that, talking hurriedly, panicked, as they stress smoked cigarettes.

A butt dropped right in front of her, its cherry sizzling out in the seawater. She glanced up and saw the horrified face of a teen boy that couldn't have been more than eighteen. Darby had a hard choice to make. It took all of half a second to make that choice as she aimed her pistol up and fired. The bullet entered the soft flesh under the teen's chin and the top of his head was ripped open, sending brain, bone, and blood flying into the air.

The element of surprise gone, Darby decided to make her presence known.

***

"Clear," Max said as he stepped over three bodies and kept moving towards the engine room. "Not as many as I thought there'd be."

He turned a corner and came face to face with eight men, all holding AK-47s trained on him.

Still around the corner in the other passageway, Kinsey saw Max's body language change in a split second. Everything slowed down and she watched as Max, M-4 to his shoulder started firing as he backed away from the corner. Kinsey dove and rolled, every movement of every muscle taking an eternity.

As she came up facing the men, the world slammed back into focus and speed and she sent bullets flying with surgical precision as her cousin did the same. Flashes erupted from the barrels of the of the cartel men's rifles and Kinsey felt hot air brush her check then that distinct sting of a bullet wound. Warm blood trickled down to her chin, but she ignored it as she got to her feet and pressed the offensive, walking in lock step with Max.

He grunted and went down to a knee, but didn't stop firing. Men fell and men screamed and then there was nothing left in the hallway but smoke and blood.

"Max? Talk to me!" Kinsey barked as she kept her carbine up. "You good?"

"I'm cool, Sis," Max said, getting to his feet. "Took one in the armor. Ribs hurt like split fuck, but I'm good to go."

"You sure?"

"You know it," Max said then pointed his carbine down the passageway. "One more deck and we are there."

"These numbers aren't adding up," Kinsey said as they stepped around the corpses. "Either all the men came this way or Ballantine doesn't know how to count." She activated her com, having maintained radio silence since leaving the Toyshop. "Dad? You read me?"

"Loud and clear," Thorne said. "You two good?"

"Solid," Kinsey replied. "How many hostiles are you running into?"

"Too many," Thorne said. "I think we were sold a bill of goods on their numbers."

"That'd be like Ballantine," Kinsey said. "The guy can't help but play with people."

"I can hear you, you know," Ballantine said over the com.

"Yeah," Thorne replied. "We know."

***

"I didn't want you to think the numbers were overwhelming," Ballantine said as he watched the open entrance to the Toyshop, a suppressed Desert Eagle in each hand. "Sorry for the deception. It's from too many years as a lone wolf in the field."

"Lone wolf? Field?" Thorne asked over the com. "When we're done, I'm getting your story, Thorne."

"We'll see about that," Ballantine smiled. "It's a story long dead and buried, so it will be hard to find. Even for me."

The passageway outside the Toyshop lit up as flashlights came around the corner.

"Like you said," Thorne replied. "We'll see."

Ballantine didn't respond, just stayed quiet as he waited for the men to show themselves. He picked out three distinct voices as they whispered to themselves. He listened hard to their footfalls and slowly counted in his head as he brought up his pistols.

As soon as all three were in sight, he fired. They dropped one by one and he scrambled forward.

"Lake!" he hissed, setting the pistols on a shelf as the acting captain appeared from the shadows. "Grab one of those bodies."

They dragged the bodies in and pushed them off to the side, out of sight from the passageway. Then Ballantine picked the Desert Eagles up again. He looked at them then at Lake and smiled.

"I can see why you prefer this gun," Ballantine nodded. "Great feel."

"I have to use both hands for just one," Lake said. "And I didn't know they even made suppressors for them."

"You're learning all kinds of new things today," Ballantine replied. "I should charge you tuition."

"Ballantine?" Thorne asked over the com. "You there? What happened?"

"Getting my hands dirty just like you, Commander," Ballantine said. "No need to worry about me."

"Nothing we can do about the blood," Lake said as he stared at the smears on the floor that led from the passageway to the Toyshop.

"No, but these men aren't exactly rocket scientists," Ballantine responded as he reached down and clicked off the only flashlight left working, plunging the passageway and Toyshop back into darkness. "If anything, the blood will make them hurry to us faster."

"Ballantine," Thorne snapped. "How many men are on this ship? Did more come over while we were in the water?"

"Yes, Commander," Ballantine said. "Quite a few more. But I know you can handle them. I only hire capable people, after all."

***

Grabbing onto the side of the dock with one hand, Darby continued firing with the other as she pulled herself up out of the water, rolled across the boards, kept firing, and then came up into a crouch by the hangar wall. It was all one fluid motion from grab to roll to stop.

Men fell as she took careful aim. Then her pistol clicked empty and she popped the magazine free with her thumb, tucked the pistol into her belt, picked up a TEC-9, and opened fire. The cartel men all ran towards her, despite the automatic fire she sent at them. Darby stood and ran along the wall, heading for the office door in front of her. Bullets trailed along behind her, ripping through the hangar's sheet metal wall.

But Darby was fast, not faster than bullets, but faster than the men that controlled the rifles barking at her. She knew the pull and kick of almost every firearm in use around the world and she could tell she had about one second before the bullets caught up with her.

She let the TEC-9 fall from her fingers as she fell to her knees, her back bending backwards so the bullets flew over her. Slivers of sheet metal rained down on her face and she skidded to a stop as she pulled her MK23 from her belt and slapped a fresh magazine home. Whipping back upright, Darby squeezed off six shots, sending six men plunging into the water.

She kept her momentum going and went into a forward roll as a fresh round of gunfire splintered the wood where she had just been. Darby came out of the roll and pushed off with her feet, diving forward towards the wall perpendicular to her. And the office door.

Lowering her shoulder, Darby burst through the hollow, paper thin composite wood door.

"Move and die," Darby said as she put three bullets into the foreheads of the three men with rifles that stood there, gaping at her. She got a sick satisfaction that the last looks on their faces were so idiotic.

Her pistol then turned to Dr. Morganton and McCarthy who sat in office chairs in front of a bank of equipment.

"They didn't move," Dr. Morganton snapped. "Why did you shoot them?"

"Because I wasn't talking to them," Darby said. "I was talking to you two."

Dr. Morganton leaned forward and looked closer at Darby.

"Oh, fuck, no," she gasped. "Not you."

"Yes, me," Darby smiled. She spun and put two bullets in the man that suddenly appeared at the doorway then turned back. "Hello, Dr. Morganton. Ballantine sends his regards."

***

Thorne pointed at Shane then at the last corner that stood between them and the passageway to Gunnar's lab. Shane nodded and crouched low as he slowly walked towards the corner. Thorne stayed high and followed his nephew.

The men by the lab door were busy shouting back and forth in Spanish to Diego held inside. Thorne knew some Spanish, but not enough to catch what they were saying.

Shane held out a hand to him and stood up.

"Hola!" he called out. "Ustedes necesitan un poco de ayuda?"

The men all turned and looked at Shane, some of them even lowering their weapons. They died quickly as Shane opened up on them.

"What did you say to them?" Thorne asked.

"I asked if they needed any help," Shane said. "Then I helped them. Helped them die!"

Thorne groaned.

Diego's screams from the lab filled the passageway as Shane and Thorne walked cautiously to the hatchway.

"Gunnar?" Shane called out. "You cool?"

"Yeah," Gunnar replied.

"Pearlman?" Thorne asked.

"Solid," Mike replied.

"FUCK YOU! FUCK YOU ALL!" Diego screamed.

Thorne and Shane walked into the lab, their carbines sweeping the room. They could see Diego thrashing on the far table, and Mike below giving them the thumbs up.

"Gunnar? Where are you?" Thorne asked.

"The safest place in the room," Gunnar replied. "Behind the big, giant pile of drugs."

***

"Cougher," Kinsey said as she and Max stepped into the engine room. "It's us. You can come on out."

They walked a few more feet then a shape popped up from behind one of the diesel engines. It was actually two shapes. One was Cougher, the other was a man with his arm around Cougher's throat and a pistol to his head.

"Hey, guys," Cougher said. "Someone found me."

"We can see that, Cougher," Kinsey said. "Habla Inglés?"

"Yes, I speak English," the man snapped. "I was born in El Paso."

"Good, good," Kinsey said. "How about you let our friend go and set the gun down? We won't shoot you if you be cool, okay?"

"Bullshit," the man spat, shoving the barrel harder against Cougher's temple. "I let him go and you'll blow my head off."

"No, we won't, will we, Max?" Kinsey replied.

"As long as Cougher stays alive, you stay alive," Max said. "Scout's honor."

The man watched them for a second then turned the pistol from Cougher and towards Kinsey and Max. He got off one shot before Max put a bullet between his eyes. His body fell away from Cougher and the engineer turned and kicked the corpse.

"Fucking cocksucker," Cougher said. "Teach you to fuck with Team Grendel."

Kinsey and Max stepped forward, turning this way and that, as they made sure there was no one else in the engine room.

"Can I turn a light on?" Cougher asked. "I can't see shit."

Max fished a flashlight from his belt, turned it on, and handed it to Cougher.

"Thanks," Cougher said as he took the flashlight and walked past the operators towards a bank of switches. "Now, how about I get all the lights back on?"

He threw a switch and said, "Ta da!"

But nothing happened.

"Shit," Cougher said. "That guy's bullet must have hit something important."

"Like what?" Max asked.

"I don't know yet," he replied as he held out the flashlight. "Hold that so I can find out."

***

"What happened?" Ballantine asked.

"Bullet hit the main breaker," Kinsey reported. "Cougher's working on it now, but it could be a while before we can get the power back up."

"Can he reroute it?" Ballantine asked.

"He's trying to do that," Kinsey replied. "And it isn't going well."

"I'm sending Carlos down there," Ballantine said. "I need you or Max to come get him."

"Max is on his way," Kinsey said.

"I am?" Max responded.

"You are," Kinsey stated. "Move ass, cuz. And watch yourself in case we didn't get all the sneaky bad guys."

"I hate it when bad guys get sneaky," Max said. "Them and their sneaky sneakiness."

"We'll be waiting for you," Ballantine said. He looked over at Lake and frowned. "This throws things off."

Lake just shook his head. "If you say so. I can't keep up with your schemes and plans so I'll just let you worry about it all."

"That's my job," Ballantine said. "To worry about it all."

***

"Who the hell is Ballantine?" McCarthy asked, looking from Darby to Dr. Morganton. "Is he another cartel boss?"

"In more ways than he'd like to admit," Dr. Morganton snorted. "She's his enforcer."

"But less forgiving than Espanoza's El Serpiente," Darby replied.

She whirled around and put two bullets in a man's forehead as he ran towards her from outside the office, his rifle firing wild. Then she took out the three men that were busy reloading on the other side of the hangar. Darby spun back about and sent a bullet into the floor an inch from the gun McCarthy tried to pick up.

"Jesus Christ!" McCarthy yelled, yanking his hand back.

Standing slowly, Darby kept her attention on Dr. Morganton and McCarthy while also looking out the door for more men. There were plenty of men, just no longer alive. Confident she wasn't going to be ambushed, Darby turned fully to the two in the office.

"Talk," she said to Dr. Morganton. "And know that what you tell me determines how I deliver you to Ballantine."

"Let me guess," Dr. Morganton glared. "Alive or dead, right?"

"Wrong," Darby said. "In pain or in agony. No matter what you say or do, I'm taking you out of here alive." She looked at McCarthy. "You I don't know and don't care about. Keep out of my way and you're free to go when this is all said and done."

***

Max moved quickly from deck to deck, very aware that cartel men could still be hiding anywhere. He cleared one passageway at a time before he made it to the Toyshop.

"Someone call a taxi?" Max asked as he turned his back to the Toyshop, his eyes watching the passageway.

"I don't know why I need to go down there," Carlos complained as he walked up behind Max. "Cougher knows the engines better than I do."

"Because he could use a hand and neither Mr. Reynolds nor Ms. Thorne have the technical expertise that you do," Ballantine replied.

"Fine," Carlos grumbled. "Whatever."

"While tips are not expected, they are appreciated," Max said. "Where to, sir?"

"Why can't you take anything seriously?" Carlos snapped. "You kill people for a living!"

"You just answered your own question," Max said, his tone turning cold. "When you have the amount of blood on your hands that I do, see how far you'll go just to fight back the darkness."

"Oh...right," Carlos replied quietly.

"Plus the chicks dig the funny ones," Max chuckled. "They like it when you tickle their funny bones."

"God, I hate you," Carlos said. "Can we go now?"

"Do you have everything you need?" Ballantine asked.

Carlos patted the case he held. "All right here. I'll get the engines up soon."

"Good."

Ballantine waited until they were gone then turned to Ingrid. She nodded and hurried off into the Toyshop.

Lake looked from Ballantine to the guts of the Toyshop then back to Ballantine, unsure of what had just happened.

***

"Can someone shut him the fuck up?" Thorne asked as he struggled not to put a bullet in the screaming Diego Fernandez.

"Ballantine wants him conscious for the big reveal," Gunnar said. "Which should be coming soon, I hope."

"I can't believe that asshole killed Beau," Shane said, struggling with the noise just as much as Thorne. He squatted next to Beau's corpse and dragged him off to the side, folding the man's arms across his chest. "I get the chance and I'm killing Espanoza myself. All I need is a clean line of sight."

"I'll load the cartridge for you," Thorne said.

"What about Darren? How'd he look the last time you saw him?" Gunnar asked.

"Pretty shitty," Shane said. "Once we get the lights on you can go check him out."

"Can you take me down there now?" Gunnar asked. "I'm not needed up here."

"You're supposed to stay put," Shane said.

Gunnar slid the piece of paper out of his pocket and handed it to Shane, his finger to his lips. Shane frowned, but took the paper and opened it. He quickly read it and walked over to Thorne, handing the commander the paper.

"Actually, I better take Gun down to check on Ditcher," Shane said as Thorne looked up, eyes wide. "Unless you want to go?"

"No, you better handle this," Thorne said. "I'll stay here and keep an eye on things."

***

"Ballantine?" Darby called. "Can you read me?"

"Barely," Ballantine said over the com. "You are faint. We've had some com issues here on the Beowulf III. Hopefully they have been all sorted out."

"I can hear you fine," Darby said, looking over at Dr. Morganton. "And I found the target."

"Did you now?" Ballantine said. "Can you patch her through?"

Darby looked at McCarthy. "I'm guessing you can handle tweaking the com system. I need to patch it into mine so Ballantine can have a quick chat with the doctor here."

"Yeah, yeah, sure," McCarthy said. "What's the channel?"

"What channel?" Darby asked Ballantine.

"88A dash 64C," Ballantine replied. "Tiger protocol."

Darby repeated that to McCarthy and he set the hangar's com system to the correct channel. "You're good to go."

"Great," Darby said, looking at Dr. Morganton. "Now, start from the beginning."

***

"Sir? I'm picking up what you asked for," the ensign said to Espanoza. "I am hearing someone refer to a Darby and..." He paused, his head tilted as he listened. "Ballantine. He's finally contacting her, sir, like you said he would."

"Put it through," Espanoza said and began listening to the voices on the com. His face grew red as he heard what was being said.

***

"You were in on this too?" McCarthy said. "From the beginning? You bitch."

"Like you didn't know," Darby laughed.

"I didn't!" McCarthy insisted. "I swear! I mean, I knew Espanoza had his hand in a ton of shit, but I honestly thought the subs were for the Mexican Special Forces, not to run cocaine up and down the coast."

"Well, now you do," Darby said. "And innocent men lost their lives because of your carelessness." She looked over at Dr. Morganton. "Do you have anything else to say?"

"No," Dr. Morganton replied. "I've done what I've done and there's nothing else to be said."

"Did he pay you well?" Darby asked.

"You have no idea," Dr. Morganton.

"Bitch," Darby said as she ejected the magazine from her pistol and put in a fresh one.

"What are you doing?" McCarthy asked.

Her answer was to shove McCarthy out of the way. She raised her pistol and fired, shooting Dr. Morganton twice in the belly then twice in the chest.

"Jesus!" McCarthy said. "You fucking killed her! You said you wouldn't!"

"I lied," Darby said. "Want to be next?"

"Fuck no!"

"Then get us out of here," Darby said.

***

Espanoza had a cell phone to his ear as the shots rang out over the com. He stopped speaking and listened.

"Ballantine will pay for this. I paid good money for that woman," Espanoza snarled then turned back to the cell phone.

"Send them in! Send them all in! I want Darby alive, you hear me? I want her alive!"

***

Doors burst open and armed men streamed into the marina hangar. Darby whirled about to face the men, but McCarthy tackled her about the waist. Her pistol went flying out of her hand as the two of them hit the floor. Darby tried to get her hands up, but McCarthy was faster and slammed a fist into her face again and again.

She brought her knee up into his gut, but he was too big and heavy for her to move. She boxed his ears instead and he howled at the pain, but didn't budge.

"Don't move!" a man shouted from the doorway. Close to two dozen more men were behind him. "Move and die!"

Darby thought about it for a second, but that thought was lost as McCarthy hit her again. This time she saw stars and her body went limp.

McCarthy stood up and wiped the sweat from his forehead. Then kicked Darby in the side. He turned to the armed men and frowned.

"What does Espanoza want me to do with her?" he asked.

"Don't kill her," the man replied. "She's a bargaining chip."

McCarthy took a seat and looked over at Dr. Morganton.

"Bitch actually thought she was playing me? Probably thought she could cut me out of it all," McCarthy laughed. "Guess she learned how that works out."

***

Espanoza answered his phone and grinned. "Good. Don't hurt a hair on her head or Ballantine won't play along. I want a video feed set up so he has proof of life, understood? Call me when you are set."

Looking at the ensign, Espanoza twirled his fingers lazily.

"Get me Ballantine," he ordered. "Time to get my brother back as well as my product."

Chapter Nine- Quatro!

Far off in the ocean, a shadow moved. Schools of fish fled before it; everything fled before it. The shadow swam, its massive body pushing it through the water like a sixty foot missile.

***

"Here," Carlos said, handing Kinsey the case. "Hold this for me."

"Uh, fine," Kinsey said. "What's in it?"

"Tools," Carlos said then fished out a piece of paper from his pocket and handed it to Max. He put his finger to his lips.

Max opened the paper and his eyes went wide then he handed it to Kinsey. She set the case down and read the note, looked at Carlos, re-read the note, looked at Cougher, then shook her head.

She jammed the note into her pocket and picked up the case.

"How long do you think it will take for you two to get this going?" Kinsey asked.

"Don't know," Cougher said. "Could be a long while. Maybe an hour or so."

Kinsey looked at Max. "That's cutting it close."

"Then we better hurry," Carlos said as he stared at the two operators.

"Right," Max replied. "Better hurry. We'll be right here watching over you. Keeping you safe with our guns."

They all stared at him like he'd lost his mind. He just shrugged.

"Let's hurry," Carlos said.

"Hurrying," Cougher said and pointed towards the hatchway.

Kinsey and Max turned and hustled from the engine room.

***

"Easy, easy," Gunnar said as he and Shane maneuvered Darren up out of the whale sub's cargo hold. "Don't kill him before I can fix him."

"I'm trying not to," Shane said. "But Ditcher isn't making this easy."

Darren, still out of it, rubbed his hands across Shane's face over and over.

"You feel like rubber," Darren said. "Little rubber sniper. Ten little rubber snipers. Ten rubber snipers jumping on the bed, one shoots a target and then that target is dead. Now there are...uh..."

"Still ten snipers, dude," Shane said. "You killed the target, not a sniper."

"I wouldn't kill a sniper," Darren said as Shane finally got Darren up on top of the sub and to the side of the cargo hold hatch. Gunnar climbed out and Darren pointed at him. "I'd kill a scientist. Not you, Gunny bud bud. But some other scientist."

Darren thought about it then sat up straight and grabbed Shane by the shoulders. "A mad scientist!" he shouted. "I'd kill a mad scientist and save the world!"

"You'd be a hero, dude," Shane said.

"I would," Darren replied, leaning in conspiratorially. "I'd totally be a hero."

"And you know what heroes do?" Shane asked.

"Kill mad scientists," Darren replied. "Fucking duh, *dude*."

"Dude, did you just mock my dude?" Shane asked. "If you did then I'm not telling you what else heroes do."

"Oh, shit, I'm sorry!" Darren cried. "Shane, I'm so sorry! I'm a hero! I didn't mean to mock you!" He looked to his left then to his right then right at Shane. "It's not my fault. A mad scientist drugged me."

"That he did," Shane said, looking over and rolling his eyes at Gunnar. "Now, to be a real hero you have to let me and Gunnar here get your ass off this sub."

"It's a whale," Darren said.

"It is whatever you want it to be," Shane said. "As long as you also want to get down off it."

"I do," Darren said. "I need to pee. That little mute pixie kept making me drink water. Like a lot of water. I tried to shove her away, but she's strong, man. Like a lot of strong."

"That's pretty strong," Shane nodded.

"I know!" Darren exclaimed. "Oh, damn..."

The front of Darren's pants grew wetter and wetter.

"We'll, that's unfortunate," Shane said.

"I am so glad I didn't miss that," Kinsey said from the catwalk above.

"Hey, bro," Max nodded. "You going on the secret mission too?"

"Please tell me you already killed your com piece?" Gunnar snapped. "Otherwise if they're listening you just ruined it all."

"Oh, shit!" Max said in a high falsetto. "I'd hate to ruin it all!"

"We killed them outside the hatch," Kinsey said.

"Killed 'em dead," Max said as he got to the ladder. "Now let's figure out how to get Ditcher the fuck out of here without breaking him."

"Where's Moshi?" Kinsey asked.

A small hand stuck up out of the cockpit hatch and waved.

"Hey, Moshi, thanks for taking care of Darren," Kinsey said. She got a thumbs up in return. "Hopefully you still got what Ballantine needed you to do, well, uh, done."

Moshi wiggled her hand back and forth in a "so-so" gesture.

"She's already assured me she'll be finished in time," Gunnar said as he looked at Darren. "But he's the real problem."

"I am not a problem," Darren said. "I'm a solution. Everyone stop looking at me!"

"We could always knock him out again," Max suggested.

"Then how do we get him up the ladder?" Shane asked. "The hatch down here isn't working, remember?"

"God!" Max grinned. "Why does Ditcher always gotta be such a pain in the ass?"

***

The shadow saw movement far ahead and rocketed forward, its tail thrashing back and forth, taking it to a speed few creatures of the sea could match.

It quickly reached the source of the movement; it was large and long that smelled nothing like food. But that hand't stopped the shadow before. It had survived in the ocean by being smart and curious at the same time. It kept heading towards the large and long object that didn't smell like food.

Then it realized the large and long object was moving towards an even larger, even longer object. That object was something the shadow knew. It had come across many of those objects in its journey from ocean to ocean. Sometimes it let the objects move past, sometimes it didn't. The shadow had no rules as to which object could leave its presence or which needed to be destroyed and sent to the deep. It only acted as it wanted at that exact moment.

Except for this moment. In this moment it had been drawn to this area; drawn by something that called to it.

The shadow, not knowing if the smaller object was what called it or not, started to swim faster. It targeted the object and opened its wide, wide mouth. But, to the shadow's surprise, the larger object opened up and swallowed the not as large object.

The shadow grew angry at this, being denied its prey, but instead of taking out its aggression on the larger object, the shadow slowed and turned a different direction, its senses honing in on something else. The real something that called to it.

It began to dive and search for that something, its tail taking it deeper and deeper.

***

"Oh, for fuck's sake, Ditcher!" Shane shouted. "Just climb the fucking ladder!"

"I peed my pants," Darren said, his eyes full of tears. "You don't understand, man. I peed my pants."

"No, dude, I understand," Shane said. "And the only way we can get you clean clothes is if you climb the fucking ladder!"

"He's not climbing," Gunnar said.

"That isn't helping," Kinsey said.

"He's had cardiac trauma due to ingesting a highly dangerous substance," Gunnar said. "As medical officer I can't have you forcing him to climb a ladder. That would be idiotic."

"It's been an idiotic day," Shane replied.

"Then we'll have to knock him out and figure out a way to winch him up," Max said.

"Why do that?" Popeye asked as he stepped through the hatchway onto the catwalk, surprising everyone. "Why not use the cargo lift?"

He pointed at the far end of the catwalk and the wide platform attached to the side.

"Want me to lower it down to you?" Popeye asked.

"This is why ships have boatswains," Shane said.

"Yeah, so the soldiers don't fuck everything up," Popeye laughed.

"Good to see you back onboard, Pop," Max said.

"Pissed I even had to leave," Popeye said, waving a note around. "But Ballantine gets what Ballantine wants."

He hobbled over to the other end of the catwalk and worked the controls, sending the cargo lift down to the deck below.

"You load him on and Doc can ride up with him," Popeye said. "You folks need to get yourselves moving now."

"Thanks, Pop," Kinsey said. "We owe you one."

"And Ballantine owes me a ton," Popeye said. "Keeping everyone in the damn dark. That man needs to learn to trust more."

"Fat chance," Max said.

The Reynolds and Kinsey made their way to the hatch when Gunnar called out.

"Hold up," Gunnar yelled. "Where are your weapons? You can't go in there unarmed?"

"The M-4s may not be as reliable in the water," Kinsey said, patting the case in her hand. "But don't worry, we aren't unarmed."

"We'll pick up more when we get there," Shane smiled.

"Be careful," Gunnar said. "Come back in one piece."

"Eh, it ain't so bad missing pieces," Popeye cackled.

"We'll take your word for it, Pop," Max said as the three left the specimen bay.

"Moshi? You about done?" Gunnar called out.

Moshi stuck her hand out and held up five fingers.

"Five minutes?" Gunnar asked.

She gave a thumbs up in response.

***

"Let's make this simple, Ballantine," Espanoza said. "I want my product and I want my brother back. You send them over and I don't kill your pet."

"I don't own pets," Ballantine replied over the com. "They are an entanglement and hassle that my lifestyle doesn't allow for. Gone for weeks, many times months on end, out living a life of danger and excitement. It just wouldn't be fair to a dog or cat. Or even a goldfish for that matter. Do you think a goldfish would miss me, Ricardo?"

"Shut up, Ballantine," Espanoza said. "I am done jousting with you. These are not negotiations. This isn't a conversation where we feel each other out and look for weaknesses. I have none. You have all of them."

"I could kill your brother and dump the product overboard," Ballantine replied. "Or would that be a weakness too?"

"Stop playing," Espanoza said. "Darby means something to you. You have acted like she's nothing but a bodyguard or right hand. But I know she's not. The reason I know this is because my brother is the same to me."

"Then you would probably care if I stuck a knife in his heart," Ballantine said. "Because that is what I will do if you harm a hair on Darby's head."

"You see? That wasn't so hard was it? You showed some emotion towards another person," Espanoza laughed. "You know why the Mexican cartels cannot be stopped, Ballantine? Because we are filled with emotion! It fills every fiber in our bodies. We don't separate business from emotion. We are not cold like Americans. We feel every kill. We savor every victory and mourn every loss. We live life, Ballantine. You should try it."

"Oh, I know how to live life, Ricardo," Ballantine said. "I've been doing it since I was born. Popped right out of the womb living life to its fullest. You think I became the man I am by not wanting to live life? Tsk-tsk, Ricardo, I thought you had me all figured out."

Espanoza sighed. "My brother and my product for your Darby, whatever the fuck she is."

"How do I know she's still alive?" Ballantine asked.

"I have a video feed," Espanoza said. "Proof of life."

"Sorry, but I don't have power," Ballantine said. "Video is down. All I have is emergency power for the com. Put her on so I can have a chat. Then we'll go from there."

"Patch her through," Espanoza said to the ensign.

"Yes, sir," the ensign replied.

There was some static then McCarthy shouted, "Talk to him, bitch!"

"Ballantine?" Darby's voice asked.

"Hello, old friend," Ballantine said. "How are you holding up?"

"I'm holding," Darby replied.

"Your voice sounds thick, have they been beating you?" Ballantine asked, a slight hint of anger in his voice, but he kept it in check.

"*They* haven't," Darby said. "But *he* has."

"He? He who?" Ballantine asked.

"McCarthy," Darby said. "Son of a bitch killed Dr. Morganton too."

"What?" McCarthy screamed. "I didn't kill her! *You* did, you lying cunt!"

"McCarthy, stay off the com," Espanoza said. "We'll sort out the Dr. Morganton issue after all of this is finished."

"Ricardo, if your man McCarthy hurts Darby again I will match it blow for blow, cut for cut, shot for shot on your brother," Ballantine said. "You know I will."

"I do, Ballantine," Espanoza responded. "That's why Mr. McCarthy will not touch her again. Right, James?"

"Listen, Mr. Espanoza, you have to believe me when I say I didn't kill-"

"Just answer the question, James," Espanoza ordered. "Will you or will you not harm Ms. Darby again?"

"I-I-I-I won't," McCarthy stuttered.

"It's Darby," Darby said.

"Excuse me?" Espanoza asked.

"Not Ms. Darby, just Darby," Darby answered.

"So Darby is your first name?" Espanoza asked, curious to see if the woman would admit who she was..

"Just Darby," Darby stated flatly.

"Well, that's settled," Ballantine said. "But I still don't know if I can trust you, Ricardo."

"You have my word," Espanoza said. "That's all I can give. Do you really have any other choice, Ballantine? Think it through. You have one chance to see Just Darby again." He chuckled at his little joke. "Give me my brother and my product."

Ballantine was silent for a long while. "Fine. I'll do it. We'll send a couple Zodiacs over with the product and with your brother."

"No, no, no," Espanoza said. "You'll send over the whale sub. I want that also."

"That will take some time since we are without power," Ballantine said. "We can't open the bay doors without power, Ricardo."

"One hour," Espanoza said. "Just to show I am being fair. Every minute over an hour, just Darby loses a finger. Are we clear?"

"Crystal, Ricardo," Ballantine stated cooly.

"And one more thing."

"Don't fucking push it," Ballantine growled.

"The sub pilot, the legless SEAL," Espanoza smiled. "Send him with. He's the only one that can pilot the sub anyway. And I'd like to tie up that loose end."

"You want me to send a man to his death?" Ballantine asked.

"Of course," Espanoza replied. "That's what you do, isn't it? Send men and women to their deaths?"

He snapped his fingers and the ensign cut the com.

**

"Are we clear?" Ballantine asked.

"Yeah," Ingrid said. "I have them blocked again."

"Keep them that way for the next couple of minutes then give them access," Ballantine said. "I want it to sound like we're having technical troubles on our end. We can't make it too easy for them or they'll get suspicious. Where's Lake?"

"Standing right here," Lake said as he leaned against a shelf. "Plan on filling me in on what the fuck is going on?"

"Yes," Ballantine said. "But not yet. Too many moving parts and if I stop to explain it all, then I'll lose track of something. The margin of error is this small." Ballantine held his thumb and forefinger close together.

"I crush your head," Ingrid said. The men looked at her. "Kids In The Hall? I crush your head? You do know the lounge on this ship gets Netflix, right? Try it sometime."

"Thank you, Ingrid," Ballantine said. "When I have some free time I may just do that. Could you write down some suggestions? I hate searching through menus to figure out what to watch."

"Me too," Ingrid said. "I totally hate that. I'll get you a super cool list. But I need to go check on Lucy first."

"I would hope so," Ballantine said. "How is Ms. Durning doing?'

"She's in and out," Ingrid said. "I know she has a concussion, but I don't know how bad it is. The med bay she's in is keeping an eye on her vital signs. But I have to keep an eye on the med bay since it's a prototype and I know machines, not medicine."

"Completely understood," Ballantine smiled. "Now, Acting Captain Lake, I am going to need you to come with me to Gunnar's lab."

"What for?" Lake asked. "To get Espanoza's brother and his coke?"

"Not coke," Ballantine said, holding up a finger. "Something else, but not coke. And yes, I need your help getting that down to the sub."

"Lead the way," Lake shrugged. "But know I have no intention of letting Espanoza win."

"Oh, neither do I, Acting Captain Lake," Ballantine replied.

"Just call me Marty," Lake said. "It's kinda weird when you say Acting Captain Lake."

"Fine. Marty it is," Ballantine said as he left the Toyshop.

***

"Cool you know how to drive this thing, Sis," Shane said. "We'll have to go joyriding and do some ocean donuts when we live through this shit."

"*When* we live through this shit," Max said as he opened the case and gave a nice, long whistle. "Well, lookey here."

"You know I did say when, right?" Shane said. "I didn't say *if* we live, I said *when* we live. I'm full on optimist with this shit today."

"What's in the case?" Kinsey asked from the mini-sub's pilot's seat. "Please tell me it's laser pistols or some cool shit like that."

"Nope," Max said. "But close enough."

He pulled out four flat boxes, each about twelve inches square and two inches thick.

"Great," Shane said. "Giant metal coasters."

"Uh, nope," Max said as he picked up a note. "It says these are similar to FMG9s, but with a little more kick to them. Uses same rounds as the cartel's favorite toy, the AK-47. There are already 30 rounds in the magazine so please don't shoot yourselves when opening. That's what the note says."

"Cool," Shane said. "Gimme."

Max handed over a box and Shane inspected it then turned away from Max and pressed the button on top. He flicked his hand and the box became a snub nosed semi-automatic rifle.

"Not going to have much range or accuracy at a long distance," Shane said, getting the feel for the weapon. "This is a sniper's nightmare."

"This is an assault, not hide and seek," Kinsey said. "You'll get plenty of other opportunities to sit in a hide for a week. Embrace the fight, boys. Embrace it."

"Sometime I worry about you, Sis," Max said. "I think you embrace the fight a little too much."

"Thanks," Kinsey said. "I'm taking that as a compliment, whether you meant it or not."

"Oh, it was," Max said. "But I still worry about you."

"Worry away," Kinsey said. "And stay out of my way. Time to go get my girl, Darby."

"Hey, she's all of our girl," Shane said. "Except for Max. I think. What's up with you two?"

"I don't know," Max shrugged. "If it happens then that's cool, but for now I ain't pining."

"Yeah, I think she's noticed," Kinsey said.

"What does that mean?" Max asked.

"Nothing," Kinsey said. "Just that she noticed."

"What does that mean?" Max asked, turning to Shane.

"I don't know, bro," Shane replied. "I've given up figuring out your fickle ways. Just yesterday you wanted to bang that MILF."

"What?" Kinsey asked, looking back at the boys. "What's a MILF?"

"Oh, Sis," Shane said. "For a woman that has been to hell and back you have a lot to learn about this world."

"I didn't want to bang her," Max said. Shane raised his eyebrows. "Not that I wouldn't have liked to get to know her better." He paused. "Was that yesterday? Wasn't that like just this morning?"

"Dude, we've been out at sea for like a week," Shane grinned.

"Two weeks," Max replied.

"A month."

"It's been a year."

"Boys, shut up," Kinsey snapped. "You're killing me here."

"Somebody sounds just like her daddy," Max whispered loudly.

"I swear I will pull this sub over and kick you out right here," Kinsey laughed. "No, seriously, shut the fuck up. Time to get our heads in the game." She held up a finger. "And no jokes about games or head or anything. Quiet time."

***

The smell was overwhelming for the shadow. It raced towards the shape on the bottom of the ocean, hungry for what was inside. But rage took hold when it reached the shape and found the belly to be empty. It slammed its head against the shape over and over, trying to dislodge what little of the delicious smelling substance still lingered inside.

The shadow wedged its head inside the shape, forcing itself deeper until it was able to taste and breathe what its senses had alerted it to above. When the substance was exhausted, the shadow withdrew and began to swim back towards the surface. It would investigate the large, long shape once more. Now that it knew the smell of the substance, it was sure it had smelled it near the large, long shape.

But, as it ascended, it sensed movement from something else, something moving in the water, something new. Maybe the new thing would have the substance it wanted so bad? It changed directions and sent itself off, its tail pushing it forward as it whipped back and forth.

***

"And we can't just kill him?" Mike asked as Diego kept screaming on the table.

"No," Thorne said. "Ballantine has plans."

"I do," Ballantine said as he walked into the lab with Lake. "And how are those plans coming?"

Thorne looked up from his work and frowned. "You're sure about this?"

219

"Yes," Ballantine said.

"What if he finds it, it pisses him off and he calls in the order to kill Darby?" Thorne asked.

"I'm hoping your daughter and nephews prevent that from happening," Ballantine replied.

"Too many pieces in play, Ballantine," Lake said. "One gets out of whack and the game is up."

"I am aware of that, Marty," Ballantine said. "But at this point there is nothing I can do. What has happened has happened. We all do our parts and maybe our friends, and family, make it out alive. Can't make promises, only guesses."

"Done," Thorne said. "Now let's get this down to the sub."

"Pallet jack is right here," Lake said.

He pushed the jack over and slid it under the narrow pallet the kilos of drugs rested on. Many of the bags had to be taped up as they were punctured from the many battles the lab had seen. In fact, as Lake pulled the pallet back towards the hatchway, he figured the whole lab would have to be redone since he doubted Gunnar wanted to work in a bullet ridden space.

As Thorne and Lake struggled to get the pallet from deck to deck, having to maneuver it into three different supply lifts in order to get it down below, Ballantine and Mike took a more direct route and reached the specimen bay well before the other men.

"He going to make it?" Mike asked as he saw Gunnar and Darren sitting on the catwalk.

"He will," Gunnar said. "Physically."

Darren looked over at Ballantine and Mike and frowned.

"Bummer guy is here," Darren said, putting a finger to his lips. "Better not say what I'm thinking."

"And what is that, Captain?" Ballantine smiled. "I'm all ears."

"Don't answer that," Gunnar said to Darren then looked at Ballantine. "Not cool picking on the infirm."

"Sometimes it's therapeutic to say what's on one's mind while under the influence of mind altering substances," Ballantine said. "I spent six weeks in the Sonoran Desert with a shaman drinking fermented cactus juice and eating rattlesnake. Add a drop of the venom to the cactus juice and you have yourself a rocket ride, I can assure you."

"I'll take your word for it," Gunnar said. "And you still don't get to take advantage of Darren."

"Shouldn't you get him to the infirmary?" Mike asked as he moved his wheelchair next to Gunnar. "If he's that messed up you may want to hook him up to some machines or something."

"That your medical advice?" Gunnar laughed. "Hook him up to some machines or something?"

"I don't know," Mike frowned. "Don't be a dick."

"Sorry, it's a shit day," Gunnar said. "Darren is happy where he is and I have no energy to fight him. Right now I'm testing his cognitive responses." He turned to Darren. "Hey, Darren, do you know where you are?"

"Right next to my best friend," Darren said and hugged Gunnar. Hard.

"Ow, ow," Gunnar winced, removing Darren. "No more hugging, remember? We've talked about this."

"But I like hugging you, G-Man," Darren said. "Not in a humpy way, but like best buds forever. I'd rather hug 'Sey in a humpy way, if you know what I mean."

"I do know what you mean," Gunnar said.

"No you don't," Darren laughed. "You do guys, not girls. Your way is totally different than my way. Maybe. I guess that depends on whether you're a-"

"And we're done," Gunnar said, putting his hand over Darren's mouth. He looked at Mike and Ballantine. "Isn't this fun?"

"Actually," Ballantine said. "It is, in a way. This drug seems to really lower inhibitions and loosen the tongue. Might be some applications for that."

"Yeah, it does those things," Gunnar said. "It also heightens aggression to an extreme no one wants to witness. Not to mention the whole psychosis thing." Darren went in for another hug. "And the emotional comedown."

"We'll talk about this at a later date," Ballantine smiled as he turned and looked down at the sub below. "Moshi! Good to see you. Is the sub ready as planned?"

Moshi held up a thumb as she sat cross-legged on top of the sub, running one hand along the faux skin.

"Excellent," Ballantine said. He turned to Mike. "I'll need you to do as we discussed, please."

"You bet," Mike said.

He slid out of the wheelchair and hand-walked over to the ladder. He easily swung himself around and climbed down the ladder using only his hands. He caught Gunnar looking and gave him a wink. Gunnar rolled his eyes and went back to keeping Darren from hugging him.

Mike was able to get down to the deck and over to the sub without any problem since he'd done it plenty of times before when working with McCarthy. The thought of McCarthy and what he pulled on him and the other two pilots made Mike's blood boil and Moshi recoiled from Mike, afraid of the look on his face, as he crawled past her to the cockpit hatch.

Mike lowered himself inside. Moshi waited until the hatch was closed then double-checked the seam and looked up at Ballantine, giving another thumbs up. Everyone was silent in the bay, even Darren since Gunnar finally let him hug him. Then after a couple of minutes, Ballantine clapped and gave a huge grin.

"That enough video, Moshi?" Ballantine asked.

Moshi tapped at her tablet then looked up and nodded.

"Perfect," he said. "Let's load the cargo and we'll be done in here for a long while."

The cargo hatch at the other end of the catwalk opened and Thorne looked in. "Ready for us?"

"Your timing is impeccable," Ballantine said. "I don't know about you all, but I'm actually having fun."

"Bummer guy be fucked in the head, yo," Darren said.

"No shit," Gunnar laughed.

***

"Getting close," Kinsey said. "We should be seeing Darby's mini-sub any second."

"Time to get our mustaches on," Shane said.

"You are such a hipster," Max responded.

"Dude, don't make me shoot you."

"No one's getting shot," Kinsey said. "Knock on wood or something. It's game time. Heads straight, eyes on the prize."

"Good speech, coach," Shane said, tapping his eye patch. "But I only have one eye on the prize. Does that mean I can only score half as many points?"

"Just put your mustache on," Kinsey smiled. "We're here."

Shane and Max settled their mustaches, both gagging as the tubes extended into their nostrils, while Kinsey stopped the mini-sub, shot the bolts below, and anchored it into place. She held out her hand and Max handed her a mustache. She set it, gagging as well, and then opened the bottom hatch.

The three nodded to each other, made sure they had their box rifles, and dropped into the water.

***

"He's calling again," Ingrid said. "You can't hold him off anymore."

"I know, I know," Ballantine said. "I just want to give Kinsey and the Reynolds more time."

"I'm sure he knows we're stalling as it is," Ingrid replied. "It's almost an hour."

"I know."

"And for every minute over he'll cut off one of Darby's fingers."

"I know."

"Darby likes her fingers."

Ballantine turned to Ingrid and glared. "You are not helping."

"Then answer the com," Ingrid said.

"Fine," Ballantine replied. He took a deep breath and activated his com.

***

"I thought you had forgotten me," Espanoza said as he stared out of the bridge windows towards the Beowulf III. "You didn't forget about me, did you Ballantine?"

"How could I, Ricardo?" Ballantine responded over the com.

223

"Are you ready to give me what's mine?" Espanoza asked. "I hope so for Just Darby's sake."

"Our power is still down," Ballantine said. "We can't open the bay to release the sub until we have power."

"Bullshit," Espanoza said. "You have a very capable crew on that ship. I am sure they figured out how to reroute the power by now. Send me my sub, my product, and my brother!"

"Ricardo, if you'll give-"

"I'm giving you nothing!" Espanoza shouted. "Launch the sub in the next minute or I give the order for Darby to die!"

"Then I kill your brother," Ballantine said.

"No, you won't," Espanoza laughed. "Because I have every gun on this ship aimed at the Beowulf. You've never been in a position to bargain, Ballantine. I've humored you because we have history and because I don't want my brother to die. I may be forced to mourn my brother, but I'll do it alive. You won't even get to mourn your Just Darby."

"Fine," Ballantine said. "I'm sending your sub out to you."

"Good," Espanoza said. "I'll be waiting."

***

"Go time," Ballantine said. "Tell Cougher we're ready."

"Cougher?" Ingrid said into her com. "Turn the lights back on."

There was a brief pause then the familiar hum of the engines returned followed by the lights. Cheers could be heard from below as Ballantine stood on the upper deck and looked out at Espanoza's ship.

"Launch the sub," Ballantine said. "Make sure Mike and Thorne are set."

"They are," Ingrid replied.

"Everyone ready to abandon ship in the lifeboats if my plan completely fails?" Ballantine asked.

"Yes, sir," Ingrid said then frowned. "Um, am I like your assistant now or something?"

"No," Ballantine replied. "I don't need an assistant. I just enjoy your capable company, Ingrid."

"Oh...cool."

"Yes, it is."

Ingrid listened to her com and grinned. "Popeye says the whale sub is deployed."

"Perfect."

***

The shadow could smell the prey ahead of it and it shot forward.

Then everything changed. It didn't want the prey it had been following anymore; it wanted what was back the way it came. A sound reached its senses; a call, a siren. The call said to hurry, to return to the big, long thing, to go and get what it really hungered for.

The massive shark whipped about and raced through the water, heading directly for the Beowulf III.

***

Kinsey, Shane and Max slowly surfaced, well away from the marina hangar. They watched as guards walked back and forth on the dock. Although all three knew they could make the shots, there was no way for them to take the guards quietly with the rifles they had.

Shane pulled a knife from his belt, held it up out of the water, and pointed at the guards. Max shrugged and Kinsey nodded. They quietly slid back under the surface of the water.

***

"Show me video," Espanoza ordered over the com.

"My tech has sent you the feeds," Ballantine replied into his com, winking at Ingrid. "You should see one of the cargo hold which has your product and your brother. We did have to sedate him in order to get him into the sub since he was less than cooperative."

"I can believe that," Espanoza said. "Even wounded he is formidable."

Ballantine waited patiently for Espanoza to respond.

"I see my brother and my product," Espanoza said. "Ah, and there is the crippled SEAL piloting the sub. How fortunate that half a man can be useful today. I'll take good care of him, Ballantine, don't you worry. At least until I train a different monkey to pilot the sub."

"You come from small people, Ricardo," Ballantine said. "I'm sure you can find a cousin or nephew to pilot it for you."

"Be very careful, Ballantine," Espanoza snarled. "Insulting my family will get Just Darby killed."

"They're here," Ingrid smiled.

"Excellent," Ballantine said. "Have the sub surface between the ships."

The water between the two ships began to bubble and the sub slowly came up to the surface, its body so remarkably like an adolescent blue whale.

"Ballantine? What are you doing?" Espanoza asked. "Send that sub over to me now! One call and Darby dies!"

"I don't think so," Ballantine replied, hoping he was right. "In fact, you may want to get into a boat right now and join your brother in that sub. It might be your only chance to escape." Ballantine grinned wide as he looked over at Espanoza's ship. "How about this, Ricardo? You let Darby go and once I confirm she is safe, then I let you go. You hop in that sub with your brother and you can swim off to wherever you want. Sound good?"

"You've either gone mad or no longer care for your life or the lives of anyone around you!" Espanoza shouted. "I am now giving the order for Darby to die! You hear me, Ballantine? Your Darby dies now!"

"Hey, Ballantine," Lake said over the com. "You were right. There was a fourth. Jesus, here it comes!"

"Of course I was right," Ballantine said. "Are Thorne and Mr. Pearlman in place?"

"They are," Lake said.

"Good," Ballantine said. "Ricardo? Last chance. Join your brother or end up in prison the rest of your life."

"What? Prison?" Espanoza laughed. "You have gone mad!"

***

Espanoza put his cell phone to his ear. "Kill her."

The ensign looked over at him then turned away quickly, not wanting the Devil to meet his eye and steal his soul.

***

The first guard went down quietly as Kinsey grabbed him from behind with one hand, while reaching around and stabbing him up under the ribs with her other. The knife punctured his lung, leaving him unable to cry out as she pulled out the knife and slashed his throat. She eased him down to the dock, her eyes on the next guard.

Slowly, she crouch walked over to him, but the second guard turned just as she stood up to attack.

"Aye-" he cried out as Kinsey opened his throat.

"Well, fuck quiet," Max said as he stepped around Kinsey and snapped his box rifle open, he put it to his shoulder and opened fire.

Shane was right behind him with Kinsey pulling up the rear. The three operators sent each guard falling to the deck, their chests and heads ripped open. They rushed to the hangar door and Max grabbed the knob, looked to the others then opened it.

Kinsey took point with Shane right behind her. They stepped into the hangar and began to cut down Espanoza's men with surgical precision. They didn't worry about wasting time going for the headshots; each man received two rounds in the chest, dropping them instantly.

"Clear!" Kinsey yelled then looked towards the office. "There!"

She jumped over corpses as she raced to the office, hoping she wasn't too late. Their messy entry meant Darby could have been killed seconds after the first shot was fired.

But that wasn't the case as Kinsey moved into the office and trained her rifle on McCarthy that stood with a gun pressed to Darby's head.

"I'll fucking shoot her!" McCarthy yelled. "You get the fuck out of my way or I shoot her!"

"I have you," Kinsey said softly, but saw Darby shake her head just enough to catch her attention.

"You won't get a shot off in time!" McCarthy shouted. "Get out of my way or she dies!"

Kinsey and Darby locked eyes then Kinsey lowered her weapon slightly and stepped aside.

"Out!" McCarthy ordered as he moved forward towards the door. "Out there with your buddies! You walk to the far end of the dock and set your weapons down!"

Kinsey backed out of the office and looked at Max and Shane.

"Yeah, we heard," Max said.

He and his brother stepped over and between the corpses to the far end of the dock. Kinsey followed and they all squatted and placed their rifles down then stood and held up their hands. McCarthy cautiously walked Darby from the office, making sure her body was between him and the three operators of Team Grendel.

"I'm leaving," McCarthy said. "She's coming with. When I'm far enough away, I'll let her go. Don't even think of following me!"

"Dude, why should we believe you?" Max asked. "You get out that door and you'll just blow her head off and run."

"Are you fucking kidding?" McCarthy laughed nervously. "I know who this chick is. Now I kill her and that Ballantine guy will hunt me down and skin me alive. I'm not fucking joking. He'll skin me!"

"He will," Darby said, not offering any resistance.

"So I leave and she lives," McCarthy said as he got to the hangar door. He opened it with his free hand and grabbed Darby's arm as soon as the door was open, yanking her out onto the dock outside.

The second the door closed, Kinsey, Max and Shane picked up their rifles and sprinted towards the door. Just as they reached it, it swung open and Kinsey almost put two rounds into Darby.

"Fuck!" Kinsey snapped. "You have a death wish?"

"Where'd he go?" Max asked, stepping out onto the dock, his rifle sweeping back and forth as he searched the night for McCarthy.

"He got away," Darby said as she walked past them and back to the office. "Oh, well."

She bent down, picked up a cell phone, and dialed a number.

"What the fuck are you doing?" Kinsey asked.

Darby held up a finger as the person on the other end of the phone answered.

***

"Is it done?" Espanoza asked.

"No," Darby replied. "But you are. Better run, Espanoza, because I am coming for you."

Espanoza's blood ran cold and he turned to the ensign that was by his side suddenly. "Fire on that ship," he growled. "Blast it out of the fucking water!"

The ensign lifted a pistol at Espanoza and shook his head.

"No, sir, I don't think so," he said. "By orders of the Mexican Naval Command, you are relieved of your commission and under arrest for murder, drug trafficking, and corruption of duty as a naval officer. Everything you have said and done has been recorded and transmitted. You are done."

"What's wrong, Espanoza?" Darby asked over the phone. "Things didn't work out how you thought?"

Espanoza looked at the gun in the ensign's hand then slammed the phone into the young man's face. The gun fired, but Espanoza had stepped aside. He grabbed the ensign's arm and wrenched the pistol free, turning it on the young man and shooting him in the belly.

As the ensign crumpled, Espanoza raced around him and out of the bridge. Men were running at him from every direction. He fired over and over and the men hit the deck or ducked into hatchways. He sprinted away from the bridge and hurried down to the upper deck. Someone shouted and he spun and fired, shooting the man in the chest.

Espanoza quickly realized there was nowhere for him to go. He had to get off the ship. But where? Then, as he got to the rail, he saw the sub waiting there between the ships. He looked down at the dark water below, climbed over the railing, then jumped, holding his legs closed and arms to his sides.

He felt the impact of the water all the way up his legs and into his hips, but he knew he didn't break anything when he was able to start swimming towards the sub.

***

"And he's in the water," Ballantine said. "Ingrid, bring the com back online. Full encryption protocols. No more of this open, sometimes snooped on, cat and mouse crap."

"Yes, sir," Ingrid said.

"Lake? Where is it?" Ballantine asked.

"Closing fast," Lake said. "It'll be a race between it and Espanoza as to which one gets to the sub first."

"Com is secure, sir," Ingrid said.

"Good," Ballantine said. "Darby?"

***

"All is as it should be," Darby said into her com.

"Whoa," Shane said. "Com's on? I thought we were staying quiet?"

"And the package?" Ballantine asked.

"Wrapped and ready for delivery," Darby said, walking over to Dr. Morganton's body. She knelt down and gave the corpse a nudge.

But it wasn't a corpse.

Dr. Morganton stirred then opened her eyes and looked over at Kinsey, Max, and Shane who stood by the door.

"Who are they?" Dr. Morganton asked, sitting up.

"Team Grendel," Darby said.

"Ah, Ballantine's crew," Dr. Morganton nodded as Darby helped her to her feet. "Do you have any idea how uncomfortable it is to play dead? I'll be working out the kinks for weeks. Good thing I do yoga daily." She stepped forward and offered her hand. "Dr. Lisa Morganton. It's good to meet you."

"Uh, you too," Shane said as he shook her hand.

"Gonna need some answers, Darby," Kinsey said.

"In good time," Ballantine said over the com. "For now you stay quiet and get the package safely back here. Understood?"

"You're the boss," Kinsey said.

"Yes, he is," Darby said. "Let's go."

***

Most of the crew of the Beowulf III stood at the railing of the upper deck and watched as spotlights illuminated Espanoza swimming frenziedly towards the sub.

"It's kind of sad," Ingrid said. "He has no idea what's about to happen."

"Screw him," Gunnar said. "He killed Beau."

Everyone looked over at him and nodded.

"Here it comes!" Lake shouted from the bridge.

Espanoza reached the sub and grabbed onto the faux skin. It took him a minute, but the sub was low enough in the water that he was able to get himself up onto the back. He looked around for a second and then pounded where he thought the cargo hatch was.

"I can't look," Ingrid said and turned away.

"Not missing this for anything," Popeye said.

"Me neither," Cougher said.

Espanoza raised both hands up over his head and brought them down hard onto the cargo hatch one more time.

Then the water exploded around him and the sub was lifted into the air, clutched in the jaws of a sixty foot shark. The shark took the sub twenty feet into the air before twisting around and bringing it back to the water. Espanoza's screams could be heard all the way to the Beowulf III.

"Oh, shit!"

"Damn!"

"Holy fuck!"

"Awesome!"

"What's happening? Guys? Tell me!"

"Open your eyes!"

"Moshi," Ballantine said to the woman at his elbow. "If you'll do the honors."

Moshi swiped at her tablet, and the controls she had been remotely piloting the sub with disappeared, replaced by a single red button.

"For Beau," Moshi said and all the cheering and yells and talking stopped instantly.

They all looked at the woman that never spoke and hands went over hearts, heads lowered and as one they said, "For Beau."

Moshi pressed the button as the shark took the sub under and began to dive. The water exploded into a geyser of blood, metal, and skin, both faux and real.

The crew of the Beowulf III watched, many with tears in their eyes.

"Thorne?" Ballantine asked into his com. "You and Mr. Pearlman are up."

***

The water was chaos, but Thorne, and Mike with flippers strapped to his legs, swam hard towards the spot where the sub had exploded. Their goggles searched the waters for any sign of the giant shark.

"There!" Thorne said, pointing below them.

"Holy fuck! It's still alive?" Mike exclaimed. "What the hell are these things made of?"

"I don't really care," Thorne said. "As long as I can kill them somehow."

Both Thorne and Mike put channel rifles to their shoulders and watched as targeting sights came up in their goggles. They led the shark slightly and then each fired six rounds.

***

The shark fled, most of its jaw mangled and hanging loose. It felt its lifeblood leaving, but it didn't slow as it dove faster and faster. Then there was more pain as it was hit over and over from behind. It pushed itself to go faster, but it couldn't outrace what had already punctured it.

All twelve rounds exploded at once and the shark was sent to the bottom in a hundred pieces.

***

"Kill confirmed," Thorne said. "Heading back to the B3."

"That was crazy," Mike said. "And this is what you do all the time?"

"Not all the time," Thorne said. "Just when Ballantine calls."

"Wow," Mike said. "How do I sign up?"

"Well, we'll- LOOK OUT!" Thorne shouted as a shape came up behind Mike and grabbed him around the neck.

Mike jammed an elbow into a bleeding Espanoza's belly and swam towards Thorne. Thorne pulled his channel pistol and brought it up, taking careful aim. He fired and the round twisted through the water, nailing Espanoza right in the mouth. A second later Espanoza's headless body slowly sank towards the bottom of the ocean.

"Thanks," Mike said.

"Anytime. Stupid motherfucker thought he could take two frogmen in the water," Thorne smirked. "Now let's get inside and get dry. I'm fucking hungry and need a nap."

Chapter Ten: Home

"That's my condo," Gunnar said, pointing up at the smoking ruins of his home. "I...it wasn't like that when I left."

"Sir, the whole building has been cordoned off until the arson investigation is completed," the police officer said as he stood by the barricades that surrounded the Vista Continental Luxury Condos. "I'm sorry, but you can't go in there."

"I just need to see if there's anything left," Gunnar said. "All my clothes are in there! Everything I own!"

The officer turned and looked over his shoulder and laughed. "Man, there's nothing in there now. Three quarters of the building is scorched. And even if there was anything, I can't let you in. No one goes in until the arson investigation is completed. Please don't make me say it again."

"Did you just laugh?" Kinsey snapped as she grabbed the barricade, ready to toss it aside. "I really hope you didn't because I'd stick my foot so far up your-"

"Thank you, officer," Gunnar said, pulling Kinsey back with his one good arm. "I understand you are just doing your job. How do I find out when the investigation is finished?"

"You'll get a call," the officer said, his eyes boring into Kinsey. "Until then, just stay away."

"On my list, man," Kinsey said, her finger jabbing towards the officer. "On my list."

Gunnar winced as he yanked Kinsey away from the barricade. Kinsey ignored the nagging pain in her ribs and tried to fight him, but he just kept yanking. Six more people took their place and the officer started all over with his tired spiel as the sun rose across the late morning sky. Gunnar was already sweating heavily, mainly from the fact he hadn't taken a pain pill in a couple hours. Kinsey was about to protest the way the officer blew them off, but she saw the look on Gunnar's face and stopped.

"Shit, Gun, I'm sorry," Kinsey said, calming down instantly. "I totally forgot you were hurt."

"Not bad," Gunnar said. "I'll live."

"No, no, it is bad, *my* bad," Kinsey said and switched from being held to doing the holding as she walked Gunnar over to the long, white passenger van that sat across the street. A car honked as they crossed and Kinsey flipped the driver off.

"That guy on your list too?" Gunnar smirked.

"Shut up," Kinsey said as she got Gunnar into the van. "It sounded cooler in my head."

Popeye sat in the driver's seat. The boatswain looked as exhausted as they all did, but nowhere near as irritated. "Ballantine said it was all gone."

"I had to see," Gunnar said as he leaned into the back seat. "Why the hell did Espanoza's men do that?"

"Like Ballantine said, we're at war with the Colende cartel now," Popeye said.

"Because giant fucking sharks weren't enough," Kinsey replied. "Where are the boys?"

"On the phone," Popeye said as he pointed over at the Reynolds as they paced back and forth on the sidewalk down the street.

Both brothers were pretty much yelling into their phones, arms gesticulating. A mother jogging by with two toddlers in a double stroller looked at them with angry, reproachful eyes as she went by. Kinsey guessed the Reynolds' language wasn't child friendly. After a couple of minutes they both hung up, looked at each other, then up at the sky and screamed.

"That's not good," Kinsey said. The brothers stomped back to the van and jumped in, both red in the face and twitching with anger. "What's up, cuzzes?"

"Everything's gone," Max said as he struggled to stay under control. "Everything. Just got off the phone with the Sheriff. Our cabin, our gear, all of it was burned to the ground. Not a fucking thing is left."

"No Jeep, either," Shane said. "Impound lot was broken into. Our Jeep was torched as well as all the cars around it. Gone."

"Gone," Max echoed.

"All fucking gone," Shane said.

"Goner McGonerston," Max said.

"The gonest," Shane added.

"Stop," Gunnar said. "We get the picture."

"Back to the B3?" Popeye asked.

"My dad first," Kinsey said. "We should check on him."

Popeye nodded. "No need. He's on the ship already. His place was torched too. Lake just called."

Max's phone rang and he answered quickly. "Hey, Sheriff, what's up-" He listened for a while, his eyes darting to Shane over and over. He ran his hand down his face and sighed. "Thanks... No, I get it... Yeah, yeah, sorry... Let us know if we can help. Right...sure...you have our numbers."

"What's up?" Shane asked.

"Jerky, Smut, and Hashwad are dead," Max answered. "Sheriff got the call from the State Troopers. Their fields were poached then scorched. Each guy was found strung up and flayed open. The Sheriff is already sending guys out to our other clients' fields, but he has a feeling they'll find the same thing." Max leaned his head against the headrest and closed his eyes. "We have been asked not to come back north for a long time."

"Fuck," Shane said. "They're dead?"

"Dead."

"Well, that part of our life is done," Shane said. "What do we do now?"

"We fight," Kinsey said.

Everyone turned and looked at her.

"What?" she asked. "You think the Colende cartel is just going to call it even? They aren't. I know these fucks. Or fucks like them. It's never an eye for an eye; it's every part of your body, plus the bodies of your friends and family, for an eye."

"You're right," Max said. "They won't stop."

"So we fight," Shane said.

"Can we eat lunch first?" Gunnar asked.

"On the B3, "Kinsey said. "Popeye? Put that metal leg to the metal. Get us out of here."

"We're now boat people, aren't we?" Max laughed. "So much for the choice of the good life of smoking joints and teaching hippies to shoot."

"Sometimes the choice gets made for you," Kinsey said. "Trust me."

***

"It's been two days," Darren snapped as Lake blocked him from the bridge. "Get the fuck out of my way, Marty!"

"Ballantine said the effects of the drugs can last up to ten days," Lake said. "So until ten days are up, I'm still acting captain."

"Dude!" Darren shouted. "I'm fine!"

"Don't care," Lake said. "You have been relieved of duty for the next ten days. Go have a drink."

"Can't drink," Darren said. "Can't do shit." He balled his fists and glared at Lake. "Just let me hang out, okay? I'll stay out of the way. I'll even be your CO. How's that?"

"No," Lake said. "You have a flashback or something and I don't want to deal with it on the bridge. Plus, it's confusing to the crew, Darren. I'm acting captain for now, deal with it."

"I hate you so much," Darren growled.

"Don't hate the messenger," Lake said. "Now, are you going to go chill the fuck out or do I need to kick your ass?"

"No, I'm going," Darren said as he walked away and headed for the observation deck above the briefing room. "But I'll be back!"

"Looking forward to it," Lake said.

Darren walked up the steps to the observation deck and plopped into a deck chair next to Lucy.

"No go?" Lucy asked, lying out in a Coast Guard red bikini, soaking up the sun. She had a small bandage around her head and lowered her sunglasses as she looked over at Darren. She saw the look on Darren's face and smiled. "Welcome to convalescence. Enjoy it, D. Odds are we won't be relaxing much for a while."

Darren eased into his deck chair, wincing as he took his shirt off. His torso was a mass of black, blue, green, brown, and yellow from being crushed in the shark's jaws. Three broken ribs and an almost burst kidney, but otherwise the wetsuit did its job and kept him from any permanent damage. He looked out at the Pacific Ocean, and the San Diego coastline that was just visible, and sighed heavily.

"Prisoner on my own ship," he complained.

"Knock it off," Lucy said. "Self-pity makes you look weak. Despite your tie dyed torso there, tough guy."

Darren rolled his eyes. "I hate this."

"Yes, you've made that clear," Lucy said. "You think I like any of it? We're all stuck here. Ballantine's orders. At least you got to do some fighting before it went to shit. I got knocked out in the first round and spent the whole time sleeping." She picked up a tall glass with beads of sweat running down it. "At least there're cocktails."

"I can't drink because of that messed up shit that could still be in my bloodstream," Darren said.

"And I can't drink because of the concussion," Lucy said, jiggling the ice in the glass. "It's sweet tea."

"Sweet tea?" Darren laughed. "Where are we? Georgia?" He looked at the glass and smiled. "Gimme some."

"Just a sip," Lucy said. "I don't want to get up and get more."

Darren took a sip of the sugar sweetened tea. "Needs lemon."

"I don't like lemon," Lucy said, taking the glass back. "Get your own and put lemon in it."

A dot in the sky got larger and larger and Darren shielded his eyes.

"Looks like everyone is coming back," Darren said, pointing at the helo that moved towards the Beowulf III at a fast rate. "I better go meet them."

"Don't bother," Thorne said as he walked up onto the deck. "We're meeting in the briefing room in a few minutes. Let them get aboard and settled."

"Meeting?" Darren said. "Ballantine finally going to let us in on the plan?"

"I hope so," Thorne said. "And it better be a good one. This ship is nice, but one perk of being retired from the Navy is not having to live on a boat."

"But there's sweet tea," Lucy smiled.

Thorne shrugged. "I like mine straight. It's the West Coast in me."

The helo circled the ship twice, causing everyone to shield their eyes from the rotor wash then landed on one of the helipads.

"Damn it!" Lucy snapped. "There's crap in my tea now!"

"You can get more," Thorne said as he left the two up on the observation deck.

Thorne took off his sunglasses and rubbed them on his shirt as he descended the steps past the bridge and down to the upper deck. The new helo, another MH-65F Dolphin appropriately named Wyrm III, opened and Kinsey, the Reynolds, Gunnar, and Popeye jumped out as Darby sat in the pilot's seat and finished the power down.

"Hey, Daddy," Kinsey said.

"Was it like Ballantine said?" Thorne asked.

"Worse," Gunnar replied. "There's nothing."

"That's what Ballantine told you it would be like," Thorne said. "How was it worse?"

"I got to see it with my own eyes," Gunnar said. "I'm going to shower and fix a very stiff drink."

"Wish I could join you," Kinsey said and held up a hand at her father. "Kidding."

"No, you're not," Thorne said, his lips pursed.

"True," Kinsey shrugged. "But a girl can dream."

"Keep dreaming," Thorne said then looked at Gunnar. "Shower fast, but no drink. Ballantine has called a meeting."

"That's what Darby said," Gunnar nodded. "And I'll bring the drink to the meeting."

"Hey, Uncle Vinny," Max said as he slunk past.

"How's it going?" Shane asked then followed his brother, not waiting for an answer.

"What's up with those two?" Thorne asked. "They look like their dog died, but they don't have a dog."

"Cartel hit their clients," Kinsey said. "They aren't welcome in NorCal for a while. Too much heat."

"Which clients?" Thorne asked.

"All of them," Kinsey said. "They've been on the phone since we left Gunnar's condo trying to get a hold of people. No one has answered or called back. We're all assuming the worst."

"Good assumption," Darby said as she hopped out of the helo. "Colende is one of the Evil ones."

"Are there good cartels?" Thorne asked.

Darby shrugged. "There are bad, worse, and Evil."

Kinsey and Thorne heard the capitol E in her voice.

"Mike still onboard?" Kinsey asked.

"No choice," Thorne said. "Like the rest of us."

"Where's he at?" Kinsey asked. "He might cheer Gunnar up."

"Down in the Toyshop with the nerds and Dr. Morganton," Thorne said. "I still don't trust that woman. She had a lot to do with the shit we're in and the shit we'll stay in."

"She's was fucked before us," Darby said. "Trust me, you wouldn't want to trade places with her."

"I'll have to take your word on that," Thorne said. He looked her up and down. "What's different about you?"

"Nothing," Darby said and then walked away from the Thornes.

Kinsey waited until the woman had stepped through a hatchway and below deck before turning to her father. "She got highlights," Kinsey smiled. "In her hair."

"I know where highlights go," Thorne said. "I was married and do have a daughter." Thorne smirked at Kinsey. "Although you look like one of the boys most of the time."

"Fuck you, old man," Kinsey said, punching her father in the shoulder.

"Ow," Thorne said. "Why the hell did she get highlights?"

"Only two reasons," Kinsey said. "To impress other women or to get the attention of a guy."

"Great," Thorne said. "More fucking drama."

"Oh, I'm pretty sure Darby doesn't do drama," Kinsey said. "So don't worry about anything like that."

Thorne looked about. "No gear? You didn't stop and pick up clothing or anything?"

"Darby said that wasn't in the plan," Kinsey said. "We'll pick up what we need at our next port, wherever the fuck that is."

"Well, get down and get some chow in the mess if you're hungry," Thorne said then sighed.

"Yeah, it sucks," Kinsey said. "Food isn't the same without Beau yelling at the cooks."

"He was a good Chief Steward," Thorne said. "Maybe Darren can take his place."

"Ha ha," Kinsey said. "Darren still crying about Lake not letting him be captain?"

"Every fucking minute," Thorne said. He put his arm around Kinsey and led her to the hatchway and below deck. "And that's something we need to talk about. Ballantine and I had a chat and there will be a couple changes around here."

"Changes?" Kinsey asked.

"You'll see," Thorne said. "Let's get you to your quarters so you can clean up and be ready for the meeting."

***

"I'm sure you all are wondering-" Ballantine started, but was quickly booed quiet. "What? You haven't wanted to say that?"

"Get on with it," Max said. "Shitty day doesn't need to get shittier."

"Well, it's going to," Ballantine said as he sat down at the head of the coffee table and looked at everyone.

Thorne, Kinsey, Gunnar, Darren, the Reynolds, Lucy, and Darby sat at the table while Lake leaned against the wall. Ballantine didn't bother to tell him to take a seat, something everyone was very aware of.

"I'm going to rip the bandage off first," Ballantine said. "It has been decided that the Beowulf III will have a new captain. Everyone please congratulate, Captain Lake."

There was stunned silence as all eyes fell on Darren.

"Are you shitting me?" Darren asked, his eyes turning to Ballantine. Then to Lake. "Marty? Is this shit real?"

"It's real, Darren," Lake said. "But it wasn't my idea, just so you know."

"It's true," Thorne said. "It was my idea."

"You fucking asshole," Darren said as he stood up quickly. Then promptly sat down from the head rush and dizziness.

"That is one reason why," Thorne said. "The other reason is it won't work having the captain out on missions with the Team when he should be on the bridge. You can't do both."

"Did anyone think to ask me what job I wanted?" Darren asked. "I've been Captain for a long time now."

"And it's time you let someone else take that burden," Ballantine said, nodding at Lake. "Thank you, Captain Lake. You can get back to the bridge now. I'll make sure *Mister* Chambers understands all the reasons why the decision was made."

"You better," Lake said then looked at Darren. "I didn't ask for it. Know that."

Then he left and heads turned from Ballantine to Darren and back.

"We need you as an operator, not a captain," Ballantine said. "Things have gotten a lot more complicated for Team Grendel and the Beowulf III. Focus is the key to our survival."

"From the Colende cartel, right?" Shane asked.

"From all the cartels," Ballantine said. "And other various organizations."

"What other organizations?" Max asked.

"The company isn't the only player on the scene," Ballantine said. "We have gotten the attention of various entities that would prefer we go away."

"So we all have targets on our backs?" Kinsey asked. "Is that it?"

"The company will do what it can to keep those targets off, but yes," Ballantine nodded. "I personally have zero faith in the company to protect us any longer."

"Because we've been so safe since we started working for you," Darren laughed. "At least this time we weren't betrayed."

"Not 100% true," Dr. Morganton said as she walked into the meeting room. "Sorry I was late. Had to make a couple final adjustments on Mike's new prosthetics."

She stepped aside and Mike walked in. He was a little halting, but otherwise his gait was smooth.

"Holy C3PO," Max said as his brother whistled.

"Don't be dicks," Gunnar said as he smiled at Mike. "Nice look."

"Thanks," Mike said as he stood there looking down at the lower parts of his legs.

The prosthetics were far from Popeye's simple, yet high-tech, peg leg. From the knees down Mike's legs were solid metal, shaped like real legs. He took a step forward and there was the slight sound of gyros, but if he'd been wearing pants instead of shorts no one would have noticed he was a double amputee.

"He'll need to work with them for a good few months before I green light him for active duty," Dr. Morganton said. "But for all intents and purposes, Michael Pearlman is a whole man again."

"Except when I go to bed at night," Mike said. "Then they come off."

"We aren't at full integration technology yet," Dr. Morganton said. "But, with some help, we'll get there."

"Hopefully," Mike said. "Carlos had designed the first prototype for Popeye, but he didn't like it and wanted something simpler. Lucky for me Carlos is OCD and made a matching set."

"It is impressive technology," Dr. Morganton said. "Ballantine has been lucky to keep Carlos to himself."

Everyone at the table stared at her and she took full notice.

"I, uh, will let you carry on with your meeting," Dr. Morganton said. "I have a lot of work to do down in the Toyshop. I hope to maybe talk to each of you at dinner later."

"Of course you will," Ballantine said, giving each person at the table, except for Darby, a stern look.

"Right. Dinner," Shane said.

"Which Beau won't be in charge of," Max added.

"Yes, well..." Dr. Morganton trailed off. She nodded and left quickly.

"That was rude," Ballantine said.

"No shit," Max replied. "Isn't this all her fault?"

"No, I meant you all were rude," Ballantine said. "That woman has been in deep cover for over a year. We let McCarthy go so her family and the world hopefully, will think she's dead. Let that sink in before you blame her for anything that has happened. Without her quick thinking Espanoza wouldn't have been stopped."

"Just explain it to them," Thorne said.

Ballantine nodded and stood up. He started to pace around the briefing room.

"Lisa was in charge of our advanced bio-alternative mechanics division at the company," Ballantine said. "That included everything from prosthetics, as you saw, to full size vehicles like the whale sub. There is no one in the field with her skills or genius. Which made her a prime target for outside influence." Ballantine smiled. "But, Lisa is not one to be influenced easily, so when she was approached by Espanoza to work with McCarthy and offered an obscene amount of money, she came to me."

"How much is obscene?" max asked. "Just for reference."

"More than you can imagine," Ballantine said and pointed a finger at Max as he started to respond. "Don't say what I think you're going to say."

"You already played the Star Wars card with the 'Holy C3PO' comment," Shane said.

"I was going for a theme," Max replied.

"Boys, shut the fuck up," Thorne ordered. They did. "Keep going, Ballantine."

"It was my idea for her to take Espanoza's offer since I had an idea of what the project might lead to," Ballantine said. "McCarthy had been in the Colende cartel's pocket for years and was known for running drugs up and down the coast."

"Which I still find hard to stomach," Thorne said. "The man was a SEAL."

"We all have our price, Commander," Ballantine said. "McCarthy's was surprisingly low."

Thorne grumbled, but didn't add anything.

"Once Lisa knew what she was being hired to do, she was able to dig a little deeper," Ballantine said. "The Colende cartel had developed a formula that to the naked test looked exactly like cocaine."

"No shit," Gunnar said.

"As Gunnar figured out," Ballantine said. "But as Darren found out the hard way, it didn't act like cocaine."

"It acted more like meth on steroids," Kinsey said.

"You are closer than you think," Ballantine said. "It was designed to increase the addictive components of cocaine by nearly 100 times, but be undetectable. The cartel's plan has been to cut the cocaine they send to market with the substance so they can make even more money while also creating a new class of addict."

"Rich junkies," Kinsey laughed. "Of course. Good idea."

"Right again," Ballantine said, pointing at Kinsey. "The quality of cocaine it was to be added to wasn't going to the street, but staying in the boardrooms and bedrooms of the Southern California elite. If Espanoza had executed his plan fully, most of Hollywood, and Silicone Valley up north would have been in his clutches by the end of the year. They would have done anything for him just to get more of their drug."

"Whoa, whoa, whoa!" Darren exclaimed. "Am I addicted now? I don't feel addicted!"

"No, you didn't take the finished product," Ballantine said. "You took the additive. It certainly messed with you, as you know, but it only boosts the addictive components of cocaine once combined."

"Except for the sharks, "Gunnar said. "Their unique genetics created instant addiction. It's a compound that goes straight to the adrenal cortex while also hitting the limbic system. It drove them mad in seconds."

"So what does this have to do with the sharks attacking the subs? They did that before they got the drugs in their bodies," Kinsey said. "There were plenty of adolescent blue whales up and down the coast they could have gone after. If they hadn't hit the subs then none of this would have happened."

"Unfortunately, that was my fault," Ballantine said. "The development of the whale subs first began within the company as decoys to lure in the sharks we have been hired to hunt and kill."

"Hired by a client that created the fucking things," Thorne said.

"Quite true," Ballantine nodded. "The subs emit a signal that can be heard for hundreds of miles. With the client's help, Dr. Morganton was able to make a signal that only attracted sharks that fit a certain genetic profile."

"It only called the clones?" Max asked. "Are you shitting me?"

"I shit you not," Ballantine said. He finally stopped pacing and sat back down. "Listen, all of you, there are things about the company, and the world at large, that would drive you insane if you knew about them. I'll do my best to shield you from what you don't need to know, while also letting you in on information, whether I'm allowed to or not, that I believe you do need to know."

"How nice of you," Thorne said.

"Trust me, Commander, there are things you don't want in your head," Ballantine said.

Darby snorted and they all looked at her, but she just stared back until one by one they turned away. Except for Max.

"Hey, did you do something to your hair?" he asked. Darby barely smiled, but didn't reply.

"Ah, I thought I noticed a change," Ballantine said. "The new look becomes you, Darby."

Darby's smile faltered then left completely.

"Where was I?" Ballantine asked.

"Protecting our delicate sensibilities," Thorne said.

"Yes, thank you," Ballantine smirked. "The reality is, folks, that Team Grendel is on the radar and will stay there for who knows how long. The Beowulf III is now your home until I can rest assured that you can live normal lives, well, normal for you, without ending up dead in your sleep, in a parking lot, watching a movie, out to dinner, walking in the park, or wherever whoever may strike. It is not ideal, but then nothing rarely is."

"So what now?" Darren asked. "We just float at sea until the coast is clear?"

"No, hardly, Darren," Ballantine said. "We keep on with our jobs of finding the rest of the genetically manipulated creatures out there, while also performing that research and hunt you have spent most of your adult life obsessed with."

"No fucking way," Max said.

"We're still going to go after Moby Dick?" Shane asked.

"Don't call it that," Darren muttered.

"The whale species, as you know from our time in Somalia, is real," Ballantine said. "And is more important than I can say right now. Darren will get to do what he's wanted to do and search for another, while Team Grendel does what it's supposed to do and kill monsters. And not just sharks. Let me stress that. There are way more things out there than what swims in the sea. Mega monsters come in all shapes and sizes. And live everywhere."

"Yeah, I just shit myself a little," Max said.

"Um, so where does that leave me?" Mike asked. "You all know where you stand, but what about me?"

"You have a bullseye on you still," Ballantine said. "And with your new limbs, I figure you'd be safer and more useful here on the Beowulf III."

"Welcome to Team Grendel," Thorne said, offering his hand.

Mike hesitated then shook it.

"Thanks," Mike said.

"You say that now," Gunnar smiled. "But you haven't spent enough time with these idiots to know how wrong you are."

"Exactly what monsters are we talking about?" Shane asked.

All eyes fell on Ballantine.

"You'll find out in a couple weeks," Ballantine said. "When we reach our next destination."

"Which is where?" Kinsey asked. "And I really hope there's a GAP outlet there, because you're looking at what clothes I own. And I'm wearing my only pair of underwear."

"We know," Max frowned.

"Fuck off," Kinsey said.

"We'll get everyone outfitted before too long," Ballantine said. "Just give me a day or so to make all the arrangements. Until then, and until we reach the point of our next mission, I advise you rest up and then start training."

"Good idea," Thorne said. "What else is there?"

"Nothing," Ballantine said. "For now, at least. Relax on deck and enjoy yourselves. Next port will be in Panama, so we have some time to work everything out."

"Panama?" Darren asked. "We're going south?"

"That we are," Ballantine said. "But I'm not going to discuss it right now." He nodded to Thorne. "Commander?"

"Team Grendel is dismissed," Thorne said. Everyone sat there for a second. "Get the fuck out, people."

They didn't have to be told a third time.

***

"So..."

"So..."

Kinsey and Darren looked at each other as they sat on the observation deck, the starry night sky above them.

"Looks like we'll be sort of living together again," Darren said, turning his eyes from his ex-wife and out to the calm of the Pacific Ocean. "Kinda."

Kinsey rolled her eyes. "We'll have our own quarters, so not really even kinda."

"I guess," Darren said. "But it's the closest we'll be since before the divorce."

"Yeah," Kinsey nodded. "True."

"You cool with that?" Darren asked. "I am, by the way."

"I don't know," Kinsey said. "I haven't really had time to process much of what's going on. I guess we have time to work it out, though." Kinsey's face broke into a big grin. "And I can help you with your cocaine dependence and road to sobriety."

"I'm not addicted to cocaine," Darren snapped.

"That's what every junkie says," Kinsey replied, smiling even wider.

"You're liking this, aren't you?" Darren asked, smiling also.

"A little," Kinsey said. "You seen my cousins since the meeting?"

"Up there," Darren said, pointing to the crow's nest. "They're smoking the rest of their joints in one sitting."

"Why the hell would they do that?" Kinsey asked.

"Smoke out the old and bring in the new," Darren said.

"What the fuck does that mean?"

"Not a clue," Darren laughed. "I think they were six joints in when they came up with it."

"We should probably get them down before they fall down," Kinsey sighed.

"Nah, Lucy's up there with them as designated thinker," Darren said.

"The woman with a serious concussion is doing their thinking for them?" Kinsey asked. "Yeah, what could go wrong?"

"No shit," Darren replied. "I think part of it is so they smoke it all now and it's not around you. Those cousins love you more than weed, 'Sey."

They sat there in silence for a long while.

"You ever going to forgive me for fucking us up?" Darren asked, finally breaking the silence. He reached out and took Kinsey's hand. She didn't pull it away. "I know you don't have any reason you should. But if you do that would be cool."

"We'll see," Kinsey responded.

Again, more silence, this time hand in hand.

"Have you seen Max?" Darby asked, making them both jump as they turned their heads and found her standing behind their chairs.

"How long have you been there?" Kinsey asked.

"The whole time," Darby said then that small smile of her's crept across her lips. "Kidding. Just got here."

"Max is up there getting blitzed to high heaven," Darren said.

"Hmmm," Darby said. She nodded at them then went and climbed up to the crow's nest.

"You think she's going to kick his ass?" Darren asked.

"I don't think that's her intention," Kinsey said.

"I can't even guess what a woman like that's intentions are," Darren said.

"I can," Kinsey smiled.

She took her hand from Darren's and stood up, stretching her arms high into the night.

"I'm turning in," she said. "Sleep well, 'Ren."

"You too, 'Sey," Darren said. "Need some company?"

"Not yet," Kinsey said as she walked to the steps. She looked at him for a few seconds then sighed. "But maybe at some point." Then she laughed. "If we live to that point."

"Okay," Darren said. "Night."

"Night."

He watched her leave the observation deck then looked back across the dark waters.

"If we live," he said. "One can only hope."

There was laughter from above, and Darren was very surprised to realize that it was Darby. Then someone shouted, "Ow!" and he wasn't too surprised anymore.

"Yeah," he chuckled to himself. "If we live..."

The End

Author's Note:

My idea for the Mega series, and Team Grendel, has always been to combine the fun of the old Clive Cussler novels with the camp of today's SyFy Channel sea monster movies. With Mega 2: Baja Blood I have upped the monster shark count, as well as the body count, and made sure there was plenty of fun, excitement, horror, and intrigue. Playing with Team Grendel has been a blast and I intend to keep them fighting monsters of all sorts for many novels to come. I hope you as a reader get my intentions and know that the Mega novels will never be about science reality, but instead about adventure fun.
Hooyah!

Cheers,
Jake Bible
April 2014

Jake Bible lives in Asheville, NC with his wife and two kids.

A professional writer since 2009, Jake has a record of innovation, invention and creativity. Novelist, short story writer, independent screenwriter, podcaster, and inventor of the Drabble Novel, Jake is able to switch between or mash-up genres with ease to create new and exciting storyscapes that have captivated and built an audience of thousands.

He is the author of the bestselling Z-Burbia series for Severed Press as well as the Apex Trilogy (DEAD MECH, The Americans, Metal and Ash).

Find him at jakebible.com. Join him on Twitter and Facebook.

Made in the USA
San Bernardino, CA
03 December 2014